THIS EARTH OF OURS

This edition published 2025
by Living Book Press

ISBN: 978-1-76153-393-8 (hardcover)
         978-1-76153-394-5 (softcover)

First published in 1923.

This edition is based on the 1923 printing by T. Fisher Unwin, LTD.

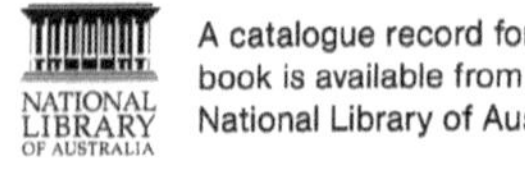

A catalogue record for this book is available from the National Library of Australia

THIS EARTH OF OURS

by

JEAN-HENRI FABRE

Contents

TRANSLATOR'S PREFACE vi

INTRODUCTION vii

1. THE TERRESTRIAL GLOBE 1
2. THE FALL OF BODIES 9
3. THE MOON FALLS 18
4. THE EARTH'S DAILY MOTION 27
5. SEASONS AND CLIMATES 39
6. THE FLATTENING OF THE EARTH AT THE POLES 52
7. THE INTERIOR OF THE EARTH 60
8. EARTHQUAKES 69
9. WHY THE CONTINENTS DO NOT SINK INTO THE OCEAN 76
10. VOLCANOES 83
11. VESUVIUS 93
12. FIRE AND WATER 101
13. MOUNTAINS 113
14. VALLEYS AND PLAINS 125
15. MONT BLANC 137
16. SAUSSURE'S ASCENT 146
17. MONT PERDU 154
18. WHERE SNOW NEVER MELTS 165
19. GLACIERS 175
20. GREAT RIVERS 184
21. LAKES AND SPRINGS 195
22. THE SEA 205
23. CORAL ISLANDS 213
24. TIDES 226
25. THE POLAR REGIONS 239

TRANSLATOR'S PREFACE

In this book we have "Uncle Paul" speaking in his own proper person; but though the dialogue form is discarded the style remains unchanged - as genially familiar and anecdotal as in the earlier volumes of the series.

No more pleasing presentation of the main facts of physical geography - or physiography, as it is now more commonly called - could be desired than is to be found in the following chapters. Especially interesting, even thrilling, are the accounts of early mountain-climbing in the Alps and in the Pyrenees - of the first ascent of Mont Blanc and Ramond's attempted ascent of Mont Perdu. The perils of polar exploration area as so vividly portrayed, and the wonders of glaciers and geysers, the terrors of volcanoes and earthquakes, and the beauties of coral islands, with much else that young readers and also their elders are sure to enjoy, will here be found set forth in the author's characteristic manner and with his wonted clearness and charm.

One further comment is called for here. Our genial author had a way of repeating himself, perhaps on the principle that one can never have too much of a good thing. Now and then a passage of greater or less length occurring in an earlier book will be found reprinted without change in one or more later books, with no apology from the author and no indication that the passage in question has already appeared elsewhere. In the present volume this eccentricity has been suppressed so far as it has been found possible to suppress it without undue mutilation of the book. What little of repetition remains will, it is hoped, be agreeably reminiscent rather than fatiguingly trite.

INTRODUCTION

This volume of the elementary science series gives a general account of the earth on which we live. Its object is to impart a little agreeable diversion to the unavoidable dryness of geography, and thus to make interesting a useful branch of learning that has too often been looked upon as devoid of interest.

In a series of familiar talks, the simplicity of which will not detract from the irresistible charm of the subject, I propose to bring within the understanding of all readers the great questions that ought to form the basis of geographical studies, but that are nearly always sacrificed in favor of a dry list of names of countries, towns, rivers, etc., having no attraction whatever for the inquiring mind. Doubtless it is well to know where on the map to find Kaffraria and Zanzibar; but it is still better to have correct ideas of the earth as a whole, the earth as God made it, with its double movement of rotation and revolution giving us our days and our seasons, with its central furnace in which continents are forged, and with its atmosphere and seas whence all life derives sustenance. It is not enough, it seems to me, to learn by rote from a geography book that a volcano is a smoking mountain, that a sea is a large body of water, that an earthquake is a trembling of the ground under our feet, and that a glacier is a valley full of snow and ice. One ought also to know in brief the mechanism of these great, natural forces and the part they play in the general scheme of things, for such studies are of inestimable worth in their power to uplift the soul and ennoble the mind by showing forth the stupendous marvels of creation.

J. H. FABRE.

CHAPTER I

THE TERRESTRIAL GLOBE

A CELEBRATED author, Bernardin de Saint-Pierre, tells us the strange notion he had, in his childhood, of the earth and sky. Judging from appearances, he thought the sun rose from behind one mountain and set behind another. He regarded the sky as a blue vault or inverted bowl resting on the outer edge of the earth, so that if he should ever manage to reach that edge it would be necessary, he imagined, to walk in a stooping posture so as not to bump his head against the firmament. One day, determined to remain no longer in doubt, he undertook to make the thing sure. Some lunch was put up for him in a basket, and he set off. He walked and walked for a long time, in the hope of soon touching the sky with his hand; but the vault, receding as he advanced, was always the same distance away, until at last fatigue overcame him and he abandoned the expedition. But, though he retraced his steps, he was still persuaded of the reality of the celestial vault; his failure to reach it and touch it being easily explained: his legs were not long enough and strong enough to carry him the necessary distance.

You, my readers, may at one time have shared this childish error and imagined the earth to be an extended tract of land broken up by mountains and covered with the blue cupola of the sky; but now you are well aware that nowhere does the sky rest on the ground, nowhere does one run the risk of bumping one's head against the firmament, because the blue sky is of the same height everywhere. You also know that by walking straight ahead you come to plains, mountains, seas, but never to any barriers marking the ends of the earth. In short, you have learned that the earth is round and that if you should continue in the same direction long enough you would finally get back to your starting-point.

The earth is an immense globe floating unsupported in space. Imagine a large ball suspended in the air by a thread, and on this ball a gnat. If this gnat should take a notion to go all over the surface, is it not true that it could come and go over the ball, above, below, on the side, without ever encountering an obstacle, without ever seeing a barrier rise up to block its passage? Is it not equally true that if it always kept on in the same direction, the gnat would end by making the tour of the ball and would come back to its starting-point? So it is with us on the surface of the earth, though we are far more insignificant when compared with the globe that bears us than is the tiniest gnat in comparison with the biggest ball you can imagine. Without ever encountering a barrier, without ever touching the cupola of the sky, we come and go in a thousand different directions, we accomplish the most distant journeys, even make the tour of the earth and return to our starting-point. The earth, then, is round; it is an immense ball that floats without support in celestial space. As to the blue vault that arches above us, it is a mere appearance caused by the blue color of the air enveloping the earth on all sides.[1]

The earth is round, as proved by the following facts. When, in order to reach the town he is journeying toward, a traveler crosses a level plain where nothing intercepts his view, from a certain distance the highest points of the town, the summits of towers and steeples, are seen first. From a lesser distance the spires of the steeples become entirely visible, then the roofs of buildings, and finally the buildings themselves; so that the view embraces a great number of objects, beginning with the highest and ending with the lowest, as the distance diminishes. This would not be so if the earth were flat. At any distance a tower, instead of becoming gradually visible from top to bottom, would be seen as a whole the moment it became visible

1   This paragraph and some subsequent ones are repeated from *The Story Book of Science*. See "Translator's Preface."

at all, as illustrated in Figure 1, which shows two observers, A and B, at very different distances from the tower at the left, but both able to see it in its full extent. On the other hand, if the ground is curved, if the earth is round, objects sufficiently far off will be hidden by the curvature of the earth's surface; and as the distance lessens they will appear by degrees, beginning with the top. Thus, to an observer at A in Figure 2, the tower is quite invisible because the curvature of the ground obstructs the view. To an observer at B the upper half of the tower is visible, while the lower half is still hidden by the curvature of the earth. Finally, when the observer arrives at the point C, the whole tower is in plain sight.

FIGURE 1

On dry land it is rare to find a surface that in extent and regularity is adapted to the observation I have just told you about. Nearly always hills, ridges, or masses of foliage intercept the view and prevent the gradual appearance, from summit to base, of the tower or steeple that one is approaching. On the sea no obstacle bars the view unless it be the convexity of the water, which follows the general curvature of the earth's surface. It is, accordingly, there especially that it is easy to study the phenomena produced by the rounded form of the earth.

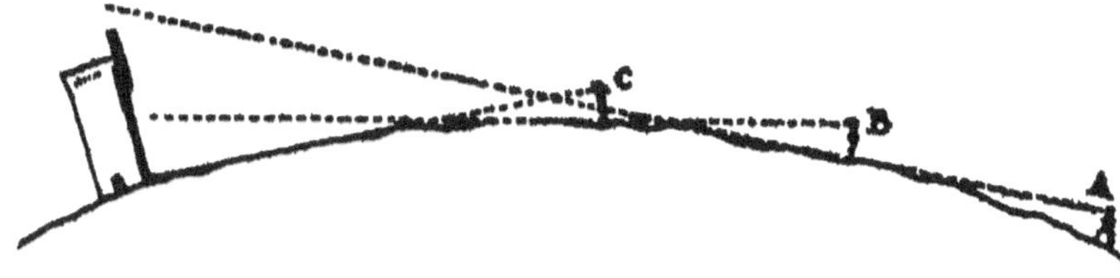

FIGURE 2

When a ship coming from the open sea approaches the coast, the first points of the shore visible to those on board are the highest points, like the summits of mountains. Later the tops of high towers come into view, then the edge of the shore itself. In the same way, an observer who watches from the shore the arrival of a vessel sees first the tops of the masts, then the topsails, then the sails next below, and finally the hull of the vessel. If the vessel were departing from the shore, the observer would see it gradually disappear and apparently sink into the water, all in reverse order; that is, the hull would be first hidden from view, then the low sails, then the high ones, and finally the top of the mainmast, which would be the last to disappear, as shown in Figure 3.

FIGURE 3

Another proof of the earth's roundness is found in the shape of the horizon. This term, taken from the Greek word meaning "to bound," is applied to the line all around us that bounds the view when one is in the open country.

It is at this line that the sky appears to join the earth. Now, on a plain, with no unevenness of ground to mar its regularity, the horizon forms a circle whose center is the observer. The circular shape of the horizon is still more marked at sea, the surface of the water presenting the appearance of a vast disk whose outline merges with the blue of the sky. If the earth were flat, our view of its surface would be limited only by the strength of our eyesight, and with a powerful enough telescope we could see almost any distance, so that there would be no boundary between the visible and the invisible portion of the earth's surface. But in reality the case is quite different: against the barrier of the horizon even the best telescopes are powerless. Hence, the earth is not flat, but round. All this will be made clear by Figure 4.

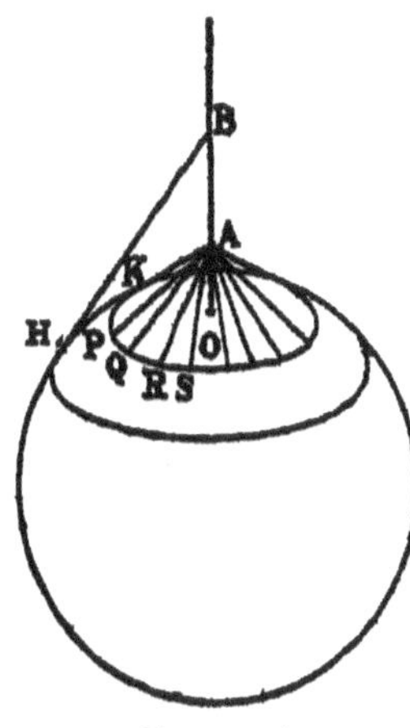

FIGURE 4

On the sphere there depicted, imagine a straight line, OB, erected, perpendicular to the surface at the point of erection. If from the point A in this line the gaze be directed all around, what portion of the sphere will be seen? The answer is easily arrived at. From A let us draw a straight line, AK, grazing the surface of the sphere at K. This straight line will serve to represent the line of vision. All between the observer and the point K where the line touches the sphere is evidently visible, while all beyond that point is invisible. If, from A, similar lines, AP, AQ, AR, AS, etc., are drawn all about the point A so as to graze the surface, each of these lines at its point of contact with the sphere will mark another point on the horizon, and all these points taken together will, if we suppose them to be infinite in number, evidently form an unbroken circle. The same result would be attained from any other point of observation. Hence, if the horizon is circular wherever it is viewed, the earth must be a sphere.

Now, this enormous globe that we call the earth is forty million meters, or ten thousand leagues, in circumference. What these numbers mean will perhaps be made clearer to you if you will follow me a little farther. If you have ever happened to climb a high tower and cast a look over the surrounding expanse, you have been struck with the great extent of territory offered to your view; and the bluish line of the horizon has seemed so far away as to remain in your mind as the best example of great distance. How far away from you really was the horizon? How far could you see from the top of the tower? That depends on two things: the height of the tower and the evenness or the unevenness of the ground. Let us look again at the figure and, instead of imagining the observer's eye at A, imagine it higher, as at B. It is clear that from this latter point the line of vision will graze the sphere's surface at a greater distance, as at H, thus giving a wider horizon. So it is that, on account of the earth's roundness, the higher you are above its surface the farther you can see.

On the other hand, the unevenness of a mountainous region cuts off the view and so restricts the horizon. Suppose, then, the ground to be even like the surface of the sea, and the place of observation to be as high as the loftiest belfry in the world, that of Strasbourg Cathedral, which is 142 meters above the pavement; under these conditions the horizon would be ten leagues from the observer. If another Bernardin de Saint-Pierre, equipped with a sturdy pair of legs, wished to reach the horizon seen from the Strasbourg Cathedral's belfry, it would be a day's walk for him; and if he succeeded in accomplishing this, he might not have the courage and the strength to start out again the next day. Well, so huge is this earth of ours that its circumference measures a thousand times ten leagues, a thousand times as far as one can see from the loftiest belfry in the world.

You have probably asked yourself by this time how it is that the earth can be said to have a rounded surface when there are so many vast mountain chains and deep valleys to break the regularity of that surface. You are willing to admit that the ocean surface is evenly curved, but the dry land, you maintain, is quite different. You see nothing but irregularity there. What indication is there, you ask, of regular curvature in this jumble of mountains, valleys, hills, plains, and precipices? How can one trace any systematic plan in ground full of these enormous irregularities? But, let me ask in turn, is an orange round? Yes, certainly, you reply. Look at it carefully, however: the skin is all wrinkled. No matter, you say; the orange is round, for the wrinkles in its skin are as nothing compared with the size of the fruit. Exactly; and so I say, in my turn, that the earth is round despite all the inequalities of its surface, because the very highest mountains are as nothing in comparison with its immense size. And I will prove it to you.

Let the earth be represented by a large, smooth ball, two meters in diameter; then, in their right proportions, picture in relief on its surface some of the principal mountains of the globe. The highest of these is Mount Everest, of the Himalayan chain in central Asia. Its granite summit towers 8,840 meters[2] above the level of the sea, being so high that it is seldom wrapped in clouds, while its base covers the space of an empire. What is man, physically considered, in face of such a giant? Well, let us represent this giant on our large ball that we imagine to be the earth. Do you know what we should need for this purpose? A tiny grain of sand that would slip through your fingers, a grain of sand 1 1/3 millimeters through! The gigantic mountain that overwhelms us with its immensity is a mere nothing when compared with the earth. The tiniest pimple on an orange is incomparably larger in comparison with the fruit. The highest mountain of Europe, Mont Blanc, which is 4,810 meters high, would be represented by a grain of sand having about half the diameter of the other. But we need not multiply these examples. You see clearly enough that by sprinkling grains of sand thus over the surface of the ball to represent the various inequalities in the earth's surface we should not really change the general shape of our ball. The earth, then, is only a larger ball strewn with grains of dust and sand proportioned to its size and known as hills and mountains.

How is the earth held poised in space? Is it suspended by some celestial chain to the vault of the firmament, as the sanctuary lamp to the vault of the temple? Or does it rest on some support, as a geographical globe on its pedestal...! Thousands of travelers have journeyed over it in all directions and have nowhere seen either suspending chain or supporting pedestal of any sort. Everywhere, as here in our own country, their view encounters only earth, air, and sea. So we must conclude that this globe of ours is isolated in space, that it swims in a void without support.

Why, then, does it not fall? Ah, that is the problem! But think a moment and perhaps you will see why the earth cannot fall. What do you see overhead? The open sky, boundless space. What would you see if you were on the opposite side of the earth, standing on the spot that we think of as directly under

---

2   That is, 29,002 feet, or nearly 5 ½ miles. The meter is equivalent to 29.37011 inches – *Translator*.

our feet? Still the open sky and boundless space. And on the spot halfway around the earth to the right or to the left? Still the same, always the same. Thus everywhere the open sky, which is the same as boundless space, surrounds the earth. Now tell me, in what direction in this space, which is the same in every direction, is the earth to fall? Tell me, if you can, which way is up and which way is down. If "up" is toward the sky, remember that the sky is also on the opposite side of the earth, that it is just the same there as here, and that it is the same everywhere. If it seems to you plain enough that the earth cannot leap up into the sky that is above us, why should you expect it to leap into the sky that is beneath us? To fall toward that sky would be to rise in the same sense that we say an arrow rises here when it is shot upward. You have never wondered why the earth does not rise toward the firmament; so do not wonder why it does not fall, for these two are one and the same.

All this will be further explained in the next chapter, in which we shall consider the cause of the fall of bodies. But first let us sum up the principal points of this chapter. The earth is round and isolated in space. It is forty million meters or ten million leagues in circumference. Its semi-diameter, or the distance from its center to its surface, is 6,366 kilometers, or a little less than 1,600 leagues. The greatest inequalities in its surface are as nothing compared with its size and do not appreciably modify its spherical shape.

CHAPTER II

THE FALL OF BODIES

WHO DOES not know the delightful fable of "The Acorn and the Pumpkin," and who is there that has not laughed at Garo's misadventure? A good man at heart, but a little pretentious, Garo the cottager thought that the pumpkin, instead of lying idly on its stomach on the ground, would be better hanging from the branches of the oak in place of the acorn. That would be just the thing, such a fruit for such a tree! While thus criticizing the works of God and taking no little satisfaction in being able to give good advice to the Creator, Garo fell asleep under an oak.

> But (rude awakening from sweet repose)
> An acorn fell and hit him on the nose.
> The injured member straight began to bleed,
> And this our Garo could not fail to heed.
> "Oh, oh!" he cried, in quite another key,
> "I wonder what would have become of me
> If there had fallen, in the acorn's place,
> A heavy pumpkin plump upon my face.
> But, heaven be praised, God did not will it so;
> And God was right, that much I've learned to know."

And you, my young readers, will agree with Garo. If the oak bore pumpkins for fruit, who would ever dare to seek its perilous shade?

If the fall of an acorn taught Garo that what is done by God is well done, the fall of an apple showed Newton that God does everything according to number, weight, and measure, and that from all time he has regulated the movements of the celestial bodies by admirable mechanical laws. Newton, who had one

9

of the keenest intellects ever known, was walking in his youth through an apple orchard, when an apple fell to the ground. You would have picked it up and eaten it, and that would have been the end of the matter. But Newton asked himself why it had fallen. Foolish question! You would have told him that it fell because, being overripe, it had become detached from the branch. But wait a moment. First answer my questions, and then perhaps you will admit that it is not so easy to brush aside the young thinker's query.

The apple fell from the top of the apple tree. Would it have fallen just the same if the apple tree had been as tall as a poplar? Yes, undoubtedly. Would it have fallen if the tree had been ten times or a hundred times as tall? Why not? We know very well that a stone falls from the top of a tower and from the summit of a mountain. Finally, would it have fallen if by some miracle the tree had grown so tall as to bear fruit at the height of a league? Yes, again, for balloons rise as high and even higher, and objects thrown out by the balloonist never fail to come back to the earth. And would the apple still have fallen from a height of ten, a hundred, or a thousand leagues? Well, you hesitate? There is nothing to hesitate about; however high you imagine the apple, it must still fall. Indeed, the greater the elevation, the faster will the fall finally become.

You and I, then, are agreed in this: though the branches of the apple tree tower above the clouds or even become lost in the depths of the firmament, the apples will always fall to the ground. But tell me; if the apple were replaced by a leaden ball, would this likewise fall to earth? Certainly, you reply; the leaden ball, being heavier than the apple, would fall so much the better, no matter from what height. Very well, then; according to you, an apple, and still more a leaden ball, must fall to earth from any height whatever. And there you reason well, for if a body falls from a given height nothing can prevent its falling from a still greater height. I even think the ball of lead would fall were it as far off as the moon. What do you think about it? This requires reflection. Yet, after all, if there is nothing in the way, why should it not fall? Yes, you say, it will fall.

And now I have caught you. The next moonlit night raise your eyes to the sky. Do you see, away up there, that enormous luminous ball unsupported by anything? Take care! According to what you have just told me, it will fall on our heads and crush us in its frightful descent. That immense ball, the moon, is a globular mass of matter equal to the fiftieth part of the terrestrial globe. Ah, bah! you exclaim; the moon fall! Yes, my young readers, the moon does actually fall; and there we have the problem that caused Newton to reflect under the apple tree. The moon falls, and if it ever reached us it would put an end to every one of us and to this poor old earth of ours, which would be shattered to fragments under the terrific shock of the heavenly body fallen from the firmament. The moon is always falling; but don't be alarmed: despite its continual fall toward the earth it always keeps at the same distance from us, which must seem to you the strangest sort of paradox. Let us, then, proceed at once to the preliminary studies that will give us an explanation of this incredible fact.

I pick up a stone; I open my hand and the stone falls, returning to the ground. Any other object, as a piece of wood, an iron ball, a drop of water, a leaden bullet, would do the same. But there are certain substances that, instead of falling toward the ground, rise and remain suspended at great heights; and among these are smoke, clouds, and balloons. Have we here a real exception to the rule that a body when left to itself falls to the ground, or is the suspension of these bodies in the air due to some cause that impedes the operation of the general law? A piece of wood held in the hand falls to the ground when released; but if, instead of standing on the earth's surface, we were immersed at a great depth in water, the piece of wood when released would not fall. Although obedient to the law of falling bodies, it would rise, on escaping from our grasp, and would return to the surface of the water; instead of descending it would ascend, because it is lighter than the water in which it is immersed.

Well, here on the earth's surface we are really on the floor of an immense ocean; we are at the bottom of the atmosphere, an ocean of air enveloping the earth on all sides. Accordingly, smoke and clouds, being lighter than the surrounding air, must rise from the bottom of the atmospheric ocean just as wood does from the bottom of the ocean of water. But if there were no air, then smoke, clouds, and balloons would not rise; everything, absolutely everything, would fall just as lead falls. And what is more, in the absence of air all bodies would fall with the same rapidity. Light down and heavy lead, stone, wood, cork, metals — all these, though of so different natures and varying weight, one from another, would reach the ground together if dropped from the same height at the same instant. A hundred-kilogram ball of lead would not go any faster in its fall than a tuft of thistledown. Here again I read in your wondering looks the signs of utter incredulity. What, you exclaim, a piece of paper, a feather, or a bit of cotton would fall as fast as a ball of lead? Nonsense! You are joking. If from an upper window we drop a leaden ball and a piece of paper at the same time, we know very well that the ball will reach the ground first and the paper will float about for some time before settling down. Agreed, I reply; but before you accuse me of error let us go over again together the experiment you propose with such assurance of triumph, according to your way of thinking.

In my turn I tell you that if the ball of metal reaches the ground before the paper, air is the cause of the difference, on account of the unequal resistance it opposes to the fall of the two bodies. This resistance is great for the paper, which has much surface and very little weight; but it is slight for the metal ball, which has little surface and much weight. Accordingly, the lead, being less impeded in its fall, must come to earth first. In racing over ground covered with dense underbrush, which of two men equally good at running on a hard road would reach the goal first, — the stronger one, who could easily thrust aside the obstructing underbrush, or the weaker one, who could do so only with difficulty? Evidently the former. Lead does the same thing: stronger than paper, or, in other words, heavier than paper, it easily pushes aside the obstacle obstructing its passage. It cleaves the air without difficulty and arrives at the goal first.

Let us return to our two men running through the thicket of

underbrush. If the weaker, the second one, instead of having to open a way for himself, ran just behind the stronger one so as to profit by the path opened by his sturdy legs, do you not think he would reach the goal on the very heels of his competitor, being as good a runner as he when no obstacles bar the way? That is clear enough, you say. Well, we are going to make the metal go first and open a way through the aerial underbrush, so to speak. Then you will see the paper rush along this course as fast as the metal. Let us take a large penny or, better still, a five-franc piece, and then with a pair of scissors cut out a round piece of paper of exactly the same size, or even a little smaller, so that its edge shall nowhere project beyond the rim of the coin. We now place this piece of paper on the coin, not pasting it on, you understand, or even wetting it first with saliva. Then, holding both coin and paper in our fingers, with the paper uppermost, we let them fall from a window at some height from the ground. Clink! It is done. Metal and paper reach the earth at the same instant. You can repeat the experiment from any height whatever, even from the top of a lofty tower, and the result will always be the same: the piece of metal and the piece of paper will reach the ground together, unless the metal turns over on the way instead of falling flat, as it started.

It cannot be said that the coin impelled or pushed the paper, since the coin started just ahead of the paper. So if the latter arrives at the goal at the same time as the former, it is because, in falling, it goes as fast as the other; and this it always will do if it meets with no resistance from the air. Hence we conclude that, with no air to offer resistance, all substances fall equally fast. Now that you are convinced of this principle, which at first seemed so strange to you, I hope that another time, before saying a thing is impossible, you will wait for the proof. How many things that seem at first impossible become quite simple upon reflection!

A falling body stops when it reaches the earth, because the solid ground bars its passage. But if the earth were to open and make way for the falling object, offering an empty well of indefinite depth for its passage, whither would it go, toward what point would it move? That is what we must now find out.

Attach a bullet to the end of a long string and you will have what is called a plumb-line or plummet. Take the other end of the string in your hand and let the bullet hang free. After swinging to and fro a number of times it will finally come to rest, and when it is quite motionless the stretched cord will indicate the direction the bullet would take if not held back; for evidently the cord could not oppose its fall and hold it stationary without being itself stretched taut in exactly the direction of the interrupted fall. Therefore, to find the direction that bodies take in falling, we have merely to note the direction indicated by the plummet. Now, if you will observe the position of a plummet over a sheet of still water like that in a wide basin, for example, you will see that in relation to the surface of the water the cord does not slant to either side but is perfectly straight; in a word, it is perpendicular. This direction of the cord is called vertical. A vertical line, then, is one that does not slant toward either side in reference to the surface of still water; or, as it is otherwise put, a vertical line is one that is perpendicular to such a surface. Finally, the surface of still water is called a horizontal surface.

This vertical direction is a matter of much importance in many cases, particularly in our buildings, which would be unstable if the builder were not careful to make sure with his plumb-line that the wall under construction went straight up instead of leaning this way or that. Suppose you wish to find out, for example, whether the corner of a house forms a perfectly vertical line. Stand before this corner with a plummet hanging in front of you from your upraised hand. The corner or edge under inspection should be completely hidden by the plumb-line; otherwise, the edge is not vertical and the house is badly built.

We have just learned that bodies fall perpendicularly in reference to the surface of still water, or, in other words, that they fall vertically. Now, for a water surface we can just as well take that of the sea in a calm as that of a lake or of a basin. In each instance, the falling body descends perpendicularly to the sheet of water. We know that the surface of the sea is rounded — that it follows, with a regularity not to be found elsewhere, the general curvature of the earth — and the same may be said

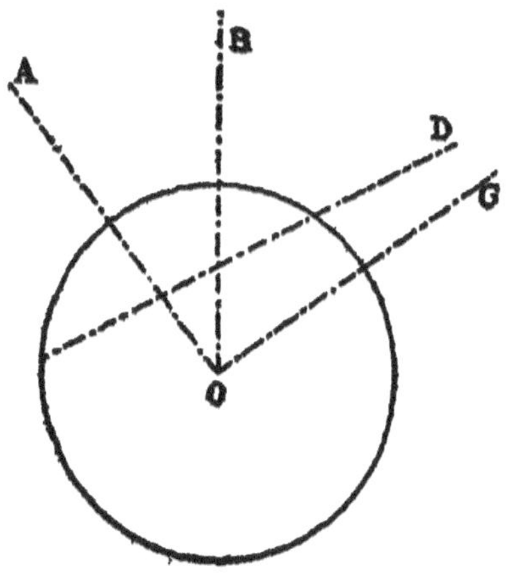

FIGURE 5

of any sheet of water, as that in a lake, or in a basin, or in a bucket. But in these latter instances, the curvature would not be appreciable on account of the small extent of the surface considered. If on the surface of a calm sea and on that of still water in general the fall of bodies is in a direction perpendicular to that surface, what conclusion shall we draw from this? In the accompanying figure, the earth is represented by a circle whose center is at O. Three straight lines, A, B, C, are drawn perpendicularly to the circumference of this circle; that is, in relation to the curve they slant neither to one side nor to the other, and all three, if sufficiently prolonged, meet at the center, O. But the line D, which slants to one side in reference to the contour of the circle, does not go through the center on being prolonged. Therefore, since everywhere bodies fall in a direction perpendicular to the curved surface of water at rest, it is plain that all falling bodies move toward the center of the earth.

What is there at this central point to make all bodies move toward it in their fall? Is there, perhaps, some powerful magnet attracting them, as an ordinary magnet attracts iron? No, there is no kind of magnet that could draw to itself objects of all sorts, no one particular thing that could cause the fall of these bodies. Just what there is at the earth's center we do not clearly know, but certainly the direction followed by falling bodies is not determined by anything at that center. If a body left unsupported falls — that is, if it returns to the ground — it is because the earth attracted it. Now, this attraction is not exerted by any one part of the earth more than by another; it is exerted by all parts equally at the same time, by those to the right, those to the left, those on the surface, and those deep within, all without distinction; and from all these attractions, of which any one acting alone would draw the body in one particular direction, there results a total attraction that directs a falling body toward the center of the earth.

Imagine a two-horse carriage. If the right-hand horse alone is harnessed to it, the carriage will go slantwise toward the right. If the left-hand horse is the one harnessed to the carriage, it will again go slantwise, but this time toward the left. If, however, both horses are harnessed to it in front, the carriage will move straight ahead. Exactly the same thing occurs when a body falls; for we can imagine the earth divided into two perfectly equal parts, one toward the right, the other toward the left of our falling body. If the right-hand half alone exerted its attraction, the body would move toward the right; if only the left-hand attracted it, it would move toward the left. But with the combined attraction of both halves, or of the total mass of the earth, the body takes a middle course and moves toward the earth's center. Consequently, if all falling bodies move toward the center of the earth, it is not on account of any special attraction belonging to this center, but simply because of the symmetrical arrangement of the earth's mass in relation to this point.

Experiment has proved that a falling body moves 4.9 meters[3] in the first second of its fall. A second, as you know, is a very short time, being only the sixtieth part of a minute, which in turn is the sixtieth part of an hour. As a body falls, it moves faster and faster, so that the distance covered in each successive second increases rapidly. This is shown in the following table.

Duration of fall expressed in seconds	Distance covered
1	4.9 meters
2	4 times 4.9 meters
3	9 times 4.9 meters
4	16 times 4.9 meters
5	25 times 4.9 meters

3   Or 16.1 feet, very nearly. – *Translator.*

<pre>
6.............................36 times 4.9 meters
7.............................49 times 4.9 meters
8.............................64 times 4.9 meters
etc   etc.
</pre>

Notice that 4 is the product of 2 multiplied by 2, 9 the product of 3 by 3, 16 the product of 4 by 4, 25 the product of 5 by 5, and so on. Therefore, to find how many meters a body falls in any given time, we multiply by itself the number of meters the fall continues, and then multiply this product by 4.9.

You can make a rather interesting application of this rule. Imagine yourself at the top of a tower, or on the edge of a precipice, or looking down into a deep dry well, and you wish to know the height of the tower or of the precipice, or the depth of the well. You take a stone and let it fall to the foot of the tower or of the precipice, or to the bottom of the dry well, counting the seconds that elapse between the dropping of the stone and the sound of its fall. To estimate this time, if you have not a watch that tells the seconds, you can count your pulse beats, which correspond approximately to the ticking of seconds. Let us suppose six seconds to elapse. Multiplying 6 by 6, we have 36, and this multiplied by 4.9 gives the height or the depth desired, or about 176 meters.

CHAPTER III

THE MOON FALLS

WE NOW come to the curious question of the falling of the moon. In Figure 6, let us imagine a cannon aimed horizontally, or in the direction of the line CA, from the top of a hillock, while facing the cannon at no very great distance is a wall. The line of aim being CA, the cannonball would seem likely to hit the wall at A. But instead of following the straight line CA, as the cannon is aimed, the ball describes a curve, CBD, and hits the wall considerably lower than the point aimed at — let us say at the point D. And this deflection indicates no lack of skill on the gunner's part. He may be as skillful as you please, yet he will never hit the spot exactly opposite the cannon's mouth, but always a spot somewhat lower; so that if he really wishes to hit the spot marked A he will have to aim at a spot correspondingly higher.

Why does not the projectile follow the line of aim, instead of hitting the wall below the point exactly opposite the cannon's mouth? The answer is plain: as soon as the ball leaves the cannon's mouth it ceases to be held up and begins to fall because, despite its initial horizontal motion, it is pulled downward by the earth just as it would be if it were at rest. That is why its actual path, CBD, inclines more and more from a straight line and forms a curved one. Moreover, the moving cannonball falls exactly as far in any given time as it would have fallen if simply dropped from the hand. Suppose, then, the ball takes three seconds to go from cannon to wall. In three seconds, a body falling freely moves, according to the table in the preceding chapter, nine times 4.9 meters, or 44.1 meters. Now, if we

Figure 6

measure the distance from point A, where the ball would have struck the wall if not pulled down by the earth's attraction, to point D, where it actually does strike, we shall find this distance to be 44.1 meters. If the ball had taken only two seconds to go from C to D, the line AD would have measured four times 4.9 meters, or 19.6 meters; and, finally, if the passage of the ball had occupied but one second, the distance from A to D would have been 4.9 meters. Hence, we conclude that the earth's attraction acts in just the same way on a moving body as on one at rest.

Here let us turn our attention to a noteworthy fact concerning the movement of a body circling about a fixed point.

In many countries, mules are used to tread out the grain at harvest time. The sheaves are disposed in a circle on the threshing floor; then a man takes his stand in the center of the circle, and with a long bridle-rein, one end of which he holds, he drives the mule at a trot over the layer of sheaves, urging the animal on with voice and whip when necessary. If the mule is unaccustomed to going thus in a circle and shows signs of dizziness, it is blindfolded so as not to be conscious of moving round and round. Then, if it describes a circle, this is because the bridle-rein that guides it prevents any straying from the beaten track. But if the man lets go of the rein, what will happen? The mule, no longer feeling the guiding hand, will follow its natural impulse and leave the threshing floor by proceeding in a straight line instead of a curve.

Tie a stone to the end of a string and, taking the other end in one hand, whirl the stone rapidly around. What keeps the stone in the circle it describes? Evidently, the string. If the string breaks or if the knot that ties the stone comes undone, you all know that the stone will go straight ahead. By a very similar mechanism, a pebble is hurled from a sling. These two examples show us that, to describe a circle about a given center, a body incapable of guiding itself must be drawn toward this center by a cord, a bridle-rein, or something similar; and they also show us that if the restraint exerted upon the circling body and confining it to its circular path suddenly relaxes, the body breaks away and darts straight ahead.

The moon circles about the earth as the stone does about the hand that holds the cord of the sling, and the circular course it follows is called its orbit. In the accompanying figure, the globe, T, represents the earth, and the circular line surrounding it at a distance represents the moon's orbit. Suppose the moon in its course about the earth to have reached the point L. On arriving at this point it is impelled by a certain force that urges it forward. It is in a situation similar to that of the cannonball as it issues from the cannon's mouth. If there were no restraining influence at the center of its orbit, the moon would go straight ahead along the line LA, which in some sort represents the line of aim in our illustration with the cannon. Imagine a vertical wall erected to an indefinite height above the earth and represented by the straight line TA. Well, the moon in its course does not reach this wall at A, the point aimed at from the position L, but lower, at B. It does not follow the straight line LA, but the curved one, LB; that is, the moon acts precisely as does the ball discharged from a cannon.

The moon, then, is attracted by the earth, and in the time it takes to go from L to the imaginary wall TA it falls the distance represented by the line AB. Likewise, on reaching B, the moon, by virtue of its forward-urging impulse, would escape from its orbit if the earth did not hold it in restraint, just as the pebble is held by the whirling sling until the moment of its release. If the moon were set free from the invisible sling that holds it to its course, it would go in a straight line to the point C in the imaginary wall TC. But the earth's attraction never relaxes its hold, and so the moon really follows the curved line BD and reaches D by a gradual fall equal in length to OD. Thus it

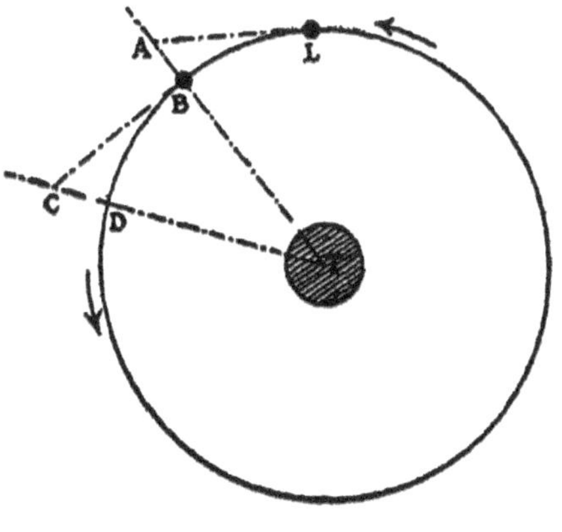

FIGURE 7

is that by an uninterrupted series of falls toward earth the moon, instead of leaving our globe forever by following the straight line along which its own impulse would drive it, revolves about us in a circular orbit. I was right, then, in saying that the moon falls, and it is precisely on account of its continual fall that it is always at the same distance from us.

The moon is held to its orbit by the earth's attraction, being by this attraction constantly brought back to the circular course that it as constantly tends to leave; and what brings it back is the very same force that makes bodies fall to the surface of our globe. The earth's attraction plays the same part in relation to the moon as the bridle-rein in relation to the mule trotting in a circle on the threshing floor, and the cord of the sling in relation to the pebble whirled around by the hand. It bends the moon's course and forces that body to come back constantly toward the earth, just as it bends the course of the cannonball and brings the projectile down to a point below the one aimed at. But the animal finds in its own bodily strength the impulse that urges it on, the pebble gets this impulse from the slinger's hand, and the cannonball owes it to the explosion of the gunpowder with which the cannon is charged. Whence, then, in its turn, does the moon derive the motive power that carries it forward? From God, whose sovereign hand has launched all the celestial bodies on their eternal courses and scattered the stars throughout the firmament even as the sower casts his seed over the plowed field. All these heavenly bodies, as says the poet Lamartine,

> Derive from God who reigns supreme the force that makes
>   them move.
> Just ponder, my young readers, on that great mysterious force,
> On that arm of power resistless that first launched them on
>   their course.
> How often have you tested, with a pebble or a ball,
> Your puny power of hurling, noting where your missiles fall,
> You say the arm that threw them was of great or little strength;
> And a cast of ten score cubits seems to you of wondrous length.
> But if such a feeble effort wins your plaudits of surprise,
> What think you of the power that moves the planets in the
>   skies,
> That makes the worlds around us go spinning on their way,

And will make them thus go spinning through eternity's long
    day.
Space relations, weight, and measure — these are nothing to that
    power
That has cast the stars o'er heaven in a scintillating shower.
Let us bow the head, my children, to that mighty One above
Who created all these wonders and who holds us in his love.

The attraction exerted by the earth on all surrounding objects, no matter how far away they may be, is not a property peculiar to itself alone. It belongs to all bodies whatsoever. The moon, for example, draws back to itself any objects that for some reason or other may have strayed away; it attracts them and makes them fall. Its attraction must reach out into the far-distant spaces of the heavens, no matter how remote, and it exerts its influence especially on this earth of ours. Consequently, the earth must be constantly falling toward the moon just as the moon is constantly falling toward the earth. But in this conflict of mutual attractions, it is clear that the more powerful body is bound to get the better of the less powerful one and to deflect it from its course far more than it is itself deflected.

When in your games two of you take hold of a rope, one at each end, and pull with all your might, each one trying to drag his opponent, victory rests with the stronger. Victory likewise rests with the stronger, the larger, of the two heavenly bodies we are considering. In other words, it rests with the one having the greater amount of matter. Now, the earth is as large as fifty moons combined; hence, it pulls the other much more powerfully than it is itself pulled, and it makes the moon fall toward the earth's center, or, otherwise expressed, it makes the moon revolve about the earth under the impulsive force originally imparted to it. If the moon were larger than the earth, these roles would be exchanged, and our terrestrial globe would be the moon's moon, revolving about it as its satellite[4], if we may use that learned term. But is there nowhere a heavenly body powerful enough to dominate

---

4   A satellite is a smaller heavenly body revolving about a larger one.

the earth and alter its course by the force of attraction, thus causing it to revolve about the larger body as a center? Yes, there is such a dominating body: it is the sun.

That small and exceedingly bright disk, which you perhaps, for fear of exaggerating, hardly venture to call as large as a mill wheel, is an immense globe, compared with which the earth, vast as it appears to us, is a mere nothing. And if the sun looks so small to us, it is because of its immense distance from us. In fact, this distance, as arrived at by the skillful calculations of learned astronomers, is no less than 34,000,000 leagues. This number means nothing to you and would slip out of your mind the next moment unless it were put into words that do have some clear meaning for you. No doubt you have seen, many times, a train of railway cars running at high speed over the rails. Imagine the train to continue at that speed — let us suppose it to be fifteen leagues an hour — indefinitely. At that rate, the train could go from one end of France to the other in a day; and yet, to accomplish the journey from the earth to the sun, if such a journey were possible, our railway train would take 289 years. For such a trip, the best and fastest locomotive ever made by the hand of man would be but as a sluggish snail undertaking to make the tour of the world.

As to the size of the sun, science tells us that it is fourteen hundred thousand times that of the earth — some more figures calling for translation into other terms to make you realize their real significance. Suppose the sun's center to coincide with that of the earth. Under these conditions, the giant would swallow the pygmy as a whale might swallow a minnow, and, extending out into space, the larger body would reach almost as far beyond the moon as the moon is beyond the earth.

Perhaps you do not even yet quite grasp the sun's immensity. Let us try another comparison. To fill the measure known as a liter[5], patient counting has proved that it takes 10,000 grains of wheat of average size. Hence, it would take 100,000

---

5   Slightly more than one quart. – *Translator*.

grains to fill a decaliter, or a ten-liter measure, and 1,400,000 to fill fourteen decaliters. Now imagine fourteen decaliters of wheat in one heap, and by its side a single grain of wheat. This solitary grain will serve to represent the earth, and the heap of fourteen decaliters will represent the sun. Are the comparative sizes now somewhat clearer to you? How small, then, is man, you will perhaps exclaim, in comparison with those vast masses! And how great and powerful must our heavenly Father be, who created both sun and earth and who holds them both as in the hollow of His hand!

You will now perceive without further explanation that upon such a giant of the heavens our diminutive earth can exert no appreciable attractive force. Accordingly, it obeys the law of the stronger and falls toward the sun. But as it is at the same time impelled by the force imparted to it at the beginning of things, its fall toward the sun combines with its forward movement to make it proceed in a curved orbit about that colossus. The earth, then, is a satellite of the sun, revolving about that body and itself accompanied by its own satellite, the moon, which follows it faithfully in its immense orbit with no interruption to its own revolution about the earth. It takes a whole year for the earth to accomplish its journey around the sun, and in this time the moon travels twelve times and somewhat more around us.

You asked, in the first of these talks of ours, why the earth, left wholly without support, does not fall. Now you can answer your own question. To fall is to approach the body that by its attraction causes the fall. If there were nothing outside of our earth, no external attraction would be exerted on our globe, and hence a fall in any direction would be impossible. Under these conditions, the earth would remain forever motionless at that point in space where the hands of the Creator had placed it; or, if once set in motion by that hand, it would go careering through space in a perfectly straight line forever and ever. But the earth feels the attraction of the sun, which turns it from its straight path and, by causing it to fall continually, makes it circle around the sun like a mettlesome steed controlled by the bridle... The force that keeps the earth suspended in the void of heaven, always at nearly the same distance from the giant luminary that attracts and threatens to swallow it, is the original impulse that launched it forth into space. Let us bow in awe, my young readers, before Him whose hand thus set our earth spinning on its course.

CHAPTER IV

THE EARTH'S DAILY MOTION

YOU SAY of the sun that it rises and sets. It rises in the east, you tell me, mounts in splendor to the top of the sky, which it reaches at midday, and then descends from the heights of the celestial vault to disappear in the west and continue its daily round on the other side of the earth. And what you say of the sun, you say also of the stars. Judging from appearances, you think they go from east to west; or, rather, you imagine that the cupola of heaven turns as a whole around the earth, the center of the universe, carrying with it in its movement the multitude of stars fixed there like silver spangles.

Well, now, are we to trust these appearances and say that the sun and the stars really revolve about the earth? If the sun, which is 34,000,000 leagues distant from us, were to revolve about our globe once every day, do you know how far it would have to travel in a minute? More than 100,000 leagues. This inconceivable speed, however, is a mere nothing to what follows. The stars are so many suns not unlike our own in size and brilliancy, but much farther away and consequently much smaller in appearance. The nearest one is about thirty thousand times farther away than the sun. Hence, in order to go around the earth in twenty-four hours, it would have to move, each minute, thirty thousand times 100,000 leagues. And how about the other stars, ten or a hundred or a thousand times as far away and nevertheless obliged to accomplish their journey around the earth always in exactly twenty-four hours? And then remember the prodigious size of the sun. You would have that immense mass, that colossus beside which our earth would look like a mere lump of clay — you would have the sun, I say, move at an impossible speed in the far-distant realms of space in order to give light and heat to the earth? And you would demand of the thousands and thousands of other suns, which we call stars, and which are equally gigantic in size or in many instances much more so, and which are immensely farther from us than our sun — you would demand of these that they all move, at a speed proportioned to their distance from us, once every day about this humble little earth of ours? Such an arrangement would be quite contrary to reason.

How, then, are we to explain the apparent motion of the heavenly bodies? Why is it that the sun and the stars and the planets appear to revolve about the earth, rising at one side of the horizon and setting at the other? It is the simplest thing in the world: the earth turns so as to present its different parts successively to the sun's rays. It spins around like a top, and that explains the whole matter.

Those of you who have ever taken a railway journey must have noticed that the trees, posts, hedges, houses, and so on, along the railway, appear to be in motion: they seem to be moving in the opposite direction to that in which you yourselves are going. You seem to yourselves to be motionless and the objects you are looking at have the appearance of rushing headlong past you. If it were not for the inevitable jolts and jars of the train, the illusion would be complete: you would think the entire landscape to be in rapid motion about you. A carriage drawn by horses, a boat carried downstream by the current, a sailing ship moving before the wind — these offer the same illusion to the passengers. In a word, then, whenever we are borne in one direction by any smoothly moving vehicle, we lose to some extent our consciousness of being in motion, and the nearby objects, which in reality are at rest, appear to us to move in the contrary direction.

Now, the earth turns on its axis from west to east, making one complete turn in twenty-four hours. We are not conscious of this motion, because it is attended by no jolts or shocks of any kind; and so, until we are taught otherwise, we firmly believe ourselves to be at rest and the various heavenly bodies to be in motion about us, their direction being from east to west, or the opposite of our own as we are carried around by the earth's daily motion. This apparent movement, then, that we attribute to sun and stars, is an illusion of precisely the same nature as that which makes trees and other objects appear to be racing past us when on a swiftly moving railway train.

Two movements, therefore, we must ascribe to this earth of ours: first, one that carries it in a curved path about the sun once every twelve months; and, secondly, one by which it turns around on its axis once in twenty-four hours. When you boys spin a top, you have a good example of two movements like those of the earth, both going on together. When your top spins on its point in one place — when it "sleeps," as you say — it has only the movement of rotation about its axis; but when you throw it in a certain peculiar way, you know better than I how it circles about on the ground at the same time that it spins on its point. Then it reproduces on a very small scale the double motion of the earth, its spinning on its point representing the earth's rotary motion on its axis, and its circling about on the ground representing the earth's wide sweep about the sun.

You can further familiarize yourselves with the earth's double motion in the following manner. Place a round table in the middle of the room, and on this table set a lighted candle to represent the sun; then circle about the table while spinning on your toes. Each spin you make corresponds to one rotation of the earth on its axis, while your movement around the table corresponds to the earth's yearly journey around the sun. Notice that in whirling about as you move, you present successively to the rays of the candle your face, your cheek, the back of your head, and your other cheek, your head taking the place of the earth in this exercise, and every part of it being in turn exposed to the rays of the candle or shaded from those rays. The earth goes through the same process on a vastly larger scale, presenting its different parts, one after another, to the rays of the sun. It is day for the region that faces the sun, night for the opposite one. Such is the very simple explanation of the regular succession of day and night. As to the movement of the earth around the sun, we shall soon see that it causes the seasons.

Suppose we wish to illustrate with an orange the rotary motion of the earth: we first run a knitting needle through the orange and then make the orange turn on the needle. The name "axis," which I have already used, we will give to our knitting needle passing through the fruit, and the name "poles" to the opposite points where the needle pierces the skin. To make the matter clearer to our mind's eye, we imagine the earth to be pierced, like the orange, with a long needle around which the daily rotation takes place. This imaginary needle is called the axis of the earth, just as the real needle passing through the orange we called the axis of the orange, and the points where the imaginary needle pierces the earth's surface are likewise known as the poles. Accordingly, the earth's axis may be defined as the imaginary line on which the earth turns once around every twenty-four hours, and the poles as the two opposite points where the axis pierces the earth's surface.

In appearance, the sky is to us the inside of a hollow globe, of which we occupy the center. On account of the earth's rotation from west to east, this celestial globe, by an illusion already explained, appears to us to turn in just the opposite direction, or from east to west, while the earth seems to remain at rest. Now, this apparent rotation of the sky takes place about the same axis as that on which the earth makes its daily turn. An example will make all this clear to you.

Imagine an orange strung like a bead on a long horizontal wire in the middle of a room, and on this orange imagine a gnat. If the orange turns around on this wire, do you suppose the insect clinging to its skin is conscious of the motion? Certainly not. The various points of the orange-skin visible to the gnat always remaining at the same distance from it, the insect will think itself motionless; but as the floor, ceiling, and walls of the room come one after another into view, the gnat will seem to itself to see the room turning around on the wire, so that the axis on which the orange really turns will be to the deluded insect the axis of the apparent rotation of the room. Imagine the wire long enough to reach from one wall of the room to the opposite wall. The two points where it touches the walls will appear motionless to the gnat, while the other parts of the walls will have the appearance of describing circles, larger or smaller according to their distance from the wire or axis.

Now let the orange be replaced by the earth, the wire by the earth's axis, the walls and ceiling of the room by the vault of heaven, and the gnat by an observer ignorant of astronomy. This observer will believe himself motionless, and will see the sky turning on the prolonged terrestrial axis in the opposite direction to his own actual movement. Each point of the celestial cupola appears to him to describe a circle around this axis — except two points that remain at rest and correspond to the two ends of the earth's axis prolonged in both directions until it touches the inner surface of our imaginary celestial globe. These two points are called the celestial poles, and each pole occupies that point on the celestial globe that is opposite the corresponding terrestrial pole.

The foregoing will enable you to understand how the position of the earth's axis can be determined, even though that axis is invisible, being purely imaginary. You merely have to notice which star it is that does not change its place, does not circle about as the night advances; or, if you can find none that appears to remain quite motionless, you note the one that describes the smallest circle. It is in the center of this circle, the smallest of all those described by the stars, that the north pole of our celestial globe is found; and it is toward this point that the earth's axis is directed. A similar scrutiny of the skies in the southern hemisphere would determine the position of the other celestial pole, which the convexity of the earth hides from us in the northern hemisphere.

The star nearest to the celestial pole within our view is called the pole star. It is not quite motionless, but describes a very small circle about the pole. To find it, one stands on a clear night in an open spot so as to face the part of the sky that would be on the left hand if one were watching the sunrise. (I take it for granted that you already know in which direction to look for the rising sun.) One thus standing will see, above the horizon, a group of stars, a constellation, called the Great Bear. This constellation is composed of four rather bright stars arranged in a kind of oblong, and three others in an irregular line at one of the corners of the oblong. By reason of its brightness and size, the Great Bear can hardly fail to arrest the attention, for in that part of the sky where it is to be seen there are no stars comparable with it for brilliancy. Moreover, because of its position near the pole it is visible at all hours of the night. In circling about the celestial axis, it is to be seen, sometimes higher, sometimes lower in the sky; but to observers in our part of the world it never disappears below the horizon. The accompanying illustration shows you the shape of the constellation we are discussing. Four stars form the body of the bear, and three others its tail.

What is this figure drawn about the seven stars of the constellation? What is the meaning of this ferocious beast, stiffening its tail in anger, showing its teeth, and raising one paw as if about to claw some prey? Never have we seen anything like that in the sky. This picture is purely imaginary. To find their way about amid the multitude of stars, astronomers have agreed to divide the firmament into various regions to which they give names that are usually arbitrary or, sometimes, drawn from a vague resemblance to certain animals and objects. In short, they have agreed, for the sake of convenience, to enclose each of these celestial regions within the outline of the animal or object that gives

FIGURE 8

its name to the star group in question. Thus the accompanying figure, representing a bear, embraces within itself the portion of the sky known by astronomers as the Great Bear. Included in this portion of celestial space are a number of stars, of which only seven are noteworthy, and they are the seven represented in our illustration. The others are left out. So it is that the name "Great Bear" applied to the part of the sky we are speaking of is merely a matter of convention. Let us even acknowledge that it is an ill-chosen name, for in order to include three of the principal stars of the constellation, we have to give the bear an unduly large tail, the animal in real life having hardly any. Another name is sometimes given to this constellation — that of "David's Chariot." In this case, the four stars grouped in an oblong form the chariot, and the three others the pole of the chariot.

Not far from the Great Bear, sometimes above it, sometimes below it, sometimes on one side or the other, according to the time of the observation, another group of seven stars can be seen, arranged in the same way as the seven we have just been talking about, only they are less bright and cover less extent. Four of them are arranged in an imperfect square, while the three others extend from one corner of this square and form a tail. This smaller constellation is called the Little Bear. Notice that the Little Bear's tail always points in a direction opposite to that of the Great Bear's tail, and also that the star P, at the end of the Little Bear's tail, is the brightest of the group.

Well, this star, P, is the pole star, the star that in our heavens remains almost at rest while the others sweep around in circles, larger or smaller, from east to west. Accordingly, it is near this star that the earth's axis, if prolonged, would touch the imaginary over-arching sky. An easy way to find the polar star, when one is familiar with the Great Bear, is as follows: Through the two stars nearest to the Great Bear's head, run an imaginary straight line, and prolong it through and beyond the Bear's back until it reaches a star that is brighter than those about it. This bright star is the polar star. Any error in this observation may be checked by noticing whether the star thus found ends the tail of a small constellation similar to the Great Bear, but in an inverse position.

The regions about the earth's two poles take their names from the constellation of the Great Bear. For instance, the ocean lying about the pole facing this constellation is called the Arctic Ocean, from the word *arctos*, which in Greek means *bear*. The ocean on the opposite side of the earth is known as the Antarctic Ocean — that is, the ocean farthest removed from the Bear. We also call the poles by the names *north* and *south*, the one nearer us being the north pole.

From the position of the earth's axis and from the apparent movement of the stars, we get our four principal points of the compass, or the four cardinal points, namely: north, south, east, and west. The earth's axis runs north and south, and the apparent movement of the stars is from east to west. When, in any given situation, we can find out which way is north, which way is south, which way is east, and which way is west, we are said to get our bearings. To do this in the daytime, we stand so as to face that part of the horizon where the sun rises, if we are so far informed; and the east will be in front of us, the west behind us, and north and south on our left hand and right hand respectively. Of course, the quarter where the sun sets will serve equally well. If we face that, we are looking toward the west, while east is behind us, north on our right, and south on our left. To get our bearings at night, if the sky is sufficiently clear, we face the pole star, or the Great Bear; and then north is before us, south behind us, east on our right, and west on our left.

Note also, in this connection, that in place of the word *east* we sometimes use the word orient, which means *rising*; and in place of west we sometimes say *occident*, which means *setting*. Likewise, we use the adjectives *oriental* and *occidental* in the sense of *eastern* and *western*, respectively. Four other important points of the compass are to be noted before we leave the subject. Northeast is halfway between north and east, southeast halfway between south and east. Without further explanation, you will readily see the meanings of northwest and southwest. Finally, on a map, north is toward the top, unless otherwise denoted, south toward the bottom, east on the right hand, and west on the left hand.

When I was telling you about the earth's rotation, I suspected that you were perplexed by a seeming problem of a puzzling nature. If in every twenty-four hours the earth turns completely around, we ought in half that time to go halfway around with the earth and find ourselves in a position the inverse of the one we maintained at the start. At first, our head was up, you say, and our feet down; but twelve hours later their position would be just the opposite: our head would be down, and our feet up. Right end up at the beginning, we should in twelve hours come to be wrong end up. In that unnatural position, why do we not feel uncomfortable? Why do we not fall off? It seems as if, in order not to do so, we should have to cling to the ground; but no one ever seems obliged to do so, and nevertheless, no accident ever happens.

Your query is a reasonable one, but only measurably so. Yes, it is true that twelve hours hence our present position will be inverted; that is, the relative position of head and feet will be reversed. Nevertheless, despite this complete overturn, there will be no danger of our falling off from the earth's surface, nor even the slightest sense of inconvenience of any kind; for the head will always be up, or toward the sky, as the sky surrounds the terrestrial globe, and the feet will be down, or planted on the ground. Understand, once for all, that in boundless space "up" and "down" lose their meanings. Which way would you call "up" and which way "down" in space that is everywhere the same? These words have no meaning except in relation to the earth, where "down" denotes the direction toward the ground, and "up" that toward the sky, which is simply the surrounding space. And so it comes about that as, notwithstanding all terrestrial movements, we are invariably held by the earth's attraction with feet on the ground and head toward the sky (unless we choose to assume or are made to assume some other attitude), we have no difficulty in maintaining our upright position, and no inconvenience or discomfort ever makes us suspect that our position in space is inverted every twelve hours.

Another question may here occur to you. By simply leaving the ground, to which we are held by the earth's attraction — by rising to a certain height in a balloon — ought we not, you will ask, to see the earth turning beneath us? Seas and their islands, continents and their empires and forests and mountains, should all pass in succession under the eye of the observer, who would thus in twenty-four hours witness one complete rotation of the earth. What a marvelous sight that must be! What a journey to take, and how far from tiresome it would be! And when this turning of the earth brings around the country we live in, we come down, and there you are! In a comparatively few hours one has seen the whole world without having to move an inch.

Yes, I agree, it would be an admirable way to see the world. But I advise you, if ever you undertake such a journey, to be prudent and go up to a very great height. There are some very lofty mountains on the earth's surface, and if one of them, carried along by the earth's rotation, should find you in its path, you would certainly have no time to get out of the way before receiving such a buffet that it would not take a second one to put you quite out of humor with journeys of that kind. You shall judge for yourselves. Every point on the earth's surface makes one complete turn around the earth's axis every twenty-four hours, though all points do not move with equal speed because the circles they describe are not of equal size. The points most distant from the axis have to make the widest turn, and consequently they move the fastest, while the points near the poles and so having to describe only small circles go slowly, the poles themselves being motionless in relation to the rest of the earth. All this can be very easily demonstrated by means of an orange turning around on a knitting-needle stuck through it. Well, the points farthest from the earth's axis, those that in twenty-four hours have to travel in a circle measuring ten thousand leagues in circumference, are carried along at a speed of about seven leagues a minute. In our part of the world, the speed is less, being about five leagues a minute. That is twenty times as fast as the ordinary speed of a fast locomotive, and almost the speed of a cannonball. Would a mountain advancing upon you at that terrific rate be likely to leave you in a pleasant frame of mind? The little journey that seemed to you so attractive turns out to be highly dangerous. To this danger may be added another consideration that may incline you to abandon the project; and that is that the thing is impossible.

The atmosphere, the layer of air enveloping the earth, is itself in motion with the terrestrial globe of which it forms a part. Consequently, it carries a balloon along with it instead of leaving it stationary as would be necessary if the balloonist were to have the various regions of the earth pass in succession under his eyes. That is now plain enough, you reply, but, all the same, you are sorry the atmosphere has to move along with the surface of the earth, because if it would only stay still one could keep a sharp lookout and dodge the advancing mountaintops, and so enjoy a mode of travel far quicker and easier than any other. It is a pity, you declare, a very great pity.

My young friends, you are reasoning here like the good La Fontaine's cottager, Garo. Let us look into the matter together and see what would happen if the atmosphere remained at rest instead of moving onward with the earth in its rotation. When you run fast you feel the air, even in a calm, caressing your face as if a light wind were blowing. On a railway train in rapid motion you can see the window shades flapping as if from a strong wind, although outside there may be not a leaf stirring. When the train stops there is no more wind; but when it starts again the wind is apparent once more, increasing in force as the train gathers speed. So we see that wind can be produced in two ways, — by movement of the air against objects at rest, and by movement of objects against the air at rest. The first way is that of ordinary wind, the second that of wind created by a railway train in motion.

You will now see that if the atmosphere were at rest, all objects on the earth's surface — excepting, of course, those at or near the poles — would strike this motionless layer of air with terrific force, and there would always be raging on the earth's surface a hurricane of extreme violence, as if the atmosphere itself were moving in one mass at a speed of seven leagues per minute for certain regions and of five for France. Now, in the most furious of hurricanes, the wind's velocity is, at most, three-quarters of a league per minute; and yet its force is such that trees are uprooted, piles of stones swept away like dust, and houses completely overturned. What, then, would be the effect of a velocity ranging from seven to nine times as great and never slackening? Nothing could withstand such a tempest, a tempest that would even make the mountains themselves tremble and totter. Tell me, now, when the earth was set in motion on its axis would it have been better to make the atmosphere motionless?

CHAPTER V

SEASONS AND CLIMATES

THE EARTH circles about the sun, which by the force of attraction holds it to one unchanging orbit; and this journey is accomplished in very nearly 365¼ days, at the end of which the same journey is begun again, and so on indefinitely. At the rate of 27,000 leagues an hour, the enormous ball goes rolling through space, without pivot or support of any kind, yet never departing from the imaginary line traced for it by a divine geometry. So swift is its motion that it makes you dizzy even to think of it; but it is at the same time so gentle that only by reflection do we arrive at any conception of it. Now, while the earth thus circles about the sun, it turns on its own axis, each of these turns taking twenty-four hours and producing day and night alternately for every part of the globe. But it does not turn with its axis always straight up and down, as one might express it, before the sun. It is slanted a little, in respect to the plane in which the earth's orbit lies, and this slant remains always the same; that is, the axis points always the same way; or, in other words, its line of direction at any point in the orbit is parallel to its line of direction at any other point.

Figure 9 shows us the four principal positions of the earth in its yearly journey about the sun. It is at A when summer begins, June 21; at B when autumn begins, September 22; at C when winter begins, December 21; and, finally, at D when spring begins, March 20. Summer is the time the earth takes to cover the part of its orbit between A and B. Autumn corresponds to the part of the orbit between B and C, winter to that between C and D, and spring to that between D and A. Note carefully

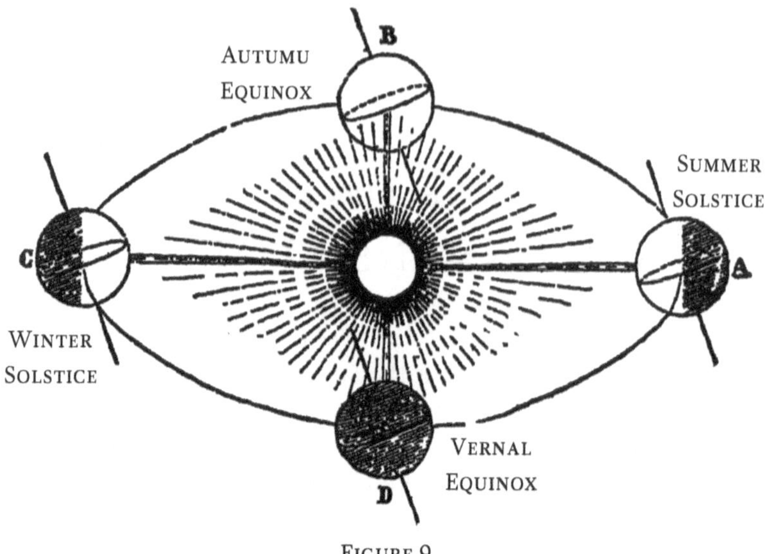

FIGURE 9

in the diagram that the imaginary line representing the earth's axis is inclined, but always the same way, always in the same direction. From this slanting of the axis and the consequent variety of positions occupied successively by the earth in relation to the sun during the earth's journey through its orbit, we have our four seasons.

Let us suppose the time of the year to be toward the end of June. At no other season does the sun rise so early. At four o'clock in the morning, for our part of the world, it appears on the eastern horizon and begins once more its daily course, flooding us with light and heat for sixteen hours. Its last rays are hardly gone by eight o'clock in the evening. At noon it is not quite over our heads, but almost, so that to see it you have to look nearly straight up. How dazzling it is then, and how hot! Its nearly perpendicular rays fairly deluge the atmosphere with light and penetrate the ground with their beneficent heat. It is the season of our longest days and shortest nights, — days of sixteen hours and nights of eight. By going farther north you would have still longer days and shorter nights. You would even come to places where the sun, rising earlier than here, is up at two o'clock in the morning and sets at ten in the evening; to others where it rises at one and sets at eleven; and to others, again, where the rising and setting occur so nearly together that the sun barely dips below the horizon and then immediately reappears. Finally, by going still nearer the pole you would witness the marvelous spectacle of a sun that does not set at all, but that circles about the observer for weeks and even months at a time without once sinking below the horizon, remaining as plainly visible at midnight as at midday. In those regions, there is then no night.

By traveling in the opposite direction, or southward, you would meet with conditions quite contrary to these: a sun of no dazzling brightness, a low temperature, short days, and nights of increasing length. Finally, at a certain point of approach toward the south pole, you would find no day, the night being continuous. Toward the end of June, therefore, the two halves of the earth, northern and southern, are experiencing opposite conditions: the northern half has long days, short nights, a bright illumination, high temperature, and continuous sunlight about the pole, while the southern half has short days, long nights, a comparatively feeble light, low temperature, and continuous night about the pole.

Nothing could be simpler than the explanation of this unequal division of sunlight between the two poles. Figure 10 shows the earth in its position with reference to the sun when at the point A of the preceding diagram — that is, on June 21. The way

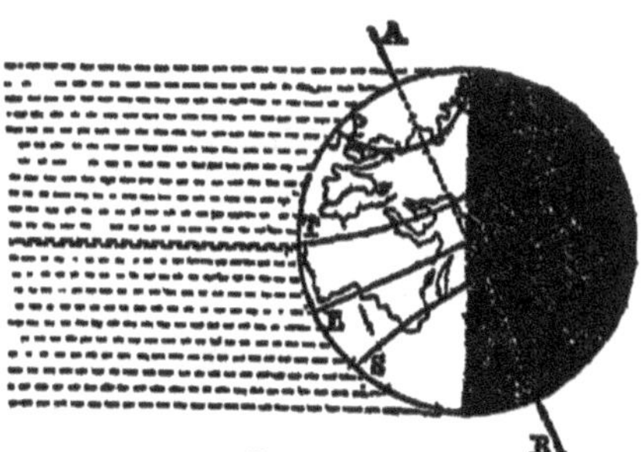

FIGURE 10

in which the earth receives the sun's rays is shown by the dotted parallel lines. As to the sun, if we wished to keep its relative size, it could not be shown here, for if drawn in correct proportions to this figure of the earth, it would be 1½ meters in diameter and placed at a distance of more than 300 meters from this figure. A drawing of such dimensions is out of the question, and so you must imagine, on your left, in the direction of the dotted lines, a globe 1½ meters through and 300 meters away. This will represent the sun, and it is under the rays of this luminous globe that the earth turns on its axis.

I have already told you, and our illustration shows it clearly, that this axis is inclined in such a way that the earth, instead of turning uniformly in an upright position before the sun, turns most of the time at an angle. Furthermore, you clearly understand that the sun can light but one half of any spherical object at a time. Hence it is that one half of the earth has daylight while the other has darkness. This division of light and darkness is shown by the two shades in our picture: the white part faces the sun and has daylight; the shaded part is hidden from the sun and hence is in the dark. On account of the inclination of the earth's axis, the line separating light and darkness, day and night, in the illustration, does not pass through the two poles, but runs in such a way as to include the north pole and exclude the south pole. Now imagine the earth to turn on its axis. Each point of the surface, except at the very poles, will turn in a circle, and this circle will be smaller the nearer it is to either pole. This turning movement at least is clear to you, is it not? Yes, you see it, but still, you think it rather puzzling.

Well, the worst is over if you can manage to see in your mind's eye what no picture can reproduce, — the rotation of a sphere on its axis. That being understood, it is obvious that the part of the earth's surface between the north pole and the circle P, which just touches the dividing line between light and darkness, does not for an instant leave the light and plunge into darkness while the earth makes a complete turn. Accordingly, with the earth's axis inclined as shown in the illustration, there is no night for the region near the north pole, and the twenty-four hours pass without a moment's interruption to the daylight. The circle P is called the Arctic Circle, and it bounds the region where there is no night on June 21.

Now let us pass somewhat farther down in our picture, to those points on the globe that describe the circle T, for instance, when the earth turns on its axis. Each of these points, at first in the region of light, moves with the earth's rotation into the region of darkness. Here, then, we have alternate day and night, but according to the picture, which you should keep constantly in mind, you see plainly enough that the time necessary for a point to traverse the dark portion is less than that occupied in passing through the light part. Hence, for that point night is shorter than day. For other points describing any of the circles not drawn in the picture, but easily imagined, day lengthens and night shortens more and more the nearer those points are to the north pole; while, on the other hand, night lengthens and day shortens more and more the nearer we approach the circle E, called the equator[6]. All that is clear enough if you but look at the picture; and it is equally clear that for any point of the equator the days and nights are of equal length, or twelve hours long, since the part of the equator included in the lighter portion of our picture is exactly equal to the part in the darker portion.

While the northern hemisphere is having long days and short nights, what is the state of affairs in the southern? The illustration will tell us at once. It says that the days are shortening and the nights lengthening as we move southward, for on the one hand the unshaded part diminishes in size, and on the other the shaded part increases. It also tells us that around the south pole is a region not brought into the light by the earth's rotation, and so getting no glimpse of the sun throughout the twenty-four hours. Hence, it is continual night there when the earth assumes the position represented in the diagram. The circle R is called the Antarctic Circle, and it bounds the region where there is no day on June 21.

The sun's rays vary in warmth with the angle at which they strike the earth. When they beat directly down upon us they give more heat than when they come obliquely. A region that receives the sun's rays from directly overhead is very hot, whereas one that receives only slanting rays is likely to be considerably cooler. To realize the truth of this you need only bear in mind that

6　　　The equator is an imaginary circle passing around the earth midway between the two poles. It divides the earth into two equal parts called hemispheres-the northern hemisphere and the southern hemisphere. The word hemisphere means half of a sphere, half of a globe.

when you wish to enjoy the full heat of an open fire you get in front of it, and then if you become too warm you can cool off by moving to one side. In the one instance the heat comes straight to you; in the other it comes obliquely, and so is less powerful. In the same way, the earth, exposed though it constantly is to the sun, does not receive the same amount of heat all over its surface: on some parts the sun's rays beat perpendicularly, or nearly so, while on others they strike more or less obliquely. Hence, at any given time of the year the earth's temperature is far from being uniform throughout; some places have intense heat, others bitter cold; here it is summer, and there it is winter.

If we know what parts of the earth receive the sun's rays from overhead on June 21, we shall know what parts are then likely to be the hottest. I take it for granted you have not forgotten that a line perpendicular to the earth's surface at any point — that is, a vertical line — is one that if prolonged would pass through the center of the earth. In the preceding diagram it is plain that a sunbeam striking the earth at T would pass through its center if prolonged. Hence, it is a vertical ray, a ray straight from the sun directly overhead, and if you stood at T you would receive the sun's heat right on your head. Therefore, at this point the heat is intense, and what is true of T is true of all points in the circle represented as passing through T, because all these points are successively brought at midday into the same position as T with reference to the sun. The circle passing through T in our diagram is called the Tropic of Cancer, and it may be defined as the circle on whose every part the sun shines vertically on June 21.

Nowhere else on the earth's surface are the sun's rays vertical at this date, and, consequently, nowhere else would the sun's rays, if prolonged, pass through the center of the earth. Everywhere else the sun's rays are oblique, and the more so the farther we go, northward or southward, from the Tropic of Cancer. Make this clear to yourselves by studying the diagram. The temperature, then, gradually becomes lower on each side of the tropic. France, lying as it does about halfway between the Tropic of Cancer and the Arctic Circle, never gets the sun's rays from directly overhead, though on June 21 the sun is more nearly overhead than at any other time of the year. Therefore at noon of that day if we wish to look at the sun we have to turn our eyes toward almost the highest point in the sky.

Six months go by and it is winter, the last part of December. What a change! To see the sun at midday you no longer look up at the highest point in the heavens, but lower down, almost straight ahead. And then it is so pale, it seems to give so little warmth! What has happened to it? Is it farther away from the earth, or is its fire dying down? Neither the one nor the other. The sun's fire is not one that dies down; always burning with the same intensity, it always sends forth into space the same abundance of light and heat. The sun is no farther away from the earth; on the contrary, it is slightly nearer[7]. And the days — have you noticed how short they are? The sun does not rise until eight o'clock in the morning, and at four o'clock in the afternoon it has already set. That makes eight hours of day to sixteen of night, or just the opposite of the arrangement in June. Farther north the nights are eighteen, twenty, twenty-two hours long, and the days correspondingly short, or six, four, and two hours long. In the neighborhood of the pole the sun has ceased to show itself and there is no day, the darkness being the same at midday as at midnight.

All this will be clear to you if you look at Figure 11, which shows the earth in the position it occupies on December 21, when it is at Point C of its orbit (Figure 9). The axis still slants at exactly the same angle, having altered not at all in the earth's long journey over the half of its orbit. But the sun's light now comes from the opposite direction because the earth is at the other end of its orbit, on the other side of the sun. No long explanation is necessary here. One sees immediately that from

7   The earth's course around the sun is not exactly circular, but slightly oval, or, in learned language, it is an ellipse of slight eccentricity; and as the sun is a little nearer one end of the oval than the other, the earth is just so much nearer the sun at a certain part of its course than at the opposite part. This part happens to be the point reached by the earth at our winter solstice (Dec. 21). In Fig. 9 the ellipse is so greatly flattened as to give an entirely false notion of the earth's comparative distances from the sun at the different seasons. – *Translator*.

the north pole to the Arctic Circle there is continual night, and that over the whole northern hemisphere the days are shorter than the nights, this difference increasing as one goes northward. It is equally plain that at the equator the days and nights are of equal length, that in the southern

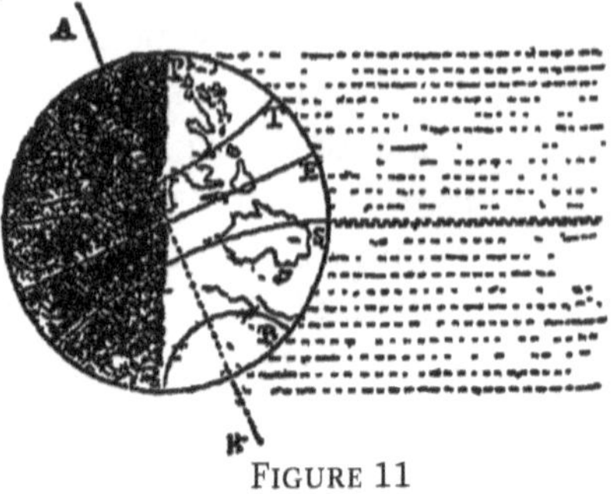

FIGURE 11

hemisphere the days are longer than the nights, and, finally, that between the Antarctic Circle and the south pole there is no night.

As to the sun's rays, you can see that they come from right overhead at the point S, and, consequently, in the course of twenty-four hours, at every other point successively in the circle passing through S; but that they deviate more and more from the vertical as one proceeds northward or southward from this circle. To this circle which passes through S and receives the sun's rays vertically on December 21 is given the name "Tropic of Capricorn."

To sum up briefly: on June 21 the day is long and warm in the northern hemisphere, and short and cold in the southern, whereas on December 21 the hemispheres exchange these conditions and we have long and warm days over the southern half of the earth, with short and cold ones over the northern.

In circling about the sun from point A of its orbit to the opposite point, C, and back again (Figure 9), the earth passes through all the intermediate positions between those we have just been considering. During this transition the dividing line between light and darkness gradually recedes from or approaches one or the other of the poles, which brings about an equally gradual decrease or increase in the length of the day and in the directness of the sun's rays. On September 22 the earth reaches point B, halfway between A and C. In this position it receives the sun's rays vertically at the equator. The dividing line between light and darkness then passes exactly through the two poles, with the result that over the whole earth day and night are of equal length, or twelve hours each. A similar situation occurs on March 20, when the earth is at point D of its orbit. September 22 we call the autumnal equinox, and March 20 the vernal equinox or the spring equinox. The word equinox indicates the equality of day and night at this time, from pole to pole.

June 21 is called the summer solstice, and December 21 the winter solstice. The word solstice denotes the halt of the sun in its apparent gradual ascent, from day to day, toward the point directly overhead. This arrest in its progress occurs, for the northern hemisphere, on June 21, when it begins to descend once more toward the south, where in turn it halts on December 21 and begins to retrace its course. It will of course be understood that this ascent and descent of the sun are only appearances caused by the earth's yearly revolution and the inclination of the earth's axis.

In regard to the distribution of the sun's heat the surface of the earth is divided into five regions or rings called zones. The equator runs through the middle of the region known as the torrid zone, which is bounded, north and south, by the tropics of Cancer and Capricorn respectively. In the torrid zone the sun at midday is always at or near the highest point in the heavens, and its rays strike the ground vertically, or nearly so, causing the high temperature characteristic of this zone. As the nights and days at the equator are throughout the year of equal length, and as they vary but little at any time for the rest of the zone, it comes about that the nightly cooling off is there almost exactly made good by the daily receipt of solar heat, so that the temperature varies but little from one season to another.

In those regions, favored thus as they are by the sun, there is summer from year's end to year's end. The trees never lose their verdure, as ours do in our cold winters, but are covered with blossoms and fruit at all seasons. Here it is that we find forests of palms whose trunks rise in lofty columns to spread their giant parasols of graceful foliage far above all neighboring vegetation; and here, too, there bloom in profusion those gorgeous flowers that adorn our greenhouses but are so sensitive to the cold that our utmost care cannot make them forget the hot sun of their native land. Even more sumptuous than the flowers are the birds that, with their brilliant plumage, vie in splendor with precious stones and costly metals. On the hummingbird's throat gleam the tints of rubies, emeralds, and polished gold. Here roam at will the elephant and the other giants of the animal kingdom that make the earth tremble under their ponderous tread; here is heard the roar of lion and tiger and panther thirsting for blood; and here may be seen the creeping forms of monstrous reptiles, of snakes and lizards cleaving a furrow through the tall grasses as would a tree trunk dragged endwise. Amid this exuberance of plant and animal life man alone cuts but a poor figure. On each side of the torrid zone lies a region known as temperate, — the north temperate zone on one side, the south temperate zone on the other. These zones are themselves bounded on one side by the tropics (Cancer and Capricorn), separating them from the torrid zone, and on the other by the circles (Arctic and Antarctic), separating them from the polar regions or zones. The inhabitants of the temperate zones never have the sun directly overhead, its rays striking the ground obliquely at all seasons, but much more so in winter than in summer. Consequently, the temperature is lower than in the torrid zone. In each temperate zone the length of the longest day of the year depends on the distance of the given place from the equator, and may be fourteen, fifteen, sixteen, and so on up to twenty-four hours long.

In this season of the longest days, the sun's heat steadily accumulates because each day's increase is not dissipated by the nightly cooling off that follows, the night being too short to use up the supply, so that the temperature mounts as the season advances. With the approach of winter, however, these conditions are reversed, and the nights gain increasingly on the days, causing a fall in temperature due to the longer and longer period of cooling in each twenty-four hours. From these two causes — the variable obliquity of the sun's rays and the difference between the length of the days and that of the nights — results the considerable variation in temperature between the hottest and the coldest seasons of the year in the temperate zones.

This difference gives us our seasons — spring with its warm breezes that make the flowers bloom, summer and its grain fields yellowing under the sun's heat, autumn with its harvest of luscious grapes, and winter as the season of rest for all vegetation. Though less rich, less varied than the products of the torrid zone, those of the temperate zones are nevertheless more valuable to us. Wheat, grapes, and the most useful of our domestic animals flourish only in a temperate climate. Moreover, it is in such a climate that man develops his greatest activity and utilizes all the resources of his mind, and here are displayed at their best the wonders of art, science, and industry. France, peer among nations, occupies the most favored region to be found in either of the temperate zones.

Beyond the polar circles (Arctic and Antarctic) lie the two remaining zones, known as the frigid zones and extending to the poles. Here the obliquity of the sun's rays and the difference in length between the days and the nights are greater than anywhere else. At the polar circles, the longest day and the longest night are each of twenty-four hours' duration. From the circles, northward and southward, this length gradually increases to six months at the poles, where the sun remains visible without interruption for one half of the year and invisible during the other half, so that the polar year is composed of one day and one night. Now, during these long days, when the sun circles about the spectator without setting, visible at midnight no less than at midday — during these long days, a single one of which amounts to many of ours, or even to weeks or months, according to position — the heat from the sun's rays, oblique though those rays are, accumulates so as to be at last hardly endurable. In some sheltered bays, navigators have even seen the tar of their vessels melt and run under the heat of this continuous sun.

But when winter comes and the nights in their turn are from twenty-four hours to six months long, the cold becomes intense. The few explorers that have passed the winter in this severe climate tell us that the mercury in the thermometer freezes, which means a temperature of at least 40° below zero. It is said that wine, beer, and other fermented liquors turn into blocks of ice in the casks; that a glass of water thrown into the air falls in frozen spray; that the breath from the lungs crystallizes into little needles of frost as it issues from the nostrils; and that a piece of metal carelessly taken hold of gives a sharp twinge of pain and destroys the skin it has touched. The sea freezes to a great depth and thus adds to the apparent extent of the dry land, from which it differs not at all to the eye, having, like it, fields of snow and crags of ice.

For weeks at a time, the sun does not show itself above the horizon, and there is no difference between day and night, or rather there is one continuous night, the same at midday as at midnight. However, when the sky is clear, the darkness is not complete by a good deal, the light from moon and stars, helped out by the shining whiteness of the snow, producing a sort of twilight sufficient for purposes of seeing. Furthermore, toward the north pole, the sky is lighted up at intervals by the splendors of the aurora borealis, an electric display that darts its rays of light upward to the zenith like some giant piece of fireworks. In this wan twilight, the tribes of these desolate regions, with the help of sledges drawn by teams of unruly dogs, hunt those fur-bearing animals whose warm white coats form an important article of commerce.

Short and thickset, the denizen of these harsh climates divides his time between hunting and fishing, the former yield-ing him skins for his clothing and the latter supplying him with food. Dried fish, kept until half-decayed, and rancid whale oil, disgusting though they would be to us, are the dishes that fur-nish a feast for his famishing stomach. Fishing also procures him fuel for his fire, which he feeds with fish bones and slices of whale blubber. In fact, wood is here quite unknown, as no trees, however hardy, can stand the rigors of winter. Willows and birches, so stunted as to be nothing but shrubbery, are the only trees found as far north as northern Lapland, where the raising of barley, one of the hardiest of cultivated plants, ceases. Beyond that, all woody shrubs come to an end, and in summer only a few scanty tufts of grass and moss are to be found hur-riedly ripening their seeds in sheltered hollows of rocks. Still farther north, there is not even a complete melting of snow and ice in the summer; hence, the ground is never bare, and no vegetation is possible.

CHAPTER VI

THE FLATTENING OF THE EARTH AT THE POLES

TTACH A cord securely to a glass half full of water and
then whirl it around like a sling, as shown in Figure 12. In
being thus whirled, the glass is sometimes upside down, sometimes more or less inclined, and yet, if it is turned fast enough,
despite its inverted or inclined position, not a drop of water is

FIGURE 12

spilled. On the contrary, the liquid is held against the bottom of the glass as if by some pressure. But if the glass were arrested in its course and made to remain a moment in an inverted or a sufficiently inclined position, it is plain that there would be an outflow of water. Therefore, it must be the whirling motion that keeps the water in the glass at every turn, by pressing it against the bottom.

Tie a stone to the end of a string and whirl it rapidly. Do you not feel the string stretching tighter and tighter as the stone goes faster? Make it go faster still, but see that no one is near. Increase the speed yet more and — crack — stretched beyond its strength, the string breaks, and away goes the stone. In its rapid whirl, the stone pulled and tugged and tried to free itself from your hand at the center of its circular motion; and that tug caused the stretching of the string. When the tug became strong enough, the string, stretched to excess, finally broke. In like manner, any object made to revolve about a center is, from the very fact of this motion, subjected to a peculiar thrust that tends to send it off from the point around which it turns. This thrust is known as centrifugal force, and it increases with the rapidity of the circular motion. It is this centrifugal force that presses the water against the bottom of the rapidly whirling glass and prevents its running out despite the inclined or even inverted position of the container. So, too, it is centrifugal force that stretches the string tied to a whirling stone, and the string finally breaks if the speed becomes too great.

Centrifugal force tends to distort a sphere rotating on its axis; and if the substance of the sphere is soft enough to yield to this outward pressure, the sphere will become enlarged at its equator and correspondingly flattened at its poles. To prove this by experiment, the difficulty lies in finding a sphere of the requisite softness; but it is a difficulty that can be overcome, as I will now explain to you. Oil poured

into water floats on the surface; poured into alcohol, it sinks. It is lighter than water, heavier than alcohol. But in a mixture of the right proportions of water and alcohol, the oil remains in the middle of the liquid and takes the form of a perfect sphere the size of an apple, we will say, supposing the quantity of oil to be sufficient. This is illustrated in Figure 13.

Gently upheld amid the enveloping liquid that acts as its support, this huge drop of oil astonishes the observer and calls to his mind the earth suspended in space. Now let us suppose the ball of oil to be pierced through its center by a long needle which some clockwork mechanism causes to turn rapidly about the imaginary line passing lengthwise through the needle's middle. The slight friction of the needle against the oil touching it starts the globe of oil little by little until it is all moving about the needle in one mass. As soon as it begins thus to turn, it is seen to flatten a little about the two opposite

FIGURE 14

points where the needle emerges — that is, at the two poles — and to swell slightly at the part midway between, or at the equator. This is shown in Figure 14. Furthermore, the polar flattening and the equatorial swelling become more pronounced as the rotation increases in velocity. Nothing of the sort would be observed if the sphere were a solid, resistant substance, because such a substance would be too hard to yield to centrifugal force unless the latter were far greater than we could produce with our simple mechanism.

It is easy enough to account for the distortion of a liquid sphere rotating on its axis. The parts at or near the equator move the fastest because they describe the largest circles, whereas those about the poles move the slowest. At the equator, therefore, centrifugal force is most powerful, while at the poles it is weakest. Hence, the equatorial portion, yielding to the outward thrust of centrifugal force, must move to a greater distance from the axis, and this displacement is made good by the adjacent matter, which hastens to fill the void thus created, so that gradually there is produced a flattening where the influence of the centrifugal thrust is least felt — that is, at the poles.

It is true that the earth is not, as is our globe of oil, composed wholly of fluid matter; but the oceans cover about three quarters of its surface, and so we may apply to this liquid portion what we have just learned about centrifugal force. We are in a position to understand that on account of the earth's rotation, the oceans have lost their perfectly rounded surface and have become depressed at the poles and swollen at the equator, where an immense ring of water has been raised and is kept in place by centrifugal force.

Nor is that all. Exact measurements have proved that the solid parts of the earth's surface — the dry land, the continents — present the same distortions as the seas; so that the earth as a whole is flattened at the poles and swollen at the equator, as if its entire mass had once been fluid and in hardening with the passage of time had preserved permanently the slightly irregular shape given to it by centrifugal force.

Let us see how this remarkable fact is proved. The earth's attraction, which causes the fall of bodies, varies in strength with the distance of the attracted body from the center of the earth. It increases if the distance diminishes and diminishes if the distance increases. To Newton is due the signal honor of discovering the law governing this variation. At the surface of the earth, the fall of a body takes place at a distance from the earth's center equal to half the diameter of the earth, and it is there that the distance covered in the first second of a body's fall is 4.9 meters. If the attracted body were removed twice as far from the earth's center, it would still fall when left without support, but its fall would be only one quarter as fast, which means that in the first second of fall, the distance covered would be only a quarter of 4.9 meters, or 1.225 meters. If removed three, four, or five times as far from the earth's center, the attracted body would fall only one ninth, one sixteenth, or one twenty-fifth (as the case might be) of 4.9 meters in its first second of fall. This law of attraction, discovered by Newton, is briefly expressed thus: The force of attraction varies inversely as the square of the distance[8].

Hence, a stone would fall faster if dropped from the hand of a man standing in a plain than from the hand of one standing on a mountain because the former would be nearer the center of the earth than the latter. This could be proved by experiment, but it would be a very delicate operation because the difference in distance of the two places from the earth's center is relatively very slight. Let us try an easier way.

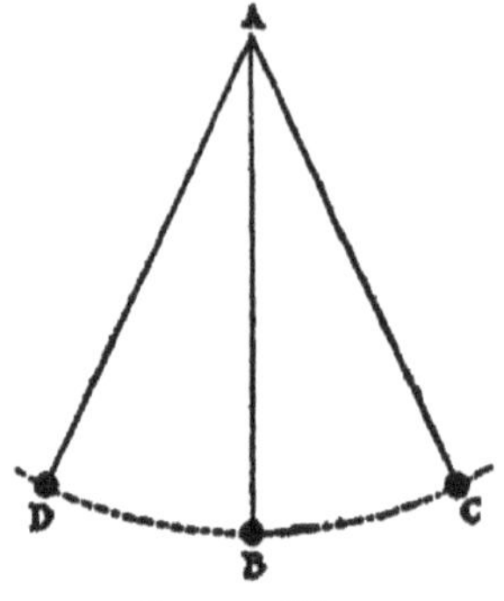

FIGURE 15

A leaden ball is tied to the end of a cord, as shown in Figure 15. If the free end of the cord is fastened somewhere, as at A, the ball, after a few movements, remains at rest, and the cord, as you will readily perceive, assumes a vertical direction. Let the line AB indicate this direction. Now move the ball to position C and release it. If the cord did not hold it, the ball would fall vertically, but on account of the cord, it cannot do this; and so, drawn by the earth's attraction in the only direction allowed by the cord holding it to the point of suspension, it slides downward through the arc of the circle CD, whose center is at the same point of suspension. Thus, it reaches position B, which it passes and ascends the arc to D. Arrived there, it falls again, or, to express it better, it slides down again and returns to position C, or very nearly to that position, which it leaves once more to come back to D; and so on for a considerable time until the resistance of the air stops its movement, a gradual process if the suspension at A is carefully made.

Each of these swings of the ball from C to D and from D back to C is called an oscillation, and the apparatus itself, the ball with its cord, is known as a pendulum. The swinging of the pendulum

8   The square of a number is the product of that number multiplied by itself. The law here given is true not only of the earth's attraction, but also of the attraction exerted by the sun, the moon, and the other heavenly bodies.

is due to the force that makes bodies fall when left unsupported; in short, it is due to the earth's attraction. Each oscillation is a kind of fall hindered by the suspending cord, and, hence, the pendulum, its length remaining the same, must swing faster with any increase in the attraction that makes it move; that is, it will swing faster if taken to a point nearer the center of the earth. On the other hand, it will swing more slowly if the force of attraction is lessened, or, in other words, if the pendulum is farther away from the earth's center. Experiment does, in fact, prove that a pendulum of a given length swings less rapidly at the top of a high mountain than down in a plain. Hence, to ascertain whether any given points of the earth's surface are equally distant from the center, all we have to do is to observe how the pendulum behaves at these points. If it swings faster at one place and slower at another, it is proof that the former is nearer the center of the earth than the latter.

Let us suppose an observer to count exactly the swings of a pendulum of a given length at various places, each at the same distance from the next, between the equator and the pole, and all at sea level. At the equator, he counts, we will say, 4000 swings in an hour; at a certain distance north of the equator, he counts 4001; still farther north, he counts 4002; then, still going northward, 4003, and, upon advancing once more, 4004. Where we live, let us suppose the number of swings to rise to 4008, and near the pole, to 4012. It is evident that if the pendulum swings back and forth more times at one place than at another, the swings must be faster. The fact that the pendulum swings more times in an hour at the poles than at the equator means that it swings faster, which in turn means that the earth's attraction at the poles is greater than at the equator, or, in other words, that the poles are nearer the earth's center than is the equator. Consequently, the earth, land as well as water, must be flattened at the poles and swollen at the equator. Therefore, it is extremely probable that the now solid portion of the terrestrial globe was originally fluid enough to be distorted by the action of centrifugal force, just as the globe of oil is distorted in the experiment I have described.

What a wonderful thing the pendulum has now taught us! Those solid rocks that form the firm crust of the earth, those mighty boulders, the very framework of continents, those blocks of granite that blunt the edge of steel tools rather than let themselves be cut, were in some former age as fluid as is iron when it is poured, molten, from a fiery furnace. Before lifting their heads above the clouds, the mountains themselves were, perhaps, part of some ocean of liquefied mineral matter, for a condition of uniform fluidity can alone explain the general distortion of the earth such as is revealed by the swinging of the pendulum.

But, you will perhaps ask, does the pendulum really tell the truth? Have not the observers counting the pendulum's swings all over the earth made some mistake in their count? No, I reply, for observations of this kind have been and still are made with the greatest care by many investigators; and always — understand, always — the pendulum's oscillations in a given time increase in number with nearer approach to either pole. Furthermore, when clockwork instead of a simple pendulum is used, the same result follows. A clock is a rather complicated mechanism with various cog-wheels geared together for the purpose of making the hands on the dial turn. A spring or a weight acts as motive power to the whole. To regulate its working, to prevent too fast or too slow a movement of the machinery, there is in every clock a very important attachment that goes back and forth at a regular rate and maintains a like regularity in the working of the machinery. In a pendulum clock, this regulator is the pendulum itself. The faster it swings, the faster goes the machinery it regulates, including the hands on the dial; and if it slows up, the machinery also will slow up.

Now, it has been found that clocks made and regulated here with the utmost exactness go too slowly when they are taken to the equator or its neighborhood, and too fast when carried toward either pole. There is no exception to this. Observed for the first time in the seventeenth century, this fact excited universal astonishment. What, it was asked, is the mysterious agency that seems to lay a finger on the mechanism to make it go slower at the equator and faster at the poles? Newton, the sublime dreamer who asked himself why apples fall, has the credit of finding the answer to this other query. He said to himself what you are now saying to yourselves: If a clock is too slow at the equator, it is because the lessened force of the earth's attraction there makes the pendulum swing more slowly; and if it is too fast at the poles, it is because the increased force of attraction there makes the pendulum swing faster. Hence, we infer that the earth is swollen at the equator and flattened at the poles.

To the proof furnished by the pendulum, other and more direct proofs have been added. At different times, extensive geometrical measurements have been undertaken, especially when it was proposed to fix for all time the length of the meter on which our metric system is based. From the total of these measurements, it was found that the pendulum had not lied, and that the earth is really distorted in the manner that the swinging of the pendulum had indicated. It has even been found possible to estimate the amount of this distortion. If we suppose the semi-diameter of the earth (that is, the distance from the earth's surface to its center) at the equator to be divided into 300 equal parts, the semi-diameter at the poles will contain only 299 of these parts. In other words, the earth's surface is about five leagues nearer its center at the poles than at the equator. This difference is more than twice the height of our highest mountain, and yet it does not appreciably alter the earth's spherical shape. On a globe two meters in diameter, the polar flattening, if made to correspond to that of the earth, would amount to only about three millimeters.

Expressed in meters, the earth's equatorial semi-diameter is 6,377,398 meters, and its polar semi-diameter is 6,356,080 meters, the difference being 21,318 meters.

CHAPTER VII

THE INTERIOR OF THE EARTH

I AM going to take you, now, down into the earth, several kilometers beneath our feet.

And what, you ask, are we going to find in the bowels of the earth? Shall we hit upon the secret of the metals, see gold in the process of filtering into the fissures of the solid rock, and see how iron, copper, and tin form themselves into layers amid the mineral substances of the earth? Are we about to witness the crystallization of precious stones and explore the treasure vaults where emeralds, carbuncles, and diamonds are made and stored? It is said that there are immense riches in the earth's capacious bosom.

No, I reply, it is not veins of gold and silver or grottoes encrusted with rubies that I propose to show you today. My plan is simply to study with you the earth's inner structure. We shall bring back from our underground journey no precious stones or costly metals, but something better — sublime conceptions of the architecture of this globe of ours and a high admiration for its divine Architect.

Man's deepest excavations for the mining of mineral wealth are insignificant compared with the distance from the surface of the earth to its center. These excavations do hardly more than scratch the earth's surface. We cannot, then, profit by the miner's labors to study by direct observation the nature of the earth's interior. But what our bodily eyes cannot accomplish, on account of our inability to descend far enough into the bowels of the earth, the mind's eye achieves at least in a general way by means of a very simple and modest instrument, but one that has many secrets to tell us. I refer to the pendulum. A leaden ball attached to a cord has shown us by its manner of swinging, slower in one place, faster in another, that the earth, molded in part by centrifugal force, is flattened at the poles and swollen at the equator. The same leaden ball will tell us what substances compose that part of the earth which is inaccessible to the miner's pick.

The pendulum's swing is due to the earth's attraction. But every molecule of the earth's substance plays its part in this attraction. Not only do the particles nearest the pendulum attract it and make it swing, but also the particles deepest down, at the earth's center, and on every side — in fact, everywhere without exception. You understand, then, that if God had chosen to make the earth contain two, three, or four times as much matter as it does now contain, the attraction exerted on the pendulum would be two, three, or four times as great, and, consequently, the pendulum would swing so much faster[9]. Its rate of swinging, therefore, when it is of a given length, depends on the quantity of matter that the earth contains.

Accordingly, it is possible, by calculations too complicated for us, to learn from the pendulum's behavior the quantity of matter composing the earth. It has thus been found that if all the substances entering into the structure of our globe — air, water, stones, metals, minerals of all kinds — were thoroughly mixed together, each cubic decimeter of this homogeneous mixture would weigh 5 ½ kilograms. But the air of our atmosphere weighs only 13/10 grams per cubic decimeter; water, 1 kilogram; marble, building stone, granite, the various kinds of soil, and nearly all the substances composing the earth's outer layer, only 2 or, at most, 3 kilograms. Consequently, the deeper layers must be of matter much heavier than these, as otherwise the average weight of 5½ kilograms per cubic decimeter could not be reached. Hence, we conclude that the earth's interior

---

9   In a general way, the attraction exerted by a body is proportioned to the quantity of matter that body contains, or in other words, to its mass. Hence, the Newtonian law already mentioned is to be completed thus: Attraction varies directly as the mass and inversely as the square of the distance.

is composed of materials of considerable weight and probably metallic in their nature. That is what the pendulum tells us.

A very simple experiment will tell us a little more. We pour into a bottle a small quantity of some very heavy liquid, as mercury, for example, otherwise known as quicksilver; or, if this is lacking, we can use a handful of common shot, small enough to be sufficiently mobile for our purpose. Into the same bottle, we next pour a like quantity of water, and then about as much oil, taking care to leave a layer of air at the top. We now cork the bottle and shake it well. The four substances it contains — lead, water, oil, and air — will all mingle so completely that while the shaking continues, we can no longer distinguish any one of them. But stop shaking, and little by little, order is restored, the various substances separating and each forming a distinct layer. The metal, on account of its greater weight, goes to the bottom; the water, being heavier than oil or air, takes its place next above the mercury (or the lead, according to which is used); the oil remains on top of the water; and the air, the lightest of the four substances, perches at the upper end of the bottle. Thus, after various fluid substances have been well mixed together, order is restored if they are allowed to stand in a state of quiet: the substances separate and take their position one over another according to their comparative weight, the heaviest going to the bottom, the lightest to the top.

The importance of a law is not proportioned to its complexity, and the simplest causes often produce the most momentous results. The very elementary principle governing the superposition of fluid substances in the order of their weight played a most important part in the arrangement of the earth's materials, as is evident if we but take the trouble to look about us. The light envelope of air, the atmosphere, is the earth's outermost layer, beneath which comes the expanse of oceans extending over the greater part of what we call the earth's surface and, finally, the solid ground, heavier than water, serves as a bed to receive and hold the oceans. Far beneath the ground the same law continues to hold good; for, as the pendulum has just told us, the substances composing the earth's interior are heavier than those at or near the surface and increase in weight the lower they lie — that is, the nearer the earth's center.

This regular arrangement, or stratification, of the earth's materials in the order of their weight is easy enough to understand in regard to fluid substances such as air and water; but how is it that the same law holds good for the solid substances, for the rocks and the minerals of all kinds constituting the earth's interior? Why is it that at a distance of some leagues beneath our feet lie substances heavier than those at the surface? Shall we explain this by saying that the regular arrangement in layers, the heavier under the lighter, after the manner of our lead, water, oil, and air in the experiment, points to an original fluid condition of all the earth's constituent substances? Did the earth spurt forth from some celestial furnace as an enormous globe of molten metal? Who knows? Let us inquire a little further.

The variations in temperature from one season to another are felt only at the earth's surface. Only a short distance underground the thermometer registers the same temperature in winter as in summer. While the thermometer indicates a decline of twenty, thirty, forty degrees[10], or even more, when winter succeeds to summer, it needs only a descent of a comparatively few meters below the surface of the earth to find a constant temperature throughout the year. This constant temperature is halfway between that of summer and that of winter at the surface; or, more exactly, it is the mean temperature of the locality.

By the mean temperature of a place is meant the temperature the place would have throughout the year if all the solar heat received annually were distributed evenly instead of unevenly and according to seasons. This is found by apportioning among all the days of the year the sum of the mean temperatures of the 365 days; that is, we divide this sum by the number of days in a

---

10   Degrees centigrade are meant here, as elsewhere in the book. The centigrade thermometer, which is thermometer used in France, as also in southern Europe generally, is so named from its division into 100 degrees between the point at which water freezes and that at which it boils, at the sea-level. In our thermometer (Fahrenheit) this range of temperature is divided into 180 (that is, 212 – 22) degrees. Hence, a degree centigrade is equal to nine fifths of a degree Fahrenheit, and a degree Fahrenheit equals five ninths of a degree centigrade. In converting centigrade reading to Fahrenheit let it be remembered that our zero is 32° Fahrenheit below the French zero. – *Translator.*

year. The mean temperature of a single day is obtained by noting the highest and lowest reading of the thermometer within the twenty-four hours and dividing their sum by two. In the north of France, the mean temperature is from 10° to 11° above zero; in the south, it rises to 14° or 15°. Now, it is precisely this mean temperature that a thermometer registers all year round if placed twenty meters underground.

In penetrating farther into the earth's interior, we find that after one leaves the layer of mean temperature, the heat increases one degree for every twenty or thirty meters of descent. The general rule of added heat at added depth holds good everywhere, having been verified in all parts of the world and in all climates; but what varies with the locality is the thickness of the layer that must be penetrated in order to attain an added degree of temperature. The nature of the soil, which is different in different places, is undoubtedly the cause of this variation. Let us cite a few examples from the innumerable observations that have been made.

A thermometer carried to the depth of 421 meters in the mines of Dolcoath[11], England, and observed at short intervals for eighteen months, remained stationary at 24°, the temperature of the upper layers being about 10°, which gives an increase of one degree of heat for every thirty meters of depth. In an oil well bored at Newcastle, the temperature at the depth of 483 meters exceeded by fourteen degrees that of the upper layers. Here the increase of heat is one degree for every thirty-four meters. Again, the increase ascertained from observations made in the oil wells of Northumberland is one degree for every twenty-four meters. The deepest excavation miners have ever made is at Kuttemberg in Bohemia. These lowest depths are no longer accessible. At the extreme depth there attained, 1151 meters, the thermometer indicated a constant temperature of 40°. Our very hottest summers never reach this point, which is attained only in the torrid zone. Thus, while above ground winter may be raging with utmost severity, there is found at the bottom of

11   Possibly Dalkeith, Scotland, is meant. – *Translator.*

the mine the insupportable heat of the equatorial regions. In the mines of Monte-Massi in Tuscany, the temperature is still higher, although the depth is less. The thermometer has been known to register 42° at the depth of no more than 370 meters. From these examples, which one might add to indefinitely without encountering a single exception to the rule they illustrate, one important fact is made clear, namely: the interior of the earth, even at a moderate depth, is a veritable furnace. At the bottom of mines, the heat indicates even to the least observant work-man the neighborhood of some immense subterranean fire.

Hot springs and artificial spouting springs, known as arte-sian wells, illustrate the same truth. An artesian well is a deep, cylindrical hole bored by means of a drill composed of strong iron rods fitted end to end and equipped with an auger at one extremity. This drill is made to penetrate the superficial layers of soil and the underlying beds of rock until it taps a subterranean water source fed by the infiltration of neighboring streams or lakes. The water gushing up from far underground, as a result of this boring, reaches the surface at very nearly the temperature of the source, and thus serves as an indicator of the diffusion of heat throughout the earth's interior.

One of the most remarkable of these wells is that in the Grenelle quarter of Paris. It attains a depth of 547 meters, and the water that gushes up is of a constant temperature of 28°. Water from ordinary wells in the same locality has a tempera-ture of only 10°, the mean temperature of the locality. There is, therefore, an increase of heat amounting to eighteen degrees for the 547 meters of depth, or about one degree for every thirty meters. The artesian well at Passy, bored at nearly a league's distance from the Grenelle well, is 586 meters deep and like-wise furnishes water having a temperature of 28°. The water of the Neu-Salzwerck artesian well in Westphalia rises from a depth of 622 meters at a temperature of 32°. The Mondorf well on the frontier between France and Luxembourg gives water from a still greater depth, 700 meters below the surface, and its temperature is 35°. Elsewhere are found subterranean springs having a temperature still higher in comparison with their depth. Thus, at 385 meters below the surface, the water of the Neuffen well in Württemberg has a temperature of 39°. Artesian wells, therefore, furnish unanimous testimony of some interior source of heat that raises the temperature of springs lying beneath the earth's surface, and they show that as a rule this increase of temperature above the mean temperature of the locality is at the rate of about one degree for every thirty meters of depth.

We know of many natural springs that, on reaching the surface, have a very high temperature, sometimes even attaining the boiling point. They are called thermal springs, or hot springs, and they, in turn, prove that at the depth they come from there prevails sufficient heat to make them warm or even boiling hot. The most famous of the hot springs of France are those at Chaudes-Aigues and at Vichy, in the department of Cantal. They are almost boiling hot. But these little springs of boiling water are nothing compared with geysers.

In the extreme north of the Atlantic Ocean and just touching the Arctic Circle, there lies a large isolated island, a hyphen between the two continents east and west of it. It is frigid Iceland, a land buried under the snow for most of the year and seeing the sun—a sun with little heat—for barely an hour on the shortest days of the year. There, however, amid frost and snow, is seen one of the strangest of spectacles, one that we owe to the high temperature of the earth's interior. While winter piles up the snowdrifts on the island, a furnace burns underground and at intervals throws up torrents of boiling water into the icy air. These spouting springs of hot water are known in that country as geysers, the word *geyser* meaning *gusher*. A hundred can be counted in an area extending about two-thirds of a league in all directions. The most powerful of these, the Great Geyser, spouts from a large basin having a diameter of between fourteen and seventeen meters and situated at the top of a hillock formed by the smooth white incrustations deposited by the spray of the ejected water. The inside of this basin narrows gradually like a funnel, ending in tortuous outlets that go downward to unknown depths.

Each eruption of this volcano of boiling water is heralded in advance by a trembling of the ground and by muffled sounds like distant detonations of some subterranean artillery. These detonations become more violent from moment to moment; the earth trembles, and from the bottom of the crater, the water rises tumultuously and fills the basin, which soon presents the appearance of a boiler heated by some invisible fire. Amid swirling steam, the water mounts still higher in a great bubbling mass. Then suddenly the geyser displays all its tremendous power: a great explosion occurs, and a column of water, sixteen meters through, shoots sixty meters upward and falls again in a boiling-hot shower after spreading outward in the form of an immense sheaf surmounted by white vapor. This formidable spouting lasts only a few minutes. Soon the liquid sheaf sinks down, the water withdraws from the basin to be swallowed up in the depths of the crater, and there comes in its place a column of furiously roaring steam which shoots upward with a noise like thunder and in its irresistible course hurls aloft the fragments of rock fallen into the crater or grinds them into bits. The whole neighborhood is flooded with swirling waters. Finally, calm is restored; the geyser's fury is appeased, but only to burst forth again later and repeat the same series of phenomena.

There is no room for doubt: inside the earth, there is maintained a very high temperature that is entirely independent of the sun's heat. Admitting, as our observations authorize us to do, that this temperature increases at the rate of one degree for every thirty meters of added depth, let us consider what must take place deeper and deeper in the earth's interior.

At three kilometers below the surface, there must be 100 degrees of heat, or the temperature of boiling water; at twenty-one kilometers, 700 degrees, or the temperature of red-hot iron, enough to melt most substances; and, finally, at the depth of forty-eight kilometers, or twelve leagues, there is a heat of 1600 degrees, the melting point of platinum, one of the hardest of metals to melt. If the rule I have stated continues in force to the center of the earth, sixteen hundred leagues from the surface, there should be at that point a heat of 210,000 degrees, or more than a hundred times the greatest heat we can produce. Nothing can give us any idea of this terrific heat, a heat more than enough to melt and even vaporize all known substances, including metals.

But it is hardly probable that the temperature continues thus to increase. When sufficient heat is attained to fuse all substances, a general equilibrium is effected; and so we may conjecture that, from the depth where there is a temperature ranging between 2000° and 3000°, which nothing can resist, there is maintained a uniform heat in the lower depths. But, after all, our uncertainty on this subject is of little importance; what we have to note is that at the depth of a dozen leagues, the earth's internal heat reaches a point sufficient to melt all known mineral substances.

Such being the case, we are to think of the earth as a globe of matter liquefied by heat with a thick crust of solid material enclosing this central ocean of molten mineral substances. From this, it is but a step to the thought of an earth that was originally all fluid. The firm crust of our time became what it is only by the cooling off of the earth's surface. In this way, everything explains itself. The polar depression, the equatorial swelling, the arrangement of the materials of the globe in layers according to their weight, are all the results of this original fluid condition of the entire earth.

CHAPTER VIII

EARTHQUAKES

ONE FEELS a certain thrill on hearing for the first time these intimate details that science reveals to us concerning the earth's structure; one cannot think without a sort of fright of the gulfs of liquid fire displayed to the mind's eye — gulfs whose waves of molten metal surge to and fro leagues beneath our feet. The comparative thinness of the crust that bears us adds still more to our fears. The distance from the surface to the center of the earth is sixteen hundred leagues, and of this distance, twelve leagues at most may be assigned to the crust of solid matter, while all the rest belongs to the molten interior.

On a globe two meters in diameter, the earth's solid crust would be represented by a layer seven millimeters thick. On our ordinary geographical globes, the crust would be scarcely more than a thin sheet of pasteboard. How, then, is it possible for an envelope relatively so slight to withstand the constant commotion that must be going on in the central liquid mass? Must not this fragile shell crack open at times, give way, and fall in? Is not the slightest wave of the fiery central ocean enough to strain, dislocate, and even rupture it? And what would happen if the waters of the sea should pour in through some crevice and empty themselves into the incandescent interior? Would there not be produced an immense volume of steam exerting an irresistible pressure? Then, shaken to their foundations, the very continents would tremble as if seized with a sudden ague, the ocean would overflow its bed in wild disorder, mountains would crumble, the solid ground would crack open, frightful abysses would yawn, and whole populations would be swallowed up. In short, there would be an earthquake.

We have all heard of these commotions that at times make the ground tremble, but in our privileged part of the world, we are far from realizing the violence they can attain and the frightful results they can produce. For us as a people, the earth is in a very real sense solid, having never given way beneath our feet. If sometimes a slight movement of the ground is felt, it is spoken of for several days as a wonderful event: this person has seen furniture displaced, that one has heard kitchen utensils jingling as they hung on the wall. Then it is all forgotten, and our confidence in the stability of the ground beneath our feet is not in the least weakened. The unknown force that has just been revealed to us by a hardly perceptible trembling seems to us unlikely ever to attain the mighty power necessary for the serious disturbance of the usual calm. Are earthquakes equally harmless everywhere? Alas, no; and God forbid that we should ever have occasion to realize this sad fact!

Of all the earthquakes ever felt in Europe, the most terrible known to us is the one that laid Lisbon low on November 1, 1755. The populous capital of Portugal, which no danger seemed to menace, was engaged in its business and other concerns, when suddenly there was heard underground a mighty noise like the continuous rolling of thunder. Then the ground, violently shaken, seemed to whirl around, rise, and fall, and in a moment the city was nothing but a heap of ruins and dead bodies. The populace still remaining had sought a refuge from the fall of shattered buildings by huddling together on a broad quay running along the waterside. All at once, this quay was swallowed up by the waves, taking with it the terrified throng, together with the boats and ships moored there. Not a single victim, not a scrap of wreckage rose to the surface. An abyss had opened that had swallowed up the waters themselves, the quay, the vessels, and the people; and then it had closed, keeping them forever. At the same time, the sea, which had at first receded from the shore, returned and piled up its waters to the height of fifteen meters above their usual level, hurling its furious waves over the town.

To the conflagration that had started among the ruins, there was added this tumultuous flood, and the greater part of what was not already destroyed disappeared. In six minutes, sixty thousand persons had perished.

While this was taking place at Lisbon and while the lofty mountains of Portugal were shaken to their foundations so that they split open and their summits broke off the same frightful disturbance was making itself felt in northern Africa. Morocco, Fez, and Mequinez were overthrown, and a town of ten thousand inhabitants was swallowed up in an abyss that suddenly opened and as suddenly closed. But the extent of the devastation was not limited to this. Almost at the same moment, violent shocks were felt from the equator to the north pole. Martinique, South Africa, Greenland, the whole of Europe even to the remotest confines of Lapland experienced a series of more or less disastrous shocks with only a few minutes' intermission between one shock and the next. Even on the sea, there was no immunity from this fearful commotion. Far out from land, where the water was of great depth, vessels received violent shocks as if they had struck on a reef. The very floor of the ocean, as was thus made evident, was also subjected to the universal disturbance, the agitation being transmitted through the water to the vessels plying on the surface.

If the Lisbon earthquake is exceptional by reason of the vast extent of territory affected, there are, unfortunately, many others comparable with it in the amount of damage done.

In 1812, at Caracas in South America, the earth was seized with violent convulsions and shook like a mass of boiling water. In three shocks, lasting five seconds, the work of destruction was completed. The first set the church bells to ringing, the second made the roofs of houses fall in with a crash, and before it was fairly realized what had happened, the third came. The town was no more, and its ten thousand inhabitants lay crushed under the ruins.

In February 1783, there began in southern Italy a long series of convulsions that lasted four years. In the first year, 949 shocks were counted, in the next year 151. The disturbance extended southward from Naples to include a great part of Sicily, raging with especial violence about the town of Oppido. The surface of the ground was so agitated that it presented the appearance of a sea stirred up by a furious storm, and the unfortunate dwellers on this undulating tract of territory were seized with nausea like that felt on the bridge of a vessel tossed about by the waves. Seasickness prevailed on dry land. At each undulation, the clouds, which were really motionless, seemed suddenly to shift their position, just as they appear to at sea when the observer is on board a ship that is pitching violently. The trees, though there was no wind, bent over so that their tops swept the ground as each wave of this commotion passed over the land.

The first shock, that of February 5, 1783, overturned in two minutes entire cities, villages, and hamlets, and the ground cracked open here and there so that it had the appearance of a vast pane of broken glass. Hills burst and split in two. Great tracts of land slid down the mountain slopes with their cultivated fields, their houses, vineyards, and olive orchards, all moving considerable distances and taking their places over other tracts of land that had remained at rest. In the little town of Polistena, several hundred houses, swept away together with the soil on which they stood, dashed pell-mell into a ravine nearly a quarter of a league distant. Even the very hills were torn from their bases. We read of some that were displaced from the sloping sides of a valley and carried to the middle of the plain, where they intercepted the course of a river.

Elsewhere the surface soil was left with no underlying support, so that it caved in, and all the inhabitants, with their houses and orchards and domestic animals, were swallowed up and disappeared forever. In still other places, deep funnels opened, full of moving sand, or vast cavities were hollowed out, which were soon turned into lakes by the inrush of water from underground sources. It is estimated that more than two hundred lakes, ponds, and swamps were thus suddenly formed where before there had been only dry land. In some districts, the ground, churned up by the waters turned from their regular channels or coming from under the surface through fissures made by the earthquake, was converted into torrents of mud, which flowed over the plains or filled the valleys. Tree-tops and the roofs of ruined farmhouses were the only objects to be seen above the surface of this sea of mud.

At intervals, sudden shocks made the ground tremble violently. So great was the commotion that paving-stones were torn from their places and flung into the air. The masonry lining the wells was thrust upward intact, like small towers ejected from beneath the ground. When the surface of the earth rose and broke, instantly houses, people, and animals were swallowed up; then, as the ground subsided, the crevice closed, and, with no vestige remaining to tell the tale, everything disappeared, crushed and held fast between the two walls of the chasm as they came together. Some time after the disaster, when excavations were made in search of buried objects of value, the workmen noticed that the engulfed buildings, with all they contained, were one compact mass, so violent had been the pressure exerted by the vise formed when the two edges of the crevice came together in closing.

A French scientist, Dolomieu[12], who visited this unfortunate country soon after the disaster, gives us an account of the heart-breaking impression made on his mind as he passed through Sicily and Calabria. He describes Messina as still presenting, from a distance, a certain appearance of its ancient splendor. All the houses were ruined, but their walls were still standing. The whole population had taken refuge in wooden barracks near the town, whose silent and deserted streets might have made one believe a pestilence had ravaged the place.

"But when I reached Calabria," he adds, "and beheld Polistena, the scene of horror that opened before me almost deprived me of the use of my faculties. My mind was prey to a feeling of terror mingled with compassion. The disaster was complete, — everything level with the ground, not a single house standing, not a scrap of wall left erect. All around lay heaps of stones,

12   A noted geologist and mineralogist (1750-1801). Dolomite takes its name from him. – *Translator*.

from whose appearance one would never have suspected that a town had once stood there."

It is estimated that eighty thousand persons lost their lives in this terrible catastrophe, most of them from the direct effect of the earthquake, but others in consequence of the epidemics occasioned by the lack of food and shelter, the inclemency of the weather, and the foul exhalations rising from the stagnant waters of the newly formed swamps. The greater number of the victims were buried alive under the ruins of their homes, others were consumed in the conflagrations that in nearly all instances followed the earthquake shocks, while still others, fleeing for safety into the open country, were swallowed up in the abysses that suddenly yawned beneath their feet.

The sight of such calamities ought to have awakened pity in the breasts of the most barbarous; and yet — who would have believed it? — excepting a few scattering deeds of heroism, the conduct of the populace, says Dolomieu, was infamous. The Calabrian peasantry flocked into the towns, not to lend aid, but to pillage. Heedless of danger, they ran through the streets, between tottering walls on each hand and amid clouds of dust, trampling on the victims and even robbing them while they were still breathing.

But enough of these tales of woe. Earthquakes occur in all lands, and there is no country whose annals do not contain the record of some of these disastrous events as terrible testimony to the existence of a tremendous central furnace that from time to time rends and shatters the earth's frail envelope.

Earthquakes are often preceded by subterranean noises announcing the catastrophe to come. First, there is the dull rumble that reminds one of distant thunder, swelling in volume, then diminishing, then swelling again, as if some storm were beginning to break far beneath the earth's surface. At this sound, so full of mysterious menace, everyone falls silent, mute with fear, and every face turns pale. Warned by their instinct, the very animals are seized with alarm: dogs howl with terror, and the plow ox stands still in the furrow and appears to brace himself by planting his hoofs wider apart. Meanwhile, the noise increases, and one seems to hear a long line of wagons, heavily laden with old iron, rumbling over a hollow roadway of brass, while a whole battery of cannon is discharged. And then the ground trembles, rises and falls, whirls around, cracks open, and a frightful abyss yawns before the terrified observer. In the presence of such scenes, the stoutest heart is panic-stricken.

These subterranean noises are not always accompanied by a quaking of the ground. Thus, in 1784, at Guanajuato in Mexico, there was heard for forty days a succession of underground rumblings interspersed with violent detonations, making the inhabitants believe an earthquake to be imminent. In wild terror, they fled from the town. One would have said that some tempest had somewhere been let loose, accompanied by sharp thunderclaps. In the galleries of neighboring mines, five hundred meters below the surface, the same detonations were heard coming from the bowels of the earth and reaching the ear in greater volume than was the case with listeners above ground. This proved the subterranean disturbances to be lower than the mines. Who knows but they may have been caused by some tumultuous commotion in the ocean of fire beating against the solid crust of the globe, by the splitting asunder of rocks, or by the caving in of certain less stable parts of the terrestrial framework? However that may have been, the people of Guanajuato escaped with nothing worse than a good scare, the underground tempest subsiding without any surface tremors.

CHAPTER IX

WHY THE CONTINENTS DO NOT SINK INTO THE OCEAN

AFTER THIS account, brief and hasty though it is, of earth-quakes and the terrible disasters due to them, a distressing thought is likely to occur to us. We ask ourselves how these dreadful catastrophes can be fitted into the plan of a beneficent Providence watching over all the events of this world, and what part in the general scheme of things can be played by the central fire which causes these catastrophes. Can it be that the fire of divine wrath lighted the subterranean furnace which, in its tempestuous moments, makes the very mountain chains dance, dismembers whole continents, and in a few seconds overthrows populous cities?

No; for the central fire is part of the great natural machinery indispensable to the very existence of things, although it sometimes inflicts upon us severe trials. Who would ever think of questioning the necessity of atmosphere and ocean — the atmosphere whose hurricanes overturn our dwellings, of the ocean whose storms swallow up our vessels? All the forces of nature cooperate for the general good being primarily the source of life and productive of prosperity, although at the same time, in obedience to the inscrutable decrees of Eternal Wisdom, they are likely to become at any moment the instruments of disaster and death. The cloud that pours rain on the harvests can also send down hail; the lightning flash, beneficial to life when it purifies the atmosphere, is also fatal to it when it strikes us; the river that irrigates the valley sometimes inundates and ravages it; and the central fire, which has thrust the continents up above the level of the surrounding waters, and which keeps them from being flooded by the seas, also shakes them with disastrous convulsions.

But Providence can turn evil to good and knows better than we the need of universal order and of human welfare. The secret designs of Providence are always wise, even amid the disasters of a region given over to the severities inflicted by underground forces, which act only with the divine permission. So let us give our confidence unreservedly to Him by whom the earth in the beginning of things was established on its burning foundations and overcanopied with the everlasting firmament. He alone dispenses life and death, He alone orders the subterranean tempests as well as the storms that rage above ground.

Like everything else in this world, the fire burning in the earth's interior has its mission to fulfill. The earthquakes that from the very first have occurred here and there on the crust of the globe have been the means of making the continents rise out of the ocean waters and take form. These ocean waters originally covered the entire surface, and without the help of the subterranean upheavals land would never have come into existence, as will be shown later.

But, you will say, now that the continents are formed and the dry land is well above the water, having been pushed upward from below by the action of the subterranean furnace, would it not be well if this roaring furnace, whose nearness to us is so dangerous, were extinguished forever?

Take care! Your wish is an imprudent one, for in course of time it would, if granted, inflict upon us disasters far worse than any earthquakes. The mechanism of the universe, you may be assured, is wisely arranged, and such modifications as we might think advisable are in reality nothing but foolishness. Sovereign Intelligence has thought out the plan, Infinite Wisdom arranged the details. Where we puny creatures see only disorder, an admirable order reigns. Extinguish the fire that burns in the earth's interior and that holds up, even though it occasionally shakes, the ground under our feet, and immediately the continents would lose their support and would sink to a lower level, allowing the waters of the ocean to sweep over them and forever obliterate them.

A slow but never-resting power is constantly eating away and leveling the dry land. This block of granite that no steel can cut is crumbled and finally reduced to powder by this power. That frowning peak rising yonder into the clouds is by this same power gradually demolished and leveled to the ground — if not in a century, then in ten; if not in ten centuries, then in a thousand — for time is as nothing to this power. Now this irresistible agency that levels mountains and demolishes continents is the unceasing action of air, water, and frost. A solid mass of rock, let us say, absorbs a slight deposit of moisture all over its surface; then frost comes and by the expansive force of the ice in the smallest cracks and crevices produces thousands of fissures crisscrossing in all directions, after which a thaw allows the surface of the rock to fall off in scales like those of old bark on a tree. Moisture and frost recur, and with every recurrence a fresh breaking down of the rock's exterior takes place until the solid mass is entirely reduced to fragments, particles, powder. In this way, all over the continents, there is constantly going on a process of demolition whose agents are the various atmospheric forces. The material thus wrested from the mountain sides and left to accumulate there finally slides down in avalanches into the valleys. Let us take an instance — one out of a thousand.

On the second day of September, 1806, after a very rainy season, the inhabitants of the valley of Goldau in central Switzerland heard a violent cracking from the neighboring heights. The surface layers of Mt. Rosenberg became detached over a stretch of four kilometers and slid down the slope with tremendous tumult and crash into the valley below. You would have thought the end of the world had come, and that the very mountains were toppling over. In five minutes the valleys of Goldau and Busingen were buried under sixty and seventy meters' depth of stones and gravel and other matter. More than fifty million cubic meters of this material had come dashing down from the upper slopes of Mt. Rosenberg, burying five villages under the avalanche and causing the death of nearly five hundred persons.

Whole mountains are in this way gradually demolished. Nor is this all. The dry land is traversed in every direction by innumerable streams of water necessary to its fertility, and all — from the brook one can jump, to the river leagues in width — wash away great quantities of surface matter and carry it to the sea in the shape of stones, gravel, sand, and mud. It has been calculated that the earthy matter thus annually borne to the sea by a single river, the Ganges, amounts to 180,000,000 cubic meters. Many hills that we regard as of considerable size have not this volume, and one of these the Ganges would sweep away entirely as its annual tribute to the ocean.

This conveyance of solid material to the sea, at the expense of the land, being thus in constant progress on a prodigious scale, with all the rivers and other watercourses doing their part, it is clear that the result must be a general though gradual leveling of the earth's surface. The ocean bed, in which is accumulated this material carried seaward by the streams, must in time, one would think, become completely filled up, and the continents thus worn away would seem to be in danger of being at last reduced to one common level, especially as atmospheric forces do their part also in the unceasing attrition. If this process were to go on unhindered, the sea, which already covers three times as much of the earth's surface as does the land, would every day gain a little in extent, so that in a more or less distant future its waves would wash the entire surface of the globe.

This possible disappearance of all the dry land may seem to you an utter absurdity. But think of the immensity of the ocean expanse and the almost insignificant height of the land above the water. Remember, also, that even our loftiest mountains are but as grains of sand on a globe two meters in diameter. How, then, can these grains of sand — and, still more, how can the plains on which they rest — withstand the unceasing action of the atmosphere that eats them away, of the streams that wear them down, and of the oceans that beat against the shores with every flow of the tide and every outbreak of storm? If anything should astonish us, it is that the dry land is able to resist these destructive forces and that the sea has not long since regained all the territory it once covered.

Yes, I mean it, the territory it once covered; for the lowest layers of the soil, the strata of stone at the bottom of quarries, and the entire bulk of mountains are often found to contain fossil remains of shellfish. The sea once covered everything, and everywhere it has deposited, along with its shellfish, its mud and slime that have hardened in the course of centuries and become converted into stone. And so this general submersion not only is seen to be possible, but was once really a fact, as is proved by the innumerable evidences left by the receding ocean waters[13].

The earth's interior fire caused our present continents to rise out of the sea, bringing about this result very gradually, and it now safeguards them from the invading waters and prevents any general leveling such as would otherwise result from the combined action of atmosphere and ocean. Underground disturbances — making more pronounced, as they do, the surface inequalities of the earth's crust — have a twofold effect: first, that of deepening the hollows that serve the sea for a bed; and, secondly, that of making more prominent the projecting parts that constitute the islands and continents. In both cases the final result is the same: if the level of the oceans is lowered by the deepening of their beds, or if the prominence of the dry land is increased by an upthrust from below, any flooding of the dry land by the oceans is rendered impossible. Thus we see that to the action of earthquakes we owe the preservation of the continents from a general submersion and the safeguarding of the peoples of the earth against extinction by flood.

If the earth had not, from the earliest times, been gradually renewed — rejuvenated, as it were — by the incessant action of the central fire, what would now be left above the waters of the sea? A few islets, perhaps, a few bare rocks, sole remaining

---

13   The submersion here referred to antedates man's appearance on the earth. It must not, therefore, be confounded with the biblical deluge, which also left on the continents unmistakable traces of its destructive actions. We agree with St. Augustine its regarding the days of Genesis not as days like ours, but as indeterminate periods. Hence, it must have taken a long succession of centuries – how long no one can say – for the dry land of our globe to emerge above the waters that had held it submerged.

vestiges of the vanished continents. Under these conditions there would be no terrestrial life. But, as things were actually ordered, the earthquakes of those prehistoric ages formed and preserved the continents for the present generation of mankind, those of our own day preserve them for future generations, and the dry land, thus forever renewed, can from its inexhaustible bosom nourish the populations of the globe to the end of time.

Let us take some examples of this increase in the prominence of the dry land caused by the central fire. In 1822, 1835, and 1837, Chile was ravaged by subterranean disturbances that very perceptibly raised the coast from Valdivia to Valparaiso, over a stretch of more than two hundred leagues. Rocks until then always under water rose to two and three meters above the level of the sea, with their tangled masses of seaweed and their deposits of sea shells. In some places the quantity of fish stranded was so great that several acres were strewn with them and the region was infected with the pestilential odor arising from their decay.

It is estimated that the disturbance of 1822 alone shook the ground over thirteen million square leagues of territory and raised its level one meter, on an average, so that the bulk thus added to the American continent — or, rather, the mass raised above the level of the sea — amounted to one hundred thousand times the Great Pyramid of Egypt, the most colossal monument ever erected by man in his moments of foolish pride. Just think, my young readers, what must be the immensity of an underground force that can raise such masses in a few seconds, whereas the labors of a whole people take years and years to build a single pyramid.

Far out to sea the ocean bottom was likewise affected by the upheaval. Forty leagues from shore a whaling vessel received a shock so violent as to dismast her. Soundings proved that where, two years before, this same vessel had anchored, there was now a lessening of depth to the extent of two and one-half meters. In the middle of Concepcion Bay, vessels that lay at anchor in thirteen meters of water suddenly found themselves stranded; the very waves beneath their keels had flowed off to seaward. In short, where ships of deep draft formerly plied without obstruction, navigation is now rendered impossible by reefs and shoals.

But these upheavals are not always so sudden and violent in their nature. Portions of the earth's crust may be raised slowly and with no shock whatsoever. That is what is taking place even now in Sweden. Observations extending over more than a century show that around the Scandinavian peninsula the waters of the Baltic and of the North Sea are gradually subsiding, at the rate of about one meter in a century; or, to be more exact, the ground is gradually rising at the same rate. In 1731 Upsala University had notches cut in the rocks at the level, and after a few years these notches were found to be several centimeters above the water. Today they are more than a meter higher than the level of the Baltic.

These two examples, which could easily be multiplied, will suffice to show that the dry land, though it may suffer submergence in some places, makes up for it in others by gaining in extent and in prominence above the sea through the action of the huge furnace forever glowing in the earth's interior. And now, if I am not much mistaken, you see at last, even in the disturbances caused by earthquakes, plain proof of a Providence that watches over the general welfare. Who can fail to recognize the work of an infinite Wisdom in this interaction of air and water, on the one hand in destroying the dry land — a process nevertheless necessary to the soil's fertility — and, on the other, of the great central fire in restoring that dry land to its former place? If the heavens declare the glory, the power, and the majesty of a God, to whom, as first cause, we ascribe all things, does not also the rent and agitated bosom of our mother earth, despite the inevitable disasters there brought about by natural forces, speak of God's never-ceasing care of His creatures?

CHAPTER X

VOLCANOES

PROBABLY NOT a day passes that does not see the earth's crust undergoing, sometimes at one spot, sometimes at another, and in the ocean bed as well as on the dry land, some disturbance necessary as an offset to the constant corrosive action of air and water. How is it, then, that disastrous earthquakes are not more frequent? How is it that the gases and the incandescent matter forever striving to lift the vault that holds them down do not burst it somewhere every day, with a tremendous noise? Why does not a terrific explosion rend the earth's crust and hurl fragments of it far out into space?

That this does not occur is due to the volcanic openings, veritable safety-valves, that furnish communication between the earth's interior and the outer space, and afford free vent for any undue excess of explosive forces. In thus furnishing a permanent vent for the confined gases that tend to escape by rupturing the earth's crust, volcanoes make earthquakes less disastrous than they otherwise would be. In volcanic regions it has been found to be the rule that every time the ground is shaken by violent commotions, an eruption is preparing in some neighboring volcano, and that these shocks cease as soon as the eruption has taken place. Volcanoes, therefore, deserve the title of providential safety-valves for modifying the violence of the central fire.

A volcano is a mountain hollowed out at the top in a large funnel-shaped excavation, more or less regular, called a crater. The bottom of the crater communicates with the interior of the earth by winding passages or chimneys, whose depth cannot be determined. Volcanoes are of widely varying heights. Some rise but a few hundred meters above the level of the sea, while others attain the altitude of a league or even more, as Antisana in South America, which is 5837 meters high. The size of the crater also varies widely. At the time of the eruption of Vesuvius in 1822 its crater was about 1 league in circumference and 300 meters deep. In the Sandwich Islands there is a volcano whose crater is between 5 and 6 leagues in circumference and 400 meters deep. But as a rule the dimensions of a volcano's mouth are much less. The European volcanoes are: Vesuvius, near Naples; Etna, in Sicily; Hekla, Skaptar-Jökul, and six others, in Iceland, where there are also several inactive volcanoes. Vesuvius is 1190 meters high, Hekla 1690, and Etna 3315.

To give you some idea of what a volcanic eruption is like, I will take Vesuvius as an excellent example, its comparative nearness making it still more interesting to us.

The approach of an eruption is usually announced by a column of smoke that fills the crater's opening and rises vertically, when the atmosphere is calm, to three times the height of the mountain. At this elevation it spreads out horizontally and hides the sun. Several days before the eruption the sheaf of smoke thickens and settles down over the volcano, covering it with a big black cloud. Then the earth all about Vesuvius begins to tremble, muffled detonations beneath the ground make themselves heard, and, growing louder every moment, soon exceed in volume of sound the most violent claps of thunder. You might take them for volleys from some tremendous artillery discharging incessantly within the bosom of the mountain.

Suddenly a sheaf of flame bursts from the mouth of the crater and shoots to the height of two or three thousand meters. The cloud hovering over the volcano glows fiery-red, and the very heavens appear to be ablaze. Millions of sparks dart upward like flashes of lightning to the top of the flaming sheaf, describe great arcs, leaving behind them trails of dazzling brilliance, and fall back in a rain of fire on the sides of the mountain. These sparks, apparently so small as seen from a distance, are in reality masses of incandescent matter, sometimes several meters through and having momentum enough to crush in their fall the most substantial buildings. Where is the machine of human construction that could hurl such masses of rock to so great a height? What our united efforts could not accomplish even once, the subterranean forces do repeatedly and without pause, as if in play. For weeks and months at a time these red-hot masses are thrown up by Vesuvius in numbers like the sparks from a display of fireworks, so that they give the appearance of a gigantic bouquet of incandescent particles over the crater.

Meanwhile, from the depths of the mountain, and doubtless from some leagues still lower, there rises through the volcano's chimney a liquid stream of molten mineral substances, a column of lava, which flows out over the crater's floor in a lake of fire as dazzling as the sun at noonday. The spectator watching from the plain, and anxiously following the progress of the eruption, is forewarned of this outburst of lava by penetrating reverberations coming from behind the smoke that hovers over the scene. Soon the crater is full, whereupon the ground suddenly trembles, the sides of the crater split open with a loud noise as of thunder, and through the crevices and over the edges of the volcano's mouth rush streams of lava.

The fiery stream of pasty matter in a state of incandescence advances slowly but irresistibly, implacably. The oncoming end of this dazzling current is as a wall of fire advancing toward the observer. A person can flee before it, but everything stationary is doomed. Century-old chestnut trees blaze up for a moment at the touch of the lava and then fall in charred remnants, the thickest walls of masonry are calcined and crumble to dust, and the hardest rocks are distorted and finally melted. But sooner or later the flow of lava ceases, and then the subterranean gases, freed from the enormous pressure of the fluid mass above them, escape with a violence even greater than any that has gone before, carrying with them great billows of ashes, or, rather, fine powder that hovers aloft in menacing clouds and finally settles down over the surrounding plain or is even borne away by the wind for hundreds of leagues. At last the terrible mountain calms down and everything returns to its former repose for another indeterminate period.

The quantity of lava thrown up by a volcano in a single eruption sometimes attains enormous proportions, as the following example proves.

On June 11, 1783, there occurred in Iceland a memorable eruption from the volcano Skaptar-Jokul. The ejected lava rushed toward a river sixty meters wide in some places and running between banks from one hundred to two hundred meters deep. The battle between fire and water was terrific but of short duration: the river, vaporized to the very last drop, gave place to the lava that hastened to fill its bed. Nor was that all: the burning torrent overflowed into the neighboring plains to a great distance, and even ousted the waters of a large lake. Then, continuing its course, it came to an old and empty river channel, into which it plunged until it was swallowed up in underground caverns whose walls softened like wax at touch of the lava that had just dried up a river and a lake.

A week later there burst from the volcano a second torrent of lava, which spread over the first one and then, after an onward rush of several days' duration, plunged into a yawning abyss hollowed out by a waterfall in the course of centuries. This being filled, the lava stream resumed its course, nor did it stop until it had advanced eighteen leagues from its starting-point. Its width on the open plain varied from four to five leagues, and its average depth was 30 meters, but in narrow ravines it attained a depth of 183 meters. It is estimated that a tract eighty square leagues in extent was covered by the lava and converted into a lake of fire. Is it to be wondered at if such masses of molten mineral matter keep their red heat for a number of years and continue to smoke thirty and forty years after issuing from the bowels of the earth?

In moments of calm the interior of certain craters can be visited without danger. It presents a gloomy chaos of calcined rocks, heaps of slag, and great blocks of lava piled up in wild disorder. Here and there puffs of suffocating vapor burst from the fissures, and through the cracks can be seen the red glow of the interior fires. At the bottom of the funnel-shaped inside of the crater is a rounded vault of congealed lava stopping up the volcanic chimney like the cover to some infernal caldron. At other times the crater is inaccessible, and the very look of it inspires fear.

The illustrious traveler, Alexander von Humboldt, has left the following record of a remarkable experience.

> In the spring of 1802, accompanied by a single Indian, I climbed the easternmost of the three rocks that surround the crater of Pichincha[14]. We were making our way upward, laboriously but with undiminished ardor, from ledge to ledge, uncertain as to our proper course, when we became enveloped in a cloud of steam, dense but inodorous. The ground was covered here and there with a crust of frozen snow that might, for all we knew, conceal some dangerous crevasse and give way under our feet. The cloud of steam made it impossible to see even a few steps ahead. We were advancing slowly and in silence over the snow and had gone but a short distance when all at once a strong smell of burning sulphur announced the nearness of the crater, and I perceived the glow of a fire burning at an immense distance beneath us. Without knowing it we had taken a few steps on a bridge of ice overhanging the abyss. I immediately seized the Indian by his coat and made him throw himself down with me on a bare rock a few meters wide.
>
> So there we both were, flat on our stomachs on a flagstone at the very brink of the crater. Just beneath us yawned the frightful abyss. There are no words in which to describe the chaos presented to our view in the depths of the crater, and I doubt whether the most fertile imagination, in its most hair-raising nightmares, could picture anything more somber, more lugubrious, than what we then saw. Imagine a circular well nearly a league in circumference, its walls vertical, its curb covered with snow. The interior is in deepest darkness, but far down in the depths of this yawning gulf can be faintly descried the tops of several mountains rising through

14   A volcano in the Andes near Quito. Its height is 15,918 feet. – *Translator*.

the gloom and out of the very heart of the interior. Some three score lurid vents were scattered over their sides, and their summits, from which issued sulphurous fumes, appeared to be four or five hundred meters below us. Judge then where their bases must have been.

Another traveler, Armand de Quatrefages, writes:

At our feet yawned the vast crater of Mt. Etna. But this was not of that nearly regular funnel-shape such as may be seen surmounting Vesuvius; it was a veritable valley, winding, deep, irregular, its steep sides bristling with masses of slag and blocks of lava heaped up, topsy-turvy, in a thousand fantastic patterns by the volcano's power or by the chances of a haphazard fall. Everywhere were colors of all sorts, with occasional big black spots and markings of deep red which served to heighten the lurid glow that tinged the whole scene. A silence as of death reigned over this chaos. Thousands of vent-holes emitted noiselessly long streamers of white vapor, which mounted slowly up the sides of the crater, bringing with them their suffocating odors. The ground under our feet, composed entirely of ashes and slag, was damp and warm, but had the appearance of being covered with a white frost. This dampness, however, was an acid that would soon have eaten into our shoes; this silvery frost sparkling with crystals was sulphur, which had been vaporized by the volcano and had then fallen in fine flakes, and salts generated by the chemical reactions continually going on in this tremendous laboratory.

We looked for a last time into the valley of the crater and then, leaving our post of observation, descended toward the base of the hillock to the east of us. But we were soon halted by our guide near a narrow and steep declivity sloping down to a sheer precipice about a hundred steps below. We saw him roll up his sleeve and hold it over his mouth, motioning to us to follow his example. Then he sprang straight across the face of the declivity, crying, "Come on! Quick!"

Without a moment's hesitation we followed him and reached the edge of a volcanic mouth that had been in eruption about ten years before. Far down in its depths, the subterranean thunder still rumbled at intervals. A vast enclosure, irregularly circular and formed of vertical walls, rose on all sides of this cavernous opening. On the left, at the foot of the enclosing wall, we saw a big vent-hole whence issued in dense eddies a fiery-red smoke. In the middle, on the right, everywhere, lay enormous blocks of lava, splintered, cracked, torn, some black, others dark red, and all showing, through their smallest fissures, the brighter tints of their inner substance. A thousand jets of white or grayish vapor crisscrossed in all directions with a deafening roar and with shrill hissing like those of a locomotive letting off steam. Unfortunately, we could cast but a glance over this strange and fearful scene. Gases of an unbearable pungency choked us, and so, reeling like drunken men, we regained the protecting slope where we could breathe at our ease.

The island of Stromboli, north of Sicily, is in reality only a volcanic mountain three leagues in circumference and about seven hundred meters high. Its volcano is the smallest of active volcanoes in Europe, but to make up for that, it is always in eruption. From its summit, one can easily observe how lava behaves inside a volcano. Three concentric enclosures, of which the two outer ones are now standing on but one side, constitute the crater of Stromboli. The innermost enclosure embraces six separate volcanic mouths, two of which emit clouds of sulphurous vapor that are always hovering over the summit of the mountain, while a third belches white smoke mixed with sparks — that is to say, red-hot stones which rise and then fall, hitting against one another unceasingly with a clinking like that of the hammers of some great forge. The three other mouths are intermittent in their eruptions.

In moments of calm, the lava can be seen, as dazzling as melted iron, rising and falling, oscillating rhythmically, pulsing and palpitating inside the volcanic chimneys, without overflowing. A noise not unlike that of a stove in which a fire is burning with a strong draft accompanies this rhythmic action. Every time the lava rises, a puff of white vapor escapes, whereupon the lava immediately subsides once more. Plainly, then, it is the uplifting force of this vapor that raises the lava and holds it suspended in the volcanic opening. Every eight minutes for two of these intermittently active mouths, and about once in a quarter of an hour for the third, which is the most powerful, these regular pulsations of the lava give place to other and more tumultuous movements. The walls of the crater tremble, the ground shakes slightly, and an ominous rumbling rises from inside the mountain. The smoke from the volcano's chimneys turns bright red, the detonations become more rapid and more violent, and finally, the lava spurts up, impelled by a blast of violet-colored vapor that escapes with a loud hissing. The principal mouth throws up its lava and its red-hot fragments of rock in an immense sheaf that rises two or three hundred meters to the level of a spectator standing on one of the highest pinnacles of the enclosing wall. It gives him the full effect of its waves of heat and of its loud reverberations; but after reaching that height, the sheaf opens wide and falls back in showers of fire, partly into the sea, partly into the abyss whence it came. Then the volcano quickly calms down and its lava sinks back again into the depths of the vent-holes. But before long, there is another rising, another series of rhythmic pulsations in the volcano's chimneys, followed by another explosive outburst.

It may not be without interest to compare the power of our mightiest machines with the energy required to raise a column of lava from the interior of the earth to the volcano's summit. We do not know exactly the depth of the volcanic chimneys, but they certainly reach down to the base of the mountain. Let us content ourselves with this modest limit. The energy of the most powerful engine ever made — a mechanism rarely put to use on account of the danger involved in handling so formidable a force — would lift a column of water having the same diameter as the column of lava in a volcano and reaching to a height of one hundred meters. But lava weighs about two and one-half times as much as water; consequently, the mechanism that would lift a column of water having a height of one hundred meters would lift a column of lava having only two-fifths of that height, or forty meters. At this rate, to push up a column of lava reaching from the base of Vesuvius to its summit would need the combined energy of 30 of these exceptionally powerful engines. It would take the united energy of 83 such engines to move the column of lava sent up by an eruption of Etna, and of 180 to perform a similar office for Aconcagua, the highest of our volcanoes.

These figures, which would certainly have to be doubled, trebled, or even more greatly multiplied if the volcanic chimneys extended downward far below the volcano's base, as well they might, prove sufficiently the tremendous force that causes lava to rise in a volcano and overcome any resistance opposed to its outflow. So great is this force that often the sides of the mountain cannot withstand it and are seamed with crevices through which the volcanic products make their escape. In these crevices, secondary craters take form, as was described in the account of Mt. Etna's eruption. Sometimes, again, the lava, on being obstructed in its ascent, will make a new vent for itself through the side of the volcano and spurt out in a flaming stream. In the course of the eruption of Vesuvius in 1794, a jet of melted rock was seen to break through a crack in the ground and describe a colossal arc under which a whole town could easily have found place.

Following is a list of some of the principal volcanoes in the order of their height[15]

Aconcagua, Argentina,	7150	meters
Antisana, Ecuador,	5833	"
Cotopaxi, Ecuador,	5755	"
Mt. Saint Elias, Alaska,	5443	"
Popocateptl, Mexico,	5400	"
Maipo, Argentina,	5386	"
Pichincha, Ecuador	4855	"

15   Later measurements have corrected some of the figures here given. Cotopaxi is at present the highest active volcano known.- *Translator*.

Mauna Loa, Hawaii	4800	"
Kliutachi, Siberia	4800	"
Pasto, Colombia,	4100	"
Peak of Teneriffe, Canary Islands,	3710	"
Erebus, Antarctica,	3700	"
Etna, Sicily,	3315	"
Hekla, Iceland,	1690	"
Vesuvius, Italy,	1190	"
Stromboli, Island of Stomboli,	700	"

CHAPTER XI

VESUVIUS

AFTER CENTURIES and centuries of activity, a volcano may
bank its fires and cease to smoke. It is as if something had
blocked up its chimney, thus cutting off communication with
the great central furnace. In this condition, it is said to be extinct. Vegetation clothes its lava stream, coarse grass covers the
sides of its crater; but under this mantle of verdure, the earth
retains ineffaceable traces of the ravages of fire, and by certain
unmistakable signs, it is always possible to recognize a volcano's
mouth, even though no eruption from it has been witnessed by
any living person.

In certain provinces of France, especially Auvergne, Vivarais,
and Velay, there are to be seen, isolated or in groups, numerous
conical hillocks cut off at the top, with each truncated summit
hollowed out in a vast funnel-shaped excavation. They are known
locally as "the wells." Sometimes the excavation has so regular,
shell-like a shape that one would think it had been fashioned
by the hand of man; and in other instances, it is without sym-
metry and shows a wide gap on one side. Again, a beautifully
limpid lake may fill the hollow, and nothing could be calmer,
nothing more smiling, than its blue waters reflecting the white
clouds overhead. But more often, the bottom of the excavation
is a level tract of grassland where sheep go to graze, or where,
lying here and there, heifers chew their cud while their bells
give forth a gentle tinkling.

These peaceful spots, so green and fresh at present, are the
craters of once active volcanoes. Where the waters of a beautiful
lake stretch smiling in the sun, there formerly boiled a cauldron

of molten lava; and where herds now lie ruminating, subterranean fires once roared and thundered. Vainly do the ruins of an old volcano seek to mask themselves under greensward and flowers; attentive scrutiny never fails to detect them. The conical hillock under its thin layer of black mold is nothing but a mass of slag, volcanic ashes, and vitrified rock. Its shell-shaped summit is the former crater, and the gap in its regular outline is the breach made by the lava in its overflow after it had failed to effect an outlet lower down, near the foot of the hillock. As to the lava stream, that is just as easy to detect: it is a well-marked trail of black and reddish rocks, with deep fissures and the traces of fire all along its serpentine course from the conical summit of the volcano to the plain below, like a strip of ground laid under a curse. Some scant tufts of grass and moss just manage to find a footing on these billows that the earth once vomited in a blazing condition. Here and there, an old lava stream of this sort exceeds in size the largest ones around Mt. Etna. All that is lacking in the volcanic cones of Auvergne and Vivarais is the sheaf of flame with its accompanying lava in a state of white heat. That flame was extinguished long ago; that incandescent lava cooled off centuries since.

The epoch in which more than a hundred craters threw out their torrents of fire and lighted up the whole of central France is so far back in the past that man, the last work of creation, was not yet in existence to witness these scenes of awful magnificence. For how many centuries, then, have the volcanoes of Auvergne been quiet and harmless? No one can say; nor can anyone say whether the terrific forces that set them in action once may not do so again one of these days.

In olden times, Vesuvius also was a peaceful mountain, an extinct volcano similar to the "wells" of Auvergne. It was not then, as it is today, capped by a smoking cone of slag, but by a slightly concave plateau, relic of an old crater almost filled up, where grew sparse grasses and wild vines. Tilled fields of great fertility covered its sides, while two populous towns, Herculaneum and Pompeii, lay at its base. This was the condition of things when, in the year 79 of our era, the ancient volcano that appeared to be silenced forever, and whose latest eruption dated back to prehistoric times, suddenly aroused itself and began to smoke. One of the most disastrous eruptions on record followed.

Herculaneum and Pompeii, being situated at the very base of Vesuvius, suffered severely. Dense clouds of ashes settled down on the two towns and buried them completely. Today, after remaining eighteen hundred years under their shroud of volcanic matter, they are being exhumed by the miner's pick and presented to view just as they were when overtaken by the great disaster. From that time to the present, Vesuvius has continued to smoke and to give forth occasional eruptions of lava.

Thus volcanoes that have long since become extinct can arouse themselves once more, just as active volcanoes can, on occasion, smother their fires. Moreover, at any spot whatever, whether amid cultivated fields, on the broad prairies, or at the bottom of the sea, a volcano may suddenly spring into being. Examples of these abrupt appearances of volcanic outlets in the most unexpected places are far from rare. I will tell you of some.

In September, 1538, after numerous tremors occurring at intervals for two years and causing great alarm to the people around Naples, a plain in the neighborhood of Pozzuoli was seen to rise in a sort of gigantic blister half a league in circumference. On September 29, at two o'clock in the morning, this blister suddenly burst with a frightful noise, forming as it did so a mouth or crater that threw up a mixture of fire, smoke, stones, and mud. Detonations like the most violent thunderclaps accompanied this eruption. The ejected stones were hurled up to a prodigious height, and then fell back either into the opening or on its edges. The mud was grayish in color, like a paste of cinders, and very fluid. In less than twelve hours, the tract of land pushed up by subterranean forces, and still further heightened by the accumulation of stones, ashes, and mud thrown out, formed a hill 144 meters high. For two days and two nights, the eruption continued without pause. The ejected mud fell back in showers so dense that Pozzuoli and its environs were fairly flooded. Naples suffered likewise, having a number of its palaces ruined by this curious kind of rain.

Awakened suddenly in the middle of the night by the first detonations of this outburst, the inhabitants of Pozzuoli fled at random, crazed with fear, covered with mud, the expectation of speedy death depicted on their faces. Some carried children in their arms or dragged sacks filled with household goods; others set out for Naples with a donkey bearing some infirm member of their family. Those who still retained a little presence of mind hastily gathered, along the way, great numbers of birds that had fallen to the ground, dead, at the beginning of the eruption, and fish that the adjacent sea, in receding a distance of two hundred paces, had left stranded on the beach.

On the third day, the eruption ceased. A few adventurous persons climbed the new mountain and found that it enclosed a vast funnel-shaped excavation having a depth of 138 meters. At the bottom of this crater, stones and slag appeared to have been tossed about like the bubbles of steam in a boiling pot. Quiet now seemed to be restored, and the curious were flocking to the spot to see the volcano when, on the seventh day of this treacherous calm, there burst forth a second eruption almost as violent as the first. A number of persons were knocked down and killed by falling stones or suffocated by smoke. For some time outbursts of steam and fire were seen to rise from the mountain; then all became quiet again, and from that time to this, perfect calm has reigned.

This singular volcanic cone that shot up out of the ground in a single night was named Monte Nuovo, which means New Mountain. Today, Monte Nuovo is covered with vegetation, and from its slumbering crater, no trace of smoke is ever seen to rise.

About the middle of the eighteenth century, there was a large and populous plain in Mexico watered by two rivers and covered with rich crops of maize, rice, sugar-cane, and indigo plants. No one had the slightest suspicion that these fertile lands were destined one day to be given over to the ravages of a volcanic outburst. Never had the faintest tremor of the ground been felt there; never, as far back as history went, had any rumblings of underground fires been heard. Consequently, the people of this peaceful plain were enjoying a sense of perfect security when, in the month of June 1759, subterranean noises were heard, followed during the next two months by violent shocks. Toward the end of September, these disturbances became much more pronounced, and over a district rather more than half a league square, the ground rose little by little, until at last it presented the appearance of an enormous swelling 168 meters high. Then the surface of this monstrous blister began to undulate like an angry sea and became covered with innumerable conical hillocks — one might call them pustules — two or three meters high, which rose, burst open, and then caved in, one after another, like the bubbles of gas in a fermenting liquid.

Finally, the top of the great protuberance opened and vomited a mixture of smoke, ashes, and calcined stones. Soon, from the depths of this abyss, sprang up six volcanic cones, amongst them Jorullo, whose summit rises 483 meters above the level of the surrounding plain. Until the following February, this new volcano continued to throw up streams of lava and masses of slag, while the conical pustules or blisters scattered over the dome emitted jets of burning gas and of acid fumes. At the time when the ground began to rise, the two small rivers that irrigated the plain covered with their waters the entire tract now occupied by Mt. Jorullo. They were finally swallowed up in the abyss that opened beneath them.

Alexander von Humboldt visited the country more than forty years after the event. The upheaved tract on which the volcano rested gave out a hollow sound under his tread, suggesting some vast underground vault. Its surface still retained a degree of warmth from the fires beneath. It is even said that in 1780, twenty years after the eruption, the lava a few inches down in the fissures was hot enough to light a cigar. The conical blisters, or little "furnaces," as they are locally known, were still emitting gas and steam. As for the two streams that had disappeared in the fiery chasm, they came to the surface again, a long distance from their original channel, in the form of vigorous hot springs. Since then, the little furnaces and Jorullo itself have ceased to smoke, the springs and the ground about them have cooled off, and thick underbrush has grown up so as to cover the devastated district.

Next, let us take an example of a volcano sprung into existence under the sea. On July 10, 1831, the captain of a vessel passing about a dozen leagues from the southern coast of Sicily noticed a considerable expanse of sea boiling and bringing to the surface great numbers of dead fish. Then a column of water eight hundred meters in circumference suddenly shot up to a height of twenty meters and as suddenly subsided. This occurred several times, dense volumes of steam accompanying each outburst and rising at least 500 meters so that the sky was obscured.

Now you will ask, what was going on there in the depths of the sea? Was it a school of monstrous whales coming to the surface and thus making the sea boil in that manner? No; it was a new volcano seeking an outlet through the deep waters of the Mediterranean and lifting its burning cone little by little from the bottom of the sea. A strong smell of sulphur bore to the coasts of Sicily tidings of what was taking place. Soon, despite the distance, there could be seen on the horizon a high column of smoke which at night became illumined now and then with bright and sudden flashes like the heat lightning we see on summer evenings. Finally, there was heard a dull rolling as of distant thunder. Had it not been for the column of smoke, still vertical on the same spot, one would have thought a storm was in progress, far away and of long duration.

On his return a week later, the same captain found, at the very spot where before he had observed the sea in so tumultuous a condition, a small and unknown island, rising only a few meters above the sea level and looking as if it had been subjected to the action of intense heat. In the center, it was hollowed out in a sort of basin in which reddish water was boiling and from which rose eddies of smoke and jets of volcanic matter. In a wide area about the little island were floating fragments of slag, masses of pumice, and numbers of dead fish. On July 24, two weeks after its sudden appearance, this strange island was visited by a learned geologist, Frederick Hoffmann.

From a distance of a quarter of a league (prudence forbade a nearer approach) Hoffmann perceived that the visible part of the little island was little more than the edge of a crater six hundred or seven hundred meters in circumference. The island as a whole might be a quarter of a league around and twenty meters high at its highest points. Furthermore, the eruption, which was still continuing, tended to raise the island more and more by the heaping up of matter ejected by the volcano. From the crater there was issuing — with some force, though noiselessly — a succession of puffs of steam, white as snow, which united and stretched upward in the calm atmosphere like a majestic column half a kilometer in height. Fragments of blazing slag shot through this steam from time to time with the speed of rockets. Side by side with this column arose a sheaf of black smoke, in which there eddied continually, with a noise not unlike that of hail, ejections of slag, ashes, and volcanic sand. At the touch of these glowing substances, the sea boiled and steamed as if brought into contact with red-hot iron. No flames issued from the crater, but with each violent renewal of the eruption bright flashes of light shot through the black sheaf of ashes, and each flash was followed by a resonant peal as of thunder, the frequent repetition of which must have sounded in the distance like a continuous rumbling. Every quarter of an hour this imposing spectacle gave place to a brief interval of calm, during which nothing was to be seen but the column of steam.

On August 4, the island was sixty meters high and one league around. Doubtless, it would have continued to increase in extent and height if the eruption had lasted longer, but a month after these volcanic disturbances began, they all ceased. Then for the first time, it was possible to visit the island without danger. It was named Graham Island, but its existence was a short one, as gradually the waves washed away the edges of the crater and by the month of December of the same year, Graham Island had virtually disappeared, being reduced to a mere reef after there had apparently been discharged, far below the surface of the water, a stream of lava through some invisible crevice. Volcanic energy, however, in this vicinity was not entirely spent, as two years later other eruptions took place but without causing any more new islands to rise above the waves. In 1863, the crater that was thought to be extinct and buried forever in the sea again reappeared full of boiling water and sulphurous gases.

From these various examples of new volcanoes suddenly appearing, it is evident that the incandescent matter inside the earth may burst forth at any moment and at any point, whether on dry land or at the bottom of the sea.

CHAPTER XII

FIRE AND WATER

REASONING FROM facts that it has observed, science infers that this earth of ours was in the beginning a globe of molten matter. But whence, you will ask, did it come? It came from the infinite resources of the Creator of all things,—

From Him who, when he wished to people space
And fill the void, had but to turn his face
And bid the nothingness to cease to be.
Forthwith the void conceived, at his decree,
Grew pregnant; and straightway was wrought
Outward expression of creative thought.

The earth was then an ocean of fire, without bed or shores, its great surges stirring up the elements that were one day to become continents and seas, — those elements forming at that time a fluid like the liquid metal that flows white-hot from the smelting furnace. Gradually, however, from the slow cooling off of its outermost layer, the earth acquired a solid envelope or shell, though this was at first as red-hot as any iron that ever came out of the blacksmith's forge.

Becoming thicker by degrees, this fiery crust lost, little by little, its excessive heat and finally ceased to glow. The earth's period of luminosity, of light-giving, was over; but its surrounding atmosphere was not yet of that limpid blue we are so familiar with in the appearance of our sky on a clear day. Thick and turbid and composed of many kinds of gases, it hardly allowed the sun's rays to penetrate to the earth's surface.

Scarcely had the solid crust of our earth been thus rudely fashioned, when a beneficent force began to act upon it, a force that was to continue through all the earth's history. I refer to the reaction of the earth's central fluid mass against its solidified outer crust. From this reaction, there came into being the earth's surface irregularities, its outstanding continents and the depressions filled by the sea, its chains of mountains and its valleys separating one mountain from another. Now, this force, that hollowed out the ocean beds and lifted the snow-clad summits of our loftiest peaks above the clouds, is like that which we today find at work in an apple that is gradually drying up and becoming wrinkled.

When recently gathered, an apple is of uniform smoothness all over its surface; its skin, tightly stretched over the juicy pulp within, shows not a single wrinkle. Later, the juice evaporates in part and the apple, losing in this way a portion of its substance, becomes slightly smaller. But the skin does not contract as the flesh contracts because the dry material composing it has nothing that can evaporate. If, then, the apple's covering keeps its size while the apple itself shrinks, it is evident that before long the covering will be too large for the thing covered, and, in order to continue sticking to the flesh, the skin must wither and wrinkle. The earth's crust has been doing this from time immemorial, so that now it is as shriveled as the skin of some dried-up old fruit.

The shrinking caused by the loss of heat is greater in liquids than in solids. Consequently, the central fluid mass of our globe, in gradually radiating its heat and losing it in surrounding space, contracts more than does the solid crust; and however small the difference between the rates of these two contractions, sooner or later the melted matter within must cease to furnish a firm support to the enclosing crust. Then one of two things will inevitably take place: either the crust, somewhat flexible as it is, will fold and wrinkle so as to remain in contact with the shrinking interior, or, if this flexibility is insufficient to allow such folding and wrinkling, the crust will break up under its own weight and pieces of it will fall in. But these fragments cannot adjust themselves well to the smaller space they now have to occupy, and hence all sorts of irregularities and roughness will be the result.

The surface of the globe will show every kind of inequality, of unevenness, in the form of depressions and elevations, gullies and ridges, valleys and mountain chains, deep abysses and lofty heights. When we view the huge mass of some alpine range, we find it hard to regard this as but an insignificant wrinkle in the earth's crust; but when we contrast the alpine range with the whole vast mass of the globe, all its imposing grandeur disappears; for the least wrinkle in the skin of an apple is greater in proportion to the size of the apple than is the whole range of the Andes in proportion to the size of the earth.

Evidently, the frequency and the degree of the irregularities in the earth's surface depend on the thickness and firmness of the hardened crust. If thin and flexible, the earth's crust must, at the slightest receding of the enclosed fluid mass, crumple up in undulating folds of only moderate depth. If thicker and more rigid, it will offer longer resistance to dislocating forces; but when the limit of resistance is reached, the crust, instead of folding in a more or less gentle manner, will suffer violent rupture, while strata that were horizontal will, in places, assume a vertical or nearly vertical position. Consequently, the irregularities of the earth's surface are more pronounced in proportion as they are more recent. In fact, observation has proved that the gently rounded tops of some of our lesser hills date back to the earliest epochs, while in more recent ages there sprang into being the enormous chains of the Andes and of the Himalayas. We shall soon learn how it can be determined with certainty that one chain of mountains is older than another, even though the tremendous forces that gave the earth its present surface inequalities operated long before the existence of man.

Breaks in the earth's crust are not sudden accidents, occurring with no previous preparation. For a long time - as long, in fact, as its flexibility permits - the solid covering keeps pace with the receding movement of the enclosed melted matter. With such slowness that only centuries can produce any visible changes, the earth's surface yields and bends, sinking here and rising there, until at last a rupture occurs along the lines of least resistance. Then oceans and continents make a fresh division of their respective domains; according to the manner and the degree in which they change their level, the ancient ocean bottom may become dry land, and the former dry land may become ocean. Finally, order is restored and a new period of calm begins, to be followed sooner or later by another disturbance. Many and many a time has this old earth of ours suffered these dislocations which alter its surface and change the outlines of continents and of seas; for everywhere we find traces of ocean waters that subsequently took their departure.

We are now in one of those periods of calm when the work of making over our continents performed by the subterranean furnace seems to have ceased. It is hard for us to believe that the face of our earth may some day present quite a different appearance; we regard the continents as firmly and permanently established on their foundations and the seas as settled for all time in their respective basins. Can it be that the interior fires are forever quieted, and has the earth entered upon an indefinite period of tranquillity? Everything points to the contrary; a thousand instances prove to us that the ground under our feet is not stable. Here, there, and everywhere there goes on slowly but unceasingly the oscillating movement that sooner or later makes the continents totter on their foundations of melted matter.

When the earth's crust has been fractured, the underlying fluid matter, being pressed down by the weight of the solid layer resting on it, is injected into the fissures so as to fill them more or less completely, sometimes coming up to the surface and even running over in considerable streams, or piling up in mounds and ridges above the crevice through which it was forced. An excellent example illustrating what takes place in these circumstances may be seen in the way water acts in winter when a sheet of ice is broken up. The water is forced up between the blocks of ice and may even rise to the surface here and there, after which, if the temperature is low enough, it freezes, welding the separate ice fragments together and sometimes projecting in a ridge along the line of rupture. In past periods of the earth's history, and especially when the terrestrial crust was still thin and was undergoing frequent fracture, the fluid matter of the interior came to the surface in this way, with more or less disturbance to the solid strata as it did so.

Our earth's first surface inequalities, the first pimples on the smooth skin stretched over the liquid matter inside, must have been chiefly due to the opening of volcanic mouths that poured forth incandescent matter which soon hardened into conical forms. Later, when the earth's skin had become less flexible and was crisscrossed with numerous fissures of some length, the interior liquid matter, being driven out more forcibly, must have taken the form of great ridges, each one the backbone of some lofty mountain chain whose saw-like profile now pierces the clouds with its granite peaks. This forcing up of the inner fluid matter through crevices in the outer crust has occurred so often through the ages that today one half of the ground we walk upon is composed of rocks that once came from the earth's interior in a melted state. The other half, as we shall see, is made up of sediment left by the waters that once flooded the land.

Mountain chains, then, represent the ridges once raised along the fracture lines of the earth's crust by the injection from below of subterranean matter in a molten condition, and also by the folding and the tilting up of strata already solidified. It is along these lines of fracture that earthquakes are most felt because here the resistance of the crust is feebler than elsewhere; it is along these lines, too, that hot springs make their appearance because the heat from below is easily transmitted through the crevices; and, finally, it is along these lines that volcanoes spring up in irregular rows like so many chimneys which, all erected on the same fissure, place the interior of the earth in communication with the exterior.

At the time ordained by the Creator, when the fiery mass of the earth had become cool enough, an event of the first importance occurred in the atmosphere enveloping our globe. Hitherto a very high temperature had prevented the formation of water, which therefore could exist only as steam floating in dense clouds above the earth's surface. Oceans were to take shape eventually, but the time for that had not yet arrived. The day when the first drop of water fell on the still burning-hot surface of the earth a new era was opened. The first rainfalls were, no doubt, nothing but slight showers that fell hissing on the hot ground and were immediately turned into steam. More abundant downfalls, constantly renewed and as often vaporized at the expense of the excessive heat then prevailing, finally made it possible for water to remain on the surface of the earth; and from that time the stores of moisture in the atmosphere fell in copious showers.

Excepting, perhaps, the hurricanes of the Antilles and the typhoons of India, which seem to exhaust the utmost resources of the elements in order to set the sky on fire with continuous lightning and open the floodgates of heaven in a veritable deluge, there is today nothing that can suggest to us the tremendous downpours with which the earth was flooded and the ocean beds filled in those far-off days when the continents were taking form and the earth was being prepared for the support of vegetable and animal life. One mass of dark clouds, heavy with moisture, then enveloped the globe. From time to time electric flashes lighted up this somber scene so vividly as to recall the earlier ages when the earth was one blazing mass of incandescent matter. The lightning played on every side, while peals of thunder reverberated as if the universe itself were crashing to its downfall. Through it all the floods descended in such cataracts as no Niagara of our time can hope to imitate. Earth and sky appeared to be united by a continuous body of falling water, and the very ground trembled under the impact of those liquid columns, those vertical rivers. Fearful tornadoes, unequaled by any tempests of our day, tore through the descending torrents, breaking and shaking and tossing them in wild fury.

When the reservoirs of heaven were at last emptied, the whole surface of the earth was covered by the sea — a strange sea, whose waters, boiling hot and thickened with mud and slime of all sorts, formed a kind of mineral pea-soup shrouded in a chaos of steaming vapors. Perhaps a few reefs, the tops of the highest ridges in the earth's irregular crust, lifted here and there their giant crests above the flood. On those scattered reefs alone did the turbid waves of that primeval ocean break and foam; everywhere else wave followed wave with no shore to offer opposition. Not until later was dry land to emerge from the deep; and when it did so, it was to be gradually and as the result of repeated breaks and readjustments in the earth's crust.

Finally, the atmosphere, freed from the burden of water that had gone to fill the ocean beds, retained no more moisture than it holds today in the form of invisible vapor or of clouds. It is thus, as nearly as science can infer the character of the majestic scenes of those ancient times by reasoning from effect to cause, from the known to the unknown, from facts observed to those inaccessible to observation — it is thus, I say, that in all probability occurred the formation of our oceans, the separation of the waters below from the waters above, the division of "the waters which were under the firmament from the waters which were above the firmament," as was related, in phrases of sublime brevity, by the sacred historian thirty-five centuries before science confirmed his words.

On receiving these copious rainfalls at a high temperature, the earth's crust was profoundly modified. Its primitive rock structure was broken up, and there was a general loosening and dissolving of particles all over the surface. Then the energetic action of the ocean waves contributed to disintegrate and pulverize what could not be dissolved. Thence resulted the enormous accumulations of sand, gravel, clay, and slime that turned the ocean into a fluid body of hot mud. When the effervescence had subsided and the lowering of the temperature of the water had lessened its dissolving power, this mud gradually settled and formed the first sedimentary deposit on the underlying granite bed.

At this epoch, or perhaps even earlier, the dry land began to emerge from the depths of the universal ocean. The terrestrial crust, wrinkling and breaking up more and more each day, raised the first stretches of ground above the waves. In the terse language of Genesis, the command was given, "Let the waters under the heaven be gathered together unto one place, and let the dry land appear: and it was so." The first dry land to appear was very far from having the extent of our present continents.

France, in particular, was only a sprinkling of archipelagos lost in the midst of the ocean's immensity. The greater part of what is now land was to remain under water for a long time, emerging little by little as time passed, and even now continuing to do so, as is clearly proved by the instances I have mentioned. In rising from the ocean depths the first land well deserved the adjective "dry" that is given to it in Genesis; for it could have been nothing but bare rock that had been subjected to the underground fires, a volcanic islet or two not unlike Graham Island, whose appearance I have already described. But at God's command life was in due time to appear and grass was to grow on these meager beginnings of our present continents.

Clarified at last, and swarming with aquatic life of all sorts, after the settling of the primitive mud, the oceans have from that day to this been piling up on their floors the mineral matter washed from the land by the action of the waves and of rivers and other streams. From the earliest times to the present day the ocean has been continually eating away its shores and depositing on the ocean floor what it has eaten away. It has never ceased receiving, from all the streams that empty into it, an immense contribution of sand, clay, mud, and so on, which have been deposited on the ocean bottom together with all sorts of dead shellfish, and have there hardened into layers of solid rock. At a later period underground forces lifted out of the water, here and there, the old ocean bottom and converted it into dry land. Thus it has come about that the rocky framework of our continents, even up to the highest mountain tops, is today often intermixed with marine shells.

The earth's crust, then, is composed of two kinds of rock corresponding to the two agencies that have been constantly at work in forming it,—fire and water. One kind emerged in a molten state from the earth's interior; the other was formed at the bottom of the ocean from the refuse of all sorts washed from the land and churned together by the waves. The first kind is known as eruptive rock, to indicate its origin by eruption or outburst in a fluid condition from the interior of the earth. It is also called Plutonian rock, from the name of the mythological god Pluto, the lord of the lower regions. The second kind is known as sedimentary rock, from a Latin word meaning to settle, because it is made of mineral matter that has settled at the bottom of the sea. Another name given to it is Neptunian rock, from Neptune, god of the sea.

Every solid substance that fuses or melts under the action of heat will crystallize in cooling if the cooling is not too rapid; that is, it will form into particles of a regular shape with flat sides or facets like little mirrors, as is seen in sugar, though its crystallization is otherwise brought about. (It may here be explained that sugar is a soluble substance and that soluble substances crystallize when the liquid in which they are dissolved evaporates. This is true both of sugar and of our common salt, which dissolve in water and form crystals when the water dries out.) Thus, the Plutonian or eruptive rocks, having emerged in a molten state from the bowels of the earth and having cooled off slowly, ought to present a crystalline appearance; and they are, in fact, often composed of an infinity of little crystals.

The most noteworthy and the commonest of these crystalline rocks is granite, the name of which is due to the granular structure so plainly noticeable in the rock. Granite is a mixture of three kinds of crystalline particles: quartz or silica, feldspar, and mica. You all know that glassy mineral that gives off sparks when struck with steel and that enters into the composition of white pebbles. Well, that is quartz, or silica. Flint is a variety of silica, as are also agate, distinguished for its rich coloring, and rock crystal, clearer than glass. Silica combines with many substances, and thus are formed a large number of minerals of divers sorts and known generally as silicates. Feldspar is a silicate containing silica and lime. It is of a white appearance, opaque and having a slightly satin-like gloss. In granite, it is conspicuous by reason of its oblong crystals. Mica also is a silicate, with clay in its composition. It forms little glittering scales, sometimes like gold or silver spangles, so that it is often mistaken for one of these precious metals; and sometimes it is black, green, or reddish. The glittering sand formerly used for drying the fresh writing ink owes its sparkle to nothing more valuable than mica.

I will not go further into this difficult subject of the composition of the Platonian rocks, but was merely add that they are all silicates, combinations of silica with a variety of other substances, and that most of them give out sparks on being struck with steel and are distinguished by their crystalline appearance and their excessive hardness.

The crystalline structure common in Plutonian or eruptive rocks is very rare in Neptunian or sedimentary rocks, which is quite what might have been expected, as the latter are formed from mineral matter in a finely divided state that has settled at the bottom of the sea and become hardened in the course of centuries. The most common of these sedimentary rocks is that which contains lime, and which we are familiar with in limestone, chalk, and marble. All these substances have essentially the same composition, containing as they do lime and an invisible gas called carbonic acid. They all have the peculiarity of foaming or effervescing when touched with an acid stronger than carbonic acid, this effervescence being due to the escape of the gas just named. Eruptive rocks never show this characteristic.

The other sedimentary rocks are formed from the various kinds of clay that are so easy to recognize from the facility with which, when water is added, they can be kneaded and molded; the marls, which are mixtures of clay and pulverized limestone; the many varieties of sand and of smooth pebbles, which are only mineral fragments of varying size wrested from the land by the action of water and worn down by friction; and, lastly, the sandstones, which are compact and hardened masses of sand.

The materials that entered into the composition of the sedimentary rocks were deposited at the bottom of the sea in regular horizontal layers or beds of varying thickness. Layers of this sort are also known as strata. From these deposits of mineral and other matter resulted a succession of strata, made of limestone, clay, sand, and so on, the oldest at the bottom, the later ones above. Remaining horizontal as long as no disturbing cause deranged them, they were afterward, in many instances, bent or broken and tilted up out of their original position but have always kept their first arrangement in parallel layers. Accordingly, one of the most striking features of the earth's crust is its stratification, its arrangement in layers, more or less regular, due to the action of the ocean waters. Eruptive rocks show nothing like it; pressed up in liquid form through fissures in the sedimentary strata, which they ruptured and disarranged in their passage, they eventually took the form of isolated peaks, of ridges, of jagged ramparts; or they may show as rounded domes, as cone-shaped hills, or as small mounds; but in no instance are they composed of regular layers. In short, they are not stratified.

Finally, sedimentary rocks very often contain in abundance the petrified remains of organic life, either animal or vegetable, that once existed in the depths of those waters where these sedimentary rocks were formed. We give the name of fossils to such petrified relics of animal and vegetable life. Most numerous are the fossil shellfish, the rock being sometimes almost wholly made of them. Nothing of this sort is ever found and evidently never can be found in eruptive rocks, as these had their origin in the great central fire far down in the bowels of the earth.

The distinctive peculiarities of the two series of rocks composing the earth's present crust may be tabulated as follows:

PLUTONIAN OR ERUPTIVE ROCKS	**NEPTUNIAN OR SEDIMENTARY ROCKS**
Forced up from the interior of the earth to the surface, passing through the mineral crust already formed.	Formed on the surface of the earth from matter deposited by the ocean waters.
Generally of crystalline structure.	Not, as a rule, of crystalline structure.
Arranged in irregular masses.	Arranged in regular layers or strata.
Never contain fossils, or the petrified remains of animal and vegetable organisms.	Often contain fossils, or the petrified remains of animal and vegetable organisms that once lived in the waters where these rocks were formed.

Composed of various silicates, never of limestone.

Never effervesce on being touched with an acid.

Composed in large part of limestone.

Effervesce, as a rule, on being touched with an acid, because of the limestone they contain.

CHAPTER XIII

MOUNTAINS

THE TERRITORY conquered by the earth's interior fires in
their strife with the waters of the prehistoric ocean — or, in
other words, the total extent of our present dry land — amounts
to about one quarter of the entire surface of the globe; the sea
claims the remaining three quarters. As the land did not emerge
from the deep all in one piece, but in successive parts by reason
of ruptures, bendings, folds, and other movements, all crisscross
in every direction, our continents exhibit various kinds of surface inequality, in which wild disorder seems to hold absolute
sway. In one section, for example, are deep ravines and frightful
chasms penetrating the very bowels of the earth and bordered
by frowning heights that tower to the clouds; in another part,
almost on a level with the sea, stretch vast plains; and elsewhere
still we find high plateaus with hardly a depression to break their
monotony. Amid this endless variety of elevation, it is impossible
to form a clear idea of the dry land as a whole, and so we must
have recourse to the following device based on measurements
of the chief inequalities in the earth's surface.

Suppose all the mountains of Europe razed to the ground
and their combined bulk used to fill the plains and valleys in
such a manner as to make the surface of this part of the world
perfectly level, just as if a gigantic rake had gone over it from
one end to the other and evened it off. Well then, after this
general leveling had been carried out, the height of Europe
above the sea would be only 205 meters. That is what we call
its mean altitude. In the same manner, it has been estimated
that the mean altitude of Asia is 350 meters and that of both

Americas 285. As for Africa, its mean altitude has not yet been determined because the interior of the Dark Continent is still insufficiently known to us.

The mean altitude of the continents above the sea level is about three hundred meters. Represented on the large globe, two meters in diameter, that has already served us as a term of comparison, it would be less than the thickness of a sheet of paper. It is on this slight epidermis, unceasingly washed by streams and eaten away by the oceans (which have thrice its surface area) — it is on this thin skin that empires rest and humanity pursues its destiny.

What would it take to wipe this insignificant scum off the face of the earth and relegate it to the ocean depths whence it came? It would need only the withdrawal of the sustaining hand that controls the mighty forces of nature, and at the first furious outbreak of the earth's interior fires, the continents would collapse and sink beneath the waves. A single earthquake in 1822 raised the soil of Chile over an extent of territory measuring 1300 square leagues, changing its level one meter on average. Three hundred such tremors beneath the sea would create entire continents similar to ours, and likewise three hundred such disturbances under the dry land would engulf the continents already existing if the combined effect of such disturbances were directed toward depressing instead of elevating the overlying surface — a result not at all impossible.

That the general stability of the dry land is never seriously endangered must be due to some mighty mechanism that preserves its equilibrium, an equilibrium constantly menaced and constantly maintained. It must be that the continents rest on some firmer support than the fluctuating surface of the interior incandescent ocean, and that a sleepless eye watches over the welfare of those patches of ground now lifted above the sea level. This mighty mechanism, this firm support, this sleepless eye — do you know what it is, my young readers? It is the eye, the support, the mechanism of Providence.

It needs no very serious reflection to perceive, also, the providential purpose manifest in the countless irregularities that diversify the face of the continents. What kind of world would this be if all the dry land, on emerging from the deep, had taken forever the form of an uninterrupted plateau like the one we have imagined in estimating the mean altitude of Europe? It would be just one monotonous stretch of territory on which a sparse population would drag out a languishing and miserable existence; or perhaps it would be a blank desert.

As a matter of fact, then, mountains not only serve to please the eye by their grandeur and to relieve the monotony of the earth's surface by the majesty of their towering peaks and the nobility of their general outline; they also have a more important, a more useful part to play, inasmuch as without them there could be no proper circulation of the waters of the globe, so that they are to be considered one of the chief causes of the soil's fertility. On their cloud-capped summits fall and accumulate the snows of winter, forming storage supplies of frozen water whose gradual melting feeds the various watercourses throughout the year; and on their sides, slowly eaten away by storms, soil suitable for vegetation is prepared, which washes down into the valleys and enriches them. From summit to base, therefore, a mountain is unceasingly at work promoting the fertility of the surrounding plains, distributing to them both the soil in which the seed is to germinate and the water that supplies that seed's first need.

Nor does this complete the tale. With its surface rendered uneven, broken up into plains and mountains and valleys, the dry land is not only productive, but it is also extremely varied in its products. The moist lowlands have their green pastures, the plains have their rich harvests, the hillsides have their vineyards, and the mountains their forests. On level ground, no such variety would be possible. So it is that, to make the earth teem with inexhaustible riches of infinite variety, providential foresight has broken up the surface in all kinds of ways by the action of the great subterranean furnace; and in those bald mountain tops condemned to sterility for the benefit of the plains below, in those towering peaks eternally covered with their mantle of snow, we see invaluable gifts bestowed upon the continents by the munificence of a bountiful Creator.

A mountain chain is a continuous range of mountains formed either by the upbending or by the uptilting of a part of the earth's crust, brought about in the first case by a folding movement, in the second by a break. Let us examine these two chief varieties of mountain chains.

Take between your fingers a dozen or more leaves of a book and press them inward. The result will be a fold, more or less rounded, in which the separate leaves, while keeping their relative arrangement, one above another, will all bend in the same way, and under the lowest of the leaves forming this vault there will be an empty space. What the leaves of a book do when thus pressed laterally, the leaves or strata of the earth's crust, formed of sedimentary rock in layers, one on another, will also do when subjected to tremendous lateral pressure in the disturbances caused by some mighty convulsion having its origin in the great subterranean furnace over which we all live. These strata fold or buckle without change in their order of superposition, and from the fold thus made, there is formed a mountain chain.

Of course the strata of the earth's crust are not so easily bent as are the leaves of a book. They consist of enormous beds of rock, sometimes a kilometer or more in thickness. No matter. Under the irresistible pressure that can rupture continents and throw islands up out of the ocean depths these strata are as pliable as wax. This folding of the earth's surface layers seems incomprehensible to us only because we involuntarily compare the forces engaged in this prodigious work with such similar means as are at our command. But what are our paltry mechanical devices, able at most to raise a block of some cubic meters in volume, when compared with the subterranean energies that can shatter the earth's crust and lift to the clouds such vast masses as the Andes and the Himalayas? But even these mountain-chains, as I cannot too often remind you, are as nothing, despite their impressive grandeur, when compared with the size of the earth. It is, then, not hard to understand that the strata of the earth's crust, massive and strong though they appear to be, nevertheless fold into mountain-chains under the tremendous lateral pressure brought to bear on them, just as the leaves of a book fold or buckle up under the pressure of our fingers.

Beneath the terrestrial layers thus bent upward in the form of a vault, there must be left, by this action, an unoccupied space not so very far, comparatively, below the surface; but evidently the melted mineral matter always seething just underneath the crust hastens to supply the mountain chain with a nucleus or heart of granite or some other kind of eruptive rock. Accordingly, if it were possible to make a vertical cut from top to bottom of one of these mountains and expose the cross-section to view, we should see, first, a succession of sedimentary rock layers all folded to conform with the mountain's outline, and under these, constituting the heart of the mountain, a mass of Plutonian or eruptive mineral matter. The Jura range offers some fine examples of mountains formed by this folding process.

But it is not always that the sedimentary strata of the earth's crust are flexible enough to bend without breaking under the violent pressure to which they are subjected. In that case, there is a fracture extending through the entire thickness of the fold, and the molten matter from within bursts forth through this fissure, overthrowing and tossing aside any and all obstacles to its egress. The crest of the mountain chain thus brought into being is formed of a ridge of eruptive rock, while the two sides are made of fractured sedimentary strata. Such is the structure of Mont Blanc, its summit being of granite and its sides and base of sedimentary material such as limestone, marl, sand, and sandstone.

Thus, in general, a mountain chain may belong to either one of two chief classes: it may represent a fairly regular fold in the earth's crust, with a series of heights having rounded outlines and composed, at least externally, of sedimentary layers more or less sharply bent; or it may be formed by the violent rupture of a fold in the earth's crust, the fold being fractured lengthwise and its two sides thrust apart by a mass of eruptive rock that constitutes the framework and the cap, so to speak, of the entire chain. Accordingly, when eruptive rocks are found on the surface, they always form the core and the crest of the mountain chain where they are thus exposed to view, while sedimentary rocks, uptilted and overthrown, make the base and the two sides. This arrangement may be observed in all mountain chains that expose to view two kinds of rock, as in the Alps and the Pyrenees. Furthermore, wherever these two kinds of rock are in immediate contact, it is proved by certain remarkable evidences that the so-called Plutonian or eruptive rock, such as granite (to name only the most important example), must have issued from the earth's interior at a very high temperature, as we have already learned, and must have poured forth in as fluid a condition as the lava ejected by volcanoes in our own day. These evidences merit our attention for a few minutes.

In passing through the strata of various kinds deposited by the seas, the eruptive matter afterward solidified as rock has left behind it the plainest proof of the high temperature it still retained on reaching the surface. This high temperature it has very legibly recorded, if we may so express it, on the limestones, the clays, and the different kinds of sand through which it has passed, just as the fire of a forge records its temperature on the burnt brick of the hearth. You will understand this more clearly from what follows.

Subjected to the action of heat, limestone decomposes, the carbonic-acid gas escaping and the lime alone remaining. The making of lime is based on this very principle. But if limestone is shut up tightly in a metal container, as in the tube of a cannon hermetically sealed, the carbonic-acid gas has no way of escaping and decomposition does not take place. In these circumstances, the limestone melts without change in its chemical composition, and after a slow cooling, which makes crystallization possible, the original limestone or common building stone, or the crumbling chalk, if this has been used in the experiment, is found transformed into a compact mass of white marble as crystalline as sugar. This curious experiment enabling us to change powdery chalk into firm marble by the application of heat was first performed by the physician Sir James Hall.

Now, upon coming into contact with molten granite or some other eruptive rock, limestone is turned into marble by the action of the extremely high temperature at which the eruptive rock touches it; and the resulting marble is sometimes pure white, sometimes marked with colored veins. These eruptive rocks, therefore, at the moment when they were forced in a liquid state through the sedimentary strata, must have had the great heat required in Hall's experiment; for they were evidently able, by their mere touch or nearness, to melt the limestone buried at a depth that forbade the escape of the carbonic acid contained in the stone. In like manner, the passage of eruptive rock wrought a notable change in the coal it chanced to find in its way, causing it to give up its gas, very much as our present gas works separate the gas from the coal. And in similar wise, once more, sand was vitrified or turned into the glassy substance we recognize as quartz. Also, clay became hardened or baked just as it is baked in the potter's oven.

From these various facts as observed in all parts of the world, an important inference is drawn, the correctness of which cannot be doubted: the granite masses that form the framework of the principal mountain chains emerged from the earth's interior in a state of incandescence, and in their present condition, they are the cooled and hardened overflow of subterranean molten matter. Before they lifted their lofty crests into the regions of eternal snow, they rolled as waves of lava in the great underground furnace.

I have already told you that the continents were not always as they are today. They made their appearance by degrees, and as successive breaks in the earth's crust, newly formed folds, and wrinkles wrought increasing changes of level and confined the seas within narrower limits. Consequently, the mountain chains are not all of the same age, but some are older than others, for they mark the various stages of our planet's progress through its successive transformations. The study of the earth, then, cannot fail to prompt the question, "How old are the mountains!"

Ah, my young readers, what an echo from remotest antiquity we hear in those five words! We willingly bow the head in token of respect before an ancient building bearing on its front the venerable dust of centuries, and the traveler is filled with awe as he stands before the pyramids of Egypt, contemporaries of the Pharaohs. Who, then, of a reflective mind, can contemplate with indifference the mountains, those gigantic monuments the like of which all mankind working together could never hope to erect, and of so venerable an age that man was not yet in existence to see the first stone laid in position? How old are the mountains? God alone can tell. He who knows how many centuries it took the sea to lay, a grain of sand at a time, each one of the strata composing its bottom. Therefore, science does not attempt to determine how many centuries ago this or that chain of mountains took form, but simply tells us whether such and such a chain was reared above the surrounding plain before or after such and such another. It is possible, I say, to determine the order in which the great mountain ranges came into being; we can, in short, tell their relative ages, but nothing more. We can assert positively that the Jura range, for example, had already lifted its peaks skyward when the substance of the future Pyrenees was being deposited on the ocean floor, and that the Pyrenees in their turn were piercing the clouds while the Alps still lay in the mud at the bottom of the sea. We can affirm that the Jura Mountains are older than the Pyrenees, and the Pyrenees older than the Alps, but nothing more definite than that. Let us inquire now how this meager though important information has been gained.

From the remotest times, mineral matter of all sorts has been settling at the bottom of the sea, and these deposits, compacted and hardened in the course of centuries, have become layers of rock, their position being in general horizontal. These layers or strata, usually of considerable thickness, are of different composition, one from another, being sometimes of limestone, sometimes of clay or sand, and differing also in the kinds of shellfish found petrified in their substance, because marine life, like animal life on the land, has at various times in the lapse of ages undergone great changes, as I shall tell you in another book. Not to make the explanation too complicated, let us imagine only three of these strata of sedimentary rock lying under the sea in the natural horizontal position they assumed

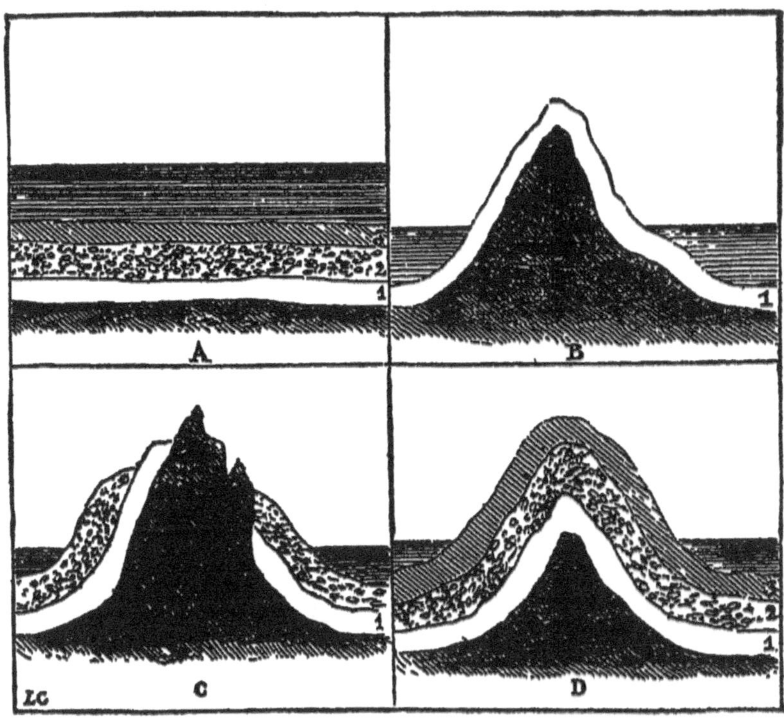

FIGURE 16

in forming. The lowest of these layers is evidently the oldest, and the uppermost is the most recent. As to the intermediate one (Number 2 in Figure 16), it was evidently deposited after Number 1 and before Number 3.

Now let us suppose the bottom of the sea to fold or buckle in such a manner as to emerge from the water and form a mountain chain. The three strata will bend in unison, as shown in Section D of our illustration, and will all together constitute the framework of the range. If in another part of the ocean bottom there had occurred an earlier upheaval, after the deposit of layers 1 and 2, but before that of Number 3, it is evident that this earlier range would have only the two strata numbered 1 and 2, these being the only ones then in existence. This is illustrated in C. Finally, layer 1 would alone constitute the framework of the mountain chain if the upheaval had occurred still earlier, before layer 2 was deposited. Section B of the illustration shows the cross-section of a mountain chain formed under these conditions. It is plain enough that of the three ranges of mountains presenting in their framework the structure indicated in the illustration, the oldest must be that shown in section B, since it lacks two layers of sedimentary rock from the fact that it emerged out of the depths before their formation. Next in age comes the range marked C, which contains one more sedimentary layer than B; and, finally, the most recent of these formations is that marked D, in which the three strata are seen all together.

As a rule, then, science tells us that one mountain chain is of earlier formation than another if it lacks one or more of the sedimentary strata found in that other. The Jura range is known to be older than the Pyrenees because it is not clothed in the complete mantle of stone with which the seas provided the Pyrenees; and the latter are known to be older than the Alps because one does not find in them all the sedimentary strata that are to be seen in the structure of the Alps. In this way, science has determined the chief stages in the disruption undergone by the earth's crust in bringing the continents to their present condition.

In the following list are arranged chronologically the names of some of the mountain chains formed by upheaval at different epochs in the earth's history. They are chiefly mountain chains of France.

1st Age. Hills of Brittany in the neighborhood of Saint – LA. Slate lands of the Ardennes.

2d Age. Mountains of the Cotes-du-Nord and of the Department of Morbihan. Ballons of the Vosges.

3d Age. Mountains at the extremity of Finisterre. Scandinavian mountains.

4th Age. Hills of Birttany between Laval and Quimper.

5th Age. Mountains of Beanjolais.

6th Age. Mountains of Thuringia.

7th Age. The Cote-d'Or Mountains. The Monts du Morvan. The Jura range. The Cevennes.

8th Age. Mountains of Dauphine.
9th Age. The Pyreness, Carpathians, and Balkans.
10th Age. Mountains of Auvergne, Corsica, and Sardinia.
11th Age. The Alps. Mont Blanc.
12th Age. Mountains of Provence and of Spain.
13th Age. Stromboli and Etna.

Following is a list of some of the principal mountains of the earth and their heights.

EUROPE

Mont Blanc, Alps (France and Italy)	4810	meters
Monte Rosa, Alps (Switzerland and Italy)	4630	"
Matterhorn, Alps (Switzerland and Italy)	4505	"
Jungfrau, Alps (Switzerland)	4180	"
Maladetta, Pyrenees (Spain)	3480	"
Monte Perdido, Pyrenees (Spain)	3405	"
Etna, volcano (Sicily)	3315	"
Pic du Midi, Pyrenees (France)	2875	"
Mont Ventoux (France)	1912	"
Mont Dore (France)	1900	"
Plomb du Cantal (France)	1855	"
La Dôle (France)	1680	"
Puy-de-Dôme (France)	1470	"
Ballon de Guebwiller (France)	1430	"

ASIA

Everest, Himalayas (Nepal)	8840	"
Kunchinjinga, Himalayas (Nepal and Sikhim)	8840	"
Elbrus, Caucasus (Russia)	5645	"
Ararat (Armenia)	5350	"
Kliutschi, volcano (Siberia)	4800	"
Yablonoi (Siberia)	4550	"

AFRICA

Kilmanjaro (German East Africa)	6100 meters
Peak of Teneriffe (Canary Islands)	3710 "
Great Atlas Mountains (Morocco)	3465 "
Piton des Neiges (Reunion Island)	3065 "
Table Mountain (Cape of Good Hope)	1350 "

NORTH AMERICA

St. Elias,16 volcano (Alaska)	5443 meters
Popocatepetl, volcano (Mexico)	5400 "
Hooker (Alberta)	5086 "

SOUTH AMERICA

Aconcagua, volcano (Chile)	7150 "
Sajama, volcano (Bolivia)	6810 "
Chimborazo, volcano (Ecuador)	6530 "
Illimani, volcano (Bolivia)	6455 "
Cotopaxi, volcano (Ecuador)	5755 "
Pichincha, volcano (Ecuador)	4855 "

OCEANICA

Mauna Loa, volcano (Hawaii)	4840 "
Ophir, volcano (Sumatra)	3950 "
Blue Mountains (Australia)	2000 "

ANTARCTICA

Erebus, volcano	3750 "
Terror, volcano	3750 "

16   Now known to be exceeded in height by the Peak of Orizaba, in Mexico, Mt. Logan, in Yukon, and Mt. McKinley, in Alaska. Since this list was made out, more careful measurements of the principal mountains of the globe have been undertaken, and their results, if embodied in the list, would modify it in several instances. — *Translator*.

CHAPTER XIV

VALLEYS AND PLAINS

WHEN HE wishes to water his plants to the best advantage, the gardener digs a series of ditches through his beds of growing vegetables or blossoming flowers, and these ditches conduct the water to the places where it is needed, instead of letting it waste itself in purposeless meanderings. The earth is the garden of mankind, and its gardener is God. As reservoirs for its running waters, it has the mountains, and for irrigation ditches, it has the valleys. Every furrow in the earth's crust serves or may serve as a channel for some one of the countless streams of all sizes irrigating that crust.

But how were these irrigating channels of the earth first made? Could the work have been done by the running streams themselves? No; for is it conceivable that a river could by its own impetus alone open a channel through the hard rock, that a torrent could eat away solid granite to the enormous depth observed in so many instances among the mountains, or that a trickling streamlet would in thousands of years manage to cut through layer after layer of the densest mineral formation? Certainly not. The vast work of adapting the continents to the requirements of their circulating systems called for some mightier power than the mere force of running water. It is true that a stream, especially if its bed descends rapidly, may lower its banks and deepen its channel; but rarely has it begun by hollowing out the valley that was to mark its course. It must then have been the violence of subterranean convulsions that, in giving to the earth the ridges we now know as mountain chains, also gave it the furrows we call valleys. It was the furious inner heat that, by folding and fracturing the outer crust, made channels in the ground, cut through the mountain chains, and effected the countless passageways through which today flow streams of sparkling water. Every river found its route traced in advance; it followed the path already prepared for it, and its work of erosion was confined to shaping a bed in the great channel of some ready-made valley.

But in soil easily furrowed by running water, the action of such water was doubtless sufficient to hollow out a course for the stream, just as at the present time we often see the surface soil plowed in little gullies by a heavy rain. Valleys thus formed by the action of running water are said to be due to erosion. They are of inconsiderable depth and of minor importance. Valleys of other formation may be due either to fractures or to folds in the earth's crust. Those made by fracture have steep sides, and sometimes the projecting parts of the two sides correspond so closely that, if the operating forces push these two sides together, the result may be a juncture so nearly exact as to leave no visible signs of separation. Valleys due to a folding of the earth's crust are merely troughs between successive folds, and their sides are commonly of gentle slope.

Take a lump of soft clay and flatten it out; then, if you tear it slightly by pulling, each tear will represent a valley formed by fracture. But if you press it gently by pushing at two opposite sides so as to make it wrinkle up in folds, each channel between two successive folds will represent a valley of the kind last described. Finally, if you run a little stream of water over the surface, the tiny gully the water hollows out will be, in miniature, a valley due to erosion. So it is with this earth of ours. It is true that its envelope is not all made of soft clay, but on the other hand, the forces acting to plow and rend it are the corrosive action of rivers and the incalculable power of the great interior furnace.

A valley separating two parallel mountain chains is called a longitudinal valley because it runs lengthwise with the ranges forming its two slopes. Such a valley may be represented by the V-shaped enclosure between two roofs joining at the eaves, each of these roofs standing for a mountain chain. Valleys that furrow the two sides of a mountain chain and run down in lines more or less nearly straight from summit to base are called transverse valleys because they cut the chain crosswise. They may be likened to the gutters that run from the ridgepole to the eaves of a roof. Most of these transverse valleys are watered by streams proportioned to their size and fed chiefly by the gradual melting of the mountain snows, just as a roof gutter is supplied in time of rain with its special streamlet. These minor watercourses all empty into a main stream that occupies the bottom of a longitudinal valley and receives from right and left the tributary waters pouring into it from the two slopes that face each other, just as the common gutter of the facing sides of two adjoining gables receives the water from the conductors of both.

The line marking the coming together of the two slopes of a mountain chain is called its ridge or divide. For the valleys, there is a corresponding line where their two sides join at their lower edge, and it is called by the German name, thalweg, which means valley-way. The thalweg of a valley, then, is the line running lengthwise along its bottom, and it may be thought of as a sort of inverted divide. The stream of water irrigating a valley always follows the course of the thalweg.

Certain valleys, especially those situated at great heights, instead of widening and gradually merging into the neighboring plain, are hemmed in by the surrounding mountains and so barred where one would naturally expect to find a broad outlet as to leave only a narrow passage called a pass or defile. The ancients called these narrow passes "gates of nations" because often in a valley thus isolated from the rest of the world there dwelt an independent tribe or nation. Among passes of this sort, the following are famous in history: the Gates of the Caucasus, the Caspian Gates, the Gates of Issus, the Warm Gates, or Thermopylae, etc. In the Andes, there are passes winding their way between mountain walls fifteen hundred meters high.

Some valleys are in the shape of vast enclosures of an irregularly circular outline, as if the ground had sunk to a great depth, leaving a high vertical wall surrounding it. Such an enclosure commonly has an outlet in the form of a wide gap. Magnificent examples of valleys of this kind are to be found in the Pyrenees, where they are known, on account of their shape, under the name of oules, which means pots or kettles. In French, they are called cirques (circuses or amphitheaters). The most noted are the following: that at Gavarnie, which I shall speak of when I tell you about cascades, and that at Héas. This latter is thus described by an illustrious scholar, Ramond, who devoted a part of his life to the study of the Pyrenees:

> On reaching the level of this majestic amphitheater, we were overcome with astonishment. The two mountain ranges that had until then hemmed us in suddenly separated, spreading out to right and left, so that from where we stood they appeared to bend into a vast crescent, one horn ending at our side in two enormous rocks jutting out like two bastions. The other horn of the crescent is formed by a long, unbroken mountain range, quite bare, and surmounted at one point by a truncated rock peak towering aloft into the clouds. Where the two horns of the crescent unite stands the Peak of Tremousse, bearing its glacier, bristling with needles, and furrowed with deep gullies down which crash falling fragments from the mountainside. The enclosed space might be called a gulf or abyss if it were not so immense, for its altitude is nowhere less than eight hundred or nine hundred meters, and its circumference is more than two leagues. It has fresh air, an open sky, and a carpet of verdure. Numerous herds graze this fine pasture, which to them is all but limitless. Three million persons would not fill it, and the entire amphitheater would seat ten million. And this spacious enclosure, this wide plain, is perched on the crest, as we might say, of the Pyrenees, at the foot of precipitous walls, where the traveler desirous of scaling the surrounding heights would have to make his perilous way up some steep path on the very face of the precipice.

Two transverse valleys running down the two slopes of a mountain chain may join at their highest point. In that case, there is at the top, where the two valleys meet, a depression or cutting, which we call a gate or notch. A notch serves as a communication between one slope and the other and is used in crossing the divide. Between two successive notches, there is a section of the ridge left upstanding and isolated, and known in French as a *cime* (summit, crest). A notch is the starting point of two opposite transverse valleys; a *cime* is the starting point of two opposite transverse ridges or minor ranges.

Plains are divided into two classes: - high plains, or plateaus, and low or ordinary plains. Plateaus are elevated stretches of territory, broad and flat upheavals of the earth's crust, often serving as bases of lofty mountains. A plateau may be regarded as the nucleus of a continent, the center around which occurred the uprising of a more or less wide extent of dry land out of the primeval ocean, the lowlands being the last to emerge. Following are the altitudes of some of the most noteworthy plateaus:

Plateau	of	Auvergne	331 meters
"	"	Bavaria	507 "
"	"	Castile	682 "
"	"	Mexico	2281 "
"	"	Quito	2905 "
"	"	Tibet	3510 "
"	"	Peru	3919 "

Let us turn our attention especially to the plateau of Auvergne as the one most interesting to us. At a very remote period, long before man made his appearance on the earth, but not so distant that science cannot reveal its secrets, what was one day to become Europe was represented merely by a few archipelagoes of eruptive rock, a few granite islands lost in an expanse of ocean. While there lay buried in the submarine ooze the future sites of the two capitals of the world, London and Paris, and while the strata that were one day to constitute Europe were being laid down on the floor of the ocean, a few islands, the beginnings of a future France, were already visible above the waves. These first beginnings of dry land, witnesses to the convulsions that produced our present Europe, and venerable mothers of

France; these bits of territory, older than the Alps, the Pyrenees, or the Jura Mountains, are now Brittany, the Ardennes, and the plateau of Auvergne. These three islands in a sea now no longer existent are today united by sedimentary tracts left exposed by the receding waves of the primeval ocean.

The plateau of Auvergne, then, is one of the earliest stretches of dry land raised above the sea level by that vast upheaval to which we owe the ground we now walk upon. Two inlets or bays broke the outline of the island of Auvergne, one opening to the north and becoming later the fertile plain of Limagne, the other wider, opening southward and forming today the sterile region of Larzac. Two promontories added to the length of this ancient island, one on the north, constituting now a part of Burgundy, the other on the south, corresponding to the Black Mountain. Its central portion was a plateau of granite formation, embracing what is today Auvergne, Velay, Forez, and Limousin. Most of the volcanoes of France, volcanoes now all extinct, are situated within the limits of these ancient beginnings of our present fatherland.

On account of their high position, plateaus are likely to be washed bare by rain and by the streams that furrow them. Their loam is easily washed away, and it goes to enrich the surrounding low plains. Consequently, some plateaus are sterile in the extreme. Such is the plateau of Larzac, west of the Cévennes. It is a high limestone plain, 120 square kilometers in extent, where the only crops to be seen are an occasional potato patch and here and there a field of oats. In some parts, you will not find, for leagues around, either a tree or a brook. Nevertheless, the plateau feeds many flocks of sheep, the produce of which suffices to maintain the inhabitants. Another effect of the high position of plateaus is a colder climate. Larzac, despite its southern location, gets so much snow in winter that guideposts are necessary at certain intervals to mark the highways.

In the tropics, plateaus often appear like lofty islands in a sea of sand, and though situated in the torrid zone, they have a temperate climate. A plateau thus situated constitutes a world apart, which in its salubrity and in the manners and civilization of its inhabitants differs to its great advantage from the adjacent low plains, where man is enervated by the heat and the air too often poisoned by the exhalations from stagnant water. Among plateaus of this kind are to be noted those of Quito, Mexico, and Peru. The first is exactly on the equator, and the snow-capped summits of Pichincha, Chimborazo, and Antisana look down upon it. There, at an altitude of 2,900 meters, which in our part of the world is above the line of perpetual snow, is situated the flourishing city of Quito. Its climate has the mildness of continual spring. On the plateau of Peru, the celebrated silver mines of Potosi are worked at an altitude of 4,165 meters, or nearly the height of Mont Blanc. The city of Mexico, capital of the country of that name, is 2,275 meters above the level of the sea. No mountain in the interior of France attains this height. It was on these three plateaus of Quito, Mexico, and Peru that European explorers found, on reaching the American continent, the most advanced civilization anywhere existing among the natives.

Low plains are of far greater aggregate extent than plateaus, they alone comprising nearly half of the dry land. Some of them consist largely of the alluvial soil deposited by the great rivers that cross them, and they are very fertile. Such are the plains watered by the Rhone, the Loire, and the Seine. As for plains of other formation, their soil is by no means always fit for agriculture. There are some made up entirely of smooth round pebbles or of sand. The most noted of the pebbly plains of France is that of Crau, near the mouth of the Rhone. It was in this region, according to ancient mythology, that Hercules was one day set upon by giants as he was returning from a distant expedition. On the extreme confines of the then-known world, he had, with one blow of his cudgel, opened the Straits of Gibraltar and thus given to navigators a free passage between the Mediterranean and the ocean. He was returning from this exploit to his home in Greece when some giants attacked him. Although capable of valiant execution with his cudgel — for he had just cleft a mountain asunder and cut a strait — he was about to succumb to superior numbers when a shower of stones fell from heaven and put the giants to flight. Ever since then, the region about Crau has been nothing but a desert of pebbles.

But science explains more simply, as well as more truthfully, the origin of this celebrated plain. It says that in very early times, one of the great rivers that then furrowed the continents, an impetuous torrent pouring down from the Alps and now but feebly represented by the Durance, came dashing and smashing through this region, bearing great quantities of pebbles in its rushing current. That old-time torrent has disappeared, but its freight of pebbles still remains and constitutes the plain of Crau. This pebbly field, despite its apparent dryness, feeds numerous flocks of sheep throughout a great part of the year. A fine grass, thin but savory, springs up between the pebbles, and the sheep know how to get at it by turning the pebbles over. With the coming of hot weather, all verdure disappears, and then the sheep migrate; they change pastures by going up toward the Alps of Dauphiné, where they find the grazing land they need.

From the Gironde to the Pyrenees extend the *landes* (moors), which have given their name to the corresponding department. It is a desert without visible limits, a flat and sandy region covered with monotonous vegetation of heather and coarse grass. Balancing themselves on their high stilts, shepherds stride over these sterile plains, following their flocks. In many other parts of France, as well as in central and southern Europe generally, are to be found similar untilled plains, moors clothed exclusively in heather bearing little pink flowers. The moors of Lüneburg in Westphalia cover an area of 25,000 square kilometers. But the stilted shepherds belong properly to the *landes* of Gascony.

From the Atlantic to the Red Sea, over an area at least thrice as great as that of the Mediterranean, northern Africa is almost wholly an immense plain commonly regarded as the bottom of a former sea — a sea-bottom raised in comparatively recent times above the waves that once washed its sands. I refer to the Desert of Sahara. Deposits of shellfish, a series of salt lakes, beds of rock-salt as white as marble, stretches of clay impregnated with saline substances — all these are but so many irrefutable proofs of the existence of a former sea. In its interior, Sahara is an ocean of shifting sand burnt by a scorching sun. Nowhere else is there to be found so vast a wilderness. Caravans can journey for whole days without meeting a single living being, without catching sight of a bird or an insect, and still less of a tree or a blade of grass. In choosing this for a habitation, an animal of any kind would have nothing but sand to eat and air to drink. It is indeed the desert, the Great Desert, where all is silence, all is death. Everywhere sand, always sand, level, or ruffled by the winds, or piled up in long ridges.

Sometimes the sun is veiled in a violet-colored fog, and a furious wind, the simoon, hot and poisonous, invades this dreary expanse and raises the sand in dense clouds which it drives before it, rolling and unrolling them like waves on the sea. When a caravan is overtaken by this storm of dust, it arranges itself in a circle with the camels outside, lying on their stomachs, and their drivers inside this living rampart. These precautions, however, are often of no avail, and both camels and drivers perish of suffocation in this atmosphere of burning-hot sand.

But if the sea of sand has its tempests and its billows, it has also its islands — that is, its patches of ground where water makes vegetation possible. Wherever water is to be found, a village is built, surrounded with vigorous plantations of date-trees, the main reliance of the Sahara tribes. These islands of verdure are called oases; and it was these occasional green spots in the midst of the desert sands that made the ancient geographers liken Sahara to the skin of a panther, the yellow background of the fur being represented by the yellow sand, the dark spots by the deep green of the oases.

But how is it, you will ask, that on those burning plains there can be any water at all, so necessary if there are to be any oases? I will explain. Like all tropical regions, the desert of Sahara has its rainy season. In a few days' time there fall great volumes of water, a veritable deluge, but of short duration. Then every ravine becomes a torrent, though not one can form a permanent river and send its waters to the sea, the desert knowing no such thing as rivers. The downpour is all eagerly drunk up by the sand. In this way, there accumulate beneath the surface great bodies of water which the Arabs call underground seas; and by digging to a moderate depth one can tap these subterranean reservoirs. In the French possession of Algeria, there is going on an active boring of artesian wells for the creation of new oases and the revival of those that now languish for lack of water.

Great plains suitable for grazing are variously called, according to the country where they occur, *steppes, llanos, savannas, pampas.* The most extensive are those about the Caspian Sea, and in Russia, Siberia, and South America. According to Alexander von Humboldt, from whom the following details are taken, the South American plains, the pampas, are so vast in extent that in the north they bear palms while in the south they are covered with perpetual snow. Although now they have a fertile surface soil and the periodical rains promote a luxuriant vegetation, these plains were a desert before the arrival of Europeans, the natives having never ventured into the treeless solitudes where no well or spring ever existed. But since the discovery of the New World, cattle-raising has flourished on the pampas, and now occasional signs of human life are not wanting, such as huts made of reeds and leather thongs and roofed with hides.

On the pampas, too, are packs of dogs that have reverted to their original wild condition and live in underground caves. With sanguinary rage, they often attack man, whom their ancestors used to defend from attack. There in the tall grass wander cattle by the million, with horses and mules that have turned wild. The multiplication of these animals imported by Europeans is all the more surprising from the fact they have to contend with innumerable dangers and hardships. On the pampas, the year is divided into two seasons, a wet one and a dry one. Under a vertical sun and a cloudless sky, the earth's green carpet becomes parched and pulverized, the baked soil cracks, the vault of heaven appears to sink, throwing over the desolate plain only a dull light, waves of stifling heat traverse the atmosphere, and the wind raises clouds of burning-hot dust. Just as with us certain animals pass the winter in a state of torpor, so here the crocodile and the boa constrictor bury themselves in the parched clay and sleep there until the return of the rainy season.

Meanwhile, horses and cattle, enveloped in thick clouds of dust and tormented with hunger and thirst, wander over the desert, the cattle lowing hoarsely and the horses, with outstretched necks and nostrils open to the passing breeze, trying to scent the neighborhood of some water-hole not yet entirely dried up. Thousands of bleaching skeletons will ere long mark the route followed by the herd in its distress. During the drought that lasted from 1827 to 1830, the province of Buenos Ayres lost a million head of cattle. Mad with thirst, horses and cattle stampeded from their native wilds to the Paraná River, in which they were drowned in such numbers that their dead bodies blocked the mouth of the Rio de la Plata.

The mule is wiser. It finds, scattered here and there, a means to quench its thirst. A rounded plant with many sharp edges and bristling with prickly spines — the cactus, in short — has at its center a succulent pith. With its forehoofs, the mule pushes aside the spines and then applies its lips carefully as it sucks up the refreshing juice. But this method of quenching thirst at a vegetable spring is not always free from danger, and these animals are often seen with their feet crippled by the cactus's terrible armor.

To the overwhelming heat of the day succeeds the grateful coolness of the night; but even then, the cattle cannot enjoy any sweet repose, for while they sleep monstrous bats suck their blood, gripping their backs and inflicting wounds that afterward ulcerate and attract swarms of stinging insects. But more terrible still, in this boundless undergrowth of thistles and dried grass, fire occasionally breaks out, and it spreads with the speed of the wind. Before the ever-advancing curtain of flame, the herds plunge headlong, crazed with fear, neighing and bellowing. If the fire hems the animals in on all sides, there is no hope for them. Such is the wretched life of these creatures when a burning sun has dried up every drop of water on the treeless plain.

But with the advent of the rainy season, the scene changes abruptly. Almost before the ground is thoroughly wet, the pampas are covered with tall grasses, in which hides the tiger of these regions, the jaguar, its tawny fur sprinkled with black spots. Watching for its prey from its hiding place, the savage beast gives one sudden bound and seizes the young bull or heifer that chances to pass that way. From time to time, on the margins of swamps, the water-soaked clay rises slowly in slabs; then with a report like the outburst of a small mud volcano, the surface soil is hurled aloft. Some gigantic water serpent or mail-clad crocodile is emerging from its temporary tomb, raised from its apparent death by the coming of the first showers.

Soon the rain falls in such sheets that the plain presents the appearance of a great inland sea. The very animals that in the first half of the year nearly died of thirst on a parched and powdery soil are now forced to adopt the habits of amphibians. The mares retire with their foals to the higher points that rise like islands above the expanse of water. The dry land shrinks day by day. In serried ranks, the animals swim for hours at a time in quest of pasturage, and only succeed in finding here and there a scanty bite in the blossoming spikes of grass that project above the surface of the brownish and putrid water. Many colts are drowned, and many others are seized by crocodiles, being first mangled by the saw-toothed tail of the reptile and then devoured. Very often, horses and cattle are seen that have escaped from these ferocious creatures, but bear on their bodies the marks of their pointed teeth.

CHAPTER XV

MONT BLANC

WHO HAS not heard, toward the close of a summer day, the martin-swallows flying high overhead in a screaming flock? They pierce the blue depths with impetuous eagerness, soaring on sportive wing into the upper regions of the atmosphere, above the clouds. At their top speed, they attain a velocity of twenty-four leagues an hour.

Birds, beloved of God, you are the monarchs of space, and to you distance is as nothing. Compared with your untiring wings, what a poor locomotive apparatus is ours! A man leaves the plain at daybreak and begins to climb a mountain. He walks and walks, with aching feet and labored breath, all day long. At nightfall, spent with fatigue, he reaches the summit. No matter; the man is content with his day's achievement; he has attained a height of two thousand meters above the plain whence he started. Justifiable pride swells his bosom as his glance sweeps complacently the wide horizon now offered him. But presently he sees, ascending from the depths of the valley below, a cluster of hardly discernible black spots. They reach him, pass the mountain-top on which he stands, and continue their upward flight until lost to view. They are martin-swallows, and in their pursuit of gnats, they have, with a single stroke of the wing, swept past the summit that the man reached only at the cost of severe bodily exertion. An instant has sufficed them for attaining these heights, and an instant will suffice for regaining their domicile in some hole in the wall of a cottage or cow-house.

Man has not the bird's strong wing, but he has something better — the strong will that laughs at obstacles. In order to vie with the swallow in swiftness of ascent, he has built for himself an airship, a balloon; and in order to study at close range the wonders of the earth's atmosphere, he has planted his observatories on mountain-tops so high that the eagle in its flight never visits them. Merely to enlarge his knowledge, he has scaled the loftiest peaks at the cost of incredible fatigue and even at the risk of life itself. He has set his foot on snow-capped summits that are lost in the clouds. With what indomitable courage, with what ardent love of learning must he not be animated to brave the dangers that confront one on those awe-inspiring heights! You can judge of this for yourselves from the little I am going to tell you about the first ascent of Mont Blanc, that colossus towering 4,810 meters into the blue sky and dominating all Europe with its snow-capped dome. It is situated on the French-Italian frontier and rears its proud head amid countless Swiss mountains. Perhaps you have seen from a distance its snow-white mantle gleaming in the sun.

To Benedict de Saussure, an illustrious scientist of Geneva, belongs the honor of being the first to conceive the audacious project of climbing to the top of Mont Blanc. He was not twenty years old when, with a scientific end in view, he began to mature his plans for scaling the giant peak. But in vain did the young naturalist proclaim to the village of Chamonix, the most favorable starting point for the ascent, and to all the neighboring parishes, that he would give a handsome prize to the guide that should first find a way to reach the top of the mountain. For many years and despite repeated endeavors, he met with no success. But at last, twenty-six years after his first announcement, a daring mountaineer, Jacques Balmat, succeeded, in the face of many dangers, in reaching the summit reputed to be inaccessible; and by his courage, he thus opened the way to science.

Balmat was then twenty-five years old. Endowed with a pair of sturdy legs and a stomach proof against extreme hunger, he trained himself until he could walk for three whole days with nothing but snow to munch for food. The conquest of Mont Blanc was a fixed idea with him; by day and by night he thought of it and dreamt of it. One morning he tied on his gaiters, took his iron-shod alpenstock, and started forth with a hunk of bread in his knapsack. Toward evening he found himself on a high plateau covered with snow and affording no kind of shelter. He stopped there for the night. After a long search, he found a spot where the rock showed through the snow and offered a small dry place for him to sit on. So there he rested, seated on his knapsack with his face wrapped in a handkerchief, and stamping his feet and slapping himself with his hands to keep a little warmth in his body. All night the snow fell. At the first peep of dawn, Balmat shook off the snow that nearly buried him and started to continue his ascent; but as Mont Blanc was veiled in mist and the weather was stormy, he saw it would be folly to attempt any further progress that day. However, not to sacrifice all advantage from what he had achieved, he explored the neighborhood and reconnoitered the likeliest passes; then, after a second night passed as he had passed the first, he made his way back to Chamonix. Only after his arrival there did his clothes thaw out.

Scarcely had he returned when he learned that other guides were undertaking the same ascent. Unwilling to be anticipated in this enterprise, he immediately renewed his provisions and started off to join them. He overtook them where the great ice-fields begin. After crossing wide stretches of snow and ice, the party found themselves confronted by a long ridge of rock running between two precipices and merging into Mont Blanc at the farther end. The others declared this rock to be impassable, but Balmat climbed up onto the dizzy edge, bestrode it, and worked his way onward, one leg hanging over the abyss on each side. Frightened at such boldness, and vexed at the coming of this new competitor, his companions returned to Chamonix.

Meanwhile, Balmat, after much strenuous endeavor, was forced to admit that he had undertaken the impossible; for an insuperable rock barred his passage when he had proceeded about a quarter of a league at the cost of several hours of time and effort. Accordingly, he inched his way back, still astride and this time moving rearward on that frightful knife edge. Not finding his companions, he was for a moment undecided whether to follow them homeward or to continue the struggle alone. A secret presentiment told him that he was destined to succeed, and so, resuming his knapsack and alpenstock, he started off in another direction.

At nightfall, he had reached the height of four thousand meters at a part known as the Great Plateau. This is a flat stretch of hardened snow, a sort of terrace about five acres in area, frequently swept by avalanches and by squalls of icy wind. On the hottest day of summer, the mercury hardly rises to zero in the sun. Arriving there, Balmat felt his eyes affected by the glare of the snow, from which he did not then know how to protect them by the use of a veil. He was seized with giddiness and could distinguish nothing clearly. Moreover, night was fast approaching. He was forced to resign himself to the necessity of remaining until morning in that fearful desert, crouching unprotected in a cranny in the ice.

One is overcome with astonishment at the thought of this daring young man's arriving at the decline of day in those awful solitudes, without shelter, without help of any sort, without even knowing whether it was possible to keep the breath of life in one's body at that altitude, and drawing on his courage alone for the strength to face such perils. He relates:

> I set down my knapsack and disposed myself as comfortably as I could for the night. After keeping my eyes closed for some time in order to rest them, I opened them and saw that the sun was setting. Never had I seen and never shall I see anything like it. Over my head the sky, although clear and cloudless, was as black as ink. Against this background of unrelieved darkness, the summit of Mont Blanc stood out dazzlingly white. Far beneath my feet, on the plains of France, a large red ball appeared to be swimming in a glowing furnace. It was the sun setting in a bank of clouds, but for a moment I had difficulty in recognizing it, so odd did it seem to have to look down in order to see it. The red ball seemed to be sinking into the earth, and long after it had disappeared it left behind it a halo of red rays reaching upward to the zenith and end-

ing in lurid streaks. Then, two or three thousand meters below me, clouds began to gather. I saw them, as they were lifted by breezes from the plain, ebb and flow like the waves of some ocean suspended in midair. Meanwhile, shadows were stealing up from the valleys, shrouding one by one the snowy summits that the last rays of daylight had tinged with roseate hues. Higher and higher the darkness mounted; it might have been taken for thick smoke. Finally, it wrapped me about, but for some time still the top of Mont Blanc, like an island of light in a sea of darkness, glowed above the expanse now completely enveloped in gloom. I watched the last gleams of daylight as they faded away on the snow-capped mountain peaks, and then all was darkness. Night had come.

At this point discouragement got the better of me. A silence as of the tomb held undisputed sway and filled me with a sort of terror. To drive away my black thoughts, I began to sing. My voice awoke no echoes in that lifeless solitude, and, more than that, it sounded so weak, so strange, that it gave me an eerie feeling. I stopped singing. I was afraid. I took my provisions out of my knapsack quite mechanically, for I was neither hungry nor thirsty. They were frozen; the bread was as hard as stone. I put them back without eating a morsel. From where I was, nothing intercepted my view of Chamonix. I had seen, as night fell, lights appearing one by one in the houses of the village, and now I saw them disappearing in the same manner. I remarked to myself that some of my companions were very likely saying at that very moment, as they pulled the bedclothes up over their ears: "I bet that crazy loon of a Balmat is stamping his feet pretty lively about now up there on the mountain. That's right, old fellow; never say die."

And I did stamp my feet in good earnest, the cold being so intense that if I had remained still a quarter of an hour, I should have frozen stiff on the spot. It was only by constantly beating my sides that I managed to keep a little warmth in my body. My strength was ebbing away, my head seemed to be clamped in a vise, a singular heaviness was creeping down from my skull to my eyelids, and I had an almost irresistible desire to sleep, while thoughts as sad as death took possession of my mind. But I fought with all my might against these sad thoughts and against the desire to sleep, for I well knew that if I gave way to this desire, I should never wake up again. The sleep induced by cold is the sleep of death.

So far the sky had been clear. Though of a deep black, it was sprinkled with stars, all appearing small and with no twinkling, but yielding sufficient light to enable me to distinguish the mountain outlines and to judge of distances. Toward midnight, the darkness became complete. The clouds I had seen forming at sunset had ascended the slopes of the mountain and shut me in. Soon, a fine stinging snow began to fall. As on the first night, I covered my face with my handkerchief and waited. The cold continued to increase. In a few seconds, my breath had frozen on the handkerchief and my clothes, already wet through with snow, were coated over with ice. The wind rose, not very strong, but so cold that under my handkerchief my face felt as if pricked with needles. I put my hand on the painful spots, and on removing it, I found my fingers had drops of blood on them. Under the biting cold, the skin had cracked like old bark on a tree.

But this was the least of my anxieties. I recalled that while it was still daylight, I had come upon a fearful crevasse running in such a direction as to end about where I was at the present moment. "Who knows," said I to myself, "whether that awful chasm is not now under my very feet, concealed by the layer of snow that I have been trampling all this time? What if the layer of snow should give way under me?" At the thought that the ground might at any moment fall away beneath my feet and that I ran the risk of being precipitated into the icy abysses far below, my hair stood on end. And yet I dared not change my position, for in the darkness that enveloped me I might, in trying to avoid a perhaps imaginary crevasse, be swallowed up in one that was real.

Amid these apprehensions, a loud cracking suddenly made the mountain tremble, and this was followed immediately by the sound of something slipping and sliding in fragments. Then everything became again as still as death. The cause of all this commotion was not unknown to me, as it was not the first time I had heard similar detonations among the mountains. Some neighboring glacier had split, and the disturbance, being communicated to the air, had dislodged certain accumulations of snow on the steep slopes and set them sliding. But all that was far from reassuring me. Several times during the night, these crackings were repeated, and I realized that I might at any moment be buried under snowdrifts sliding down from the heights above.

Fear had very nearly mastered me, and the cold had stiffened my limbs when at last, about two o'clock in the morning, the first signs of dawn came to cheer me. It was high time, for another hour or two of that fearful strain would have finished me completely. As it was, I succeeded in limbering myself up by vigorous rubbing and by the wildest sort of gymnastics, and so was able finally to resume my explorations. I began the ascent of a steep slope where the snow was so hard and slippery that I could not stand upright. However, by jabbing holes with the iron point of my alpenstock, I succeeded in hanging on, but my fatigue was extreme. Besides, it was no easy or reassuring exercise to balance on one foot over an abyss while cutting these rude steps for further ascent. Nevertheless, I at last succeeded in getting over this difficult stretch. "Oh, oh!" I exclaimed, "we are almost there now. Nothing more to bar the way between here and the summit, but all as smooth going as a sheet of ice, and no more steps to cut." But I was perishing with cold and utter fatigue, and so was forced to turn back, but with the assurance of success the next time. I returned to the village. My face was purple and swollen, the skin all chapped and blistered, and my eyes red, bleary, halfblind. I shut myself up in the barn, threw myself down on the hay, and slept for forty-eight hours at a stretch.

A month later, on August 7, 1786, Balmat started again for Mont Blanc, this time accompanied by the physician Dr. Paccard. That same evening they reached the beginning of the Bossons Glacier[17], where they passed a good night, rolled up in woolen

17   "Glacier des Bossons," Glacier of the Humps. - *Translator.*

blankets. At dawn the next morning they set out again to cross the glacier, which is here much cut up with crevasses. The doctor's first steps on this frozen sea, so furrowed with gaping cracks, were a little uncertain; but he was in a good school, and by watching Balmat he gained confidence, so that the glacier was crossed without accident. Toward noon, they arrived at the Great Plateau, and there Balmat showed his companion the spot where he had passed that famous night. The doctor made a very significant grimace, the prospect of any such experience for him failing to arouse his enthusiasm.

Balmat encouraged him as best he could, and they began to climb the steep slopes where, on his preceding trip, Balmat had cut rude steps with the iron-shod end of his alpenstock. It took them two hours to climb these slopes. Then there arose so violent a squall that the two explorers feared they should be swept away like straws. The doctor's cap, though tied on with strong strings, was torn from his head and away it went with the speed of an arrow. The wind whipped the snow until it swirled about them in blinding eddies. The two travelers fell flat on their stomachs, but the wind was so biting cold they dared not tarry lest they should freeze. Up and on, then! The doctor, now almost played out, was for giving up the expedition, and had it not been for Balmat's unremitting encouragement, he would have gone back alone to Chamonix. Finally, the wind died down. Balmat says:

> After that, the ascent was less steep and presented no great difficulty, the snow being firm, not slippery, and free from crevasses. But the air was becoming more and more difficult to breathe. Every minute or two the doctor, quite out of breath and blue with cold, would stop short and declare he could go no further, that he was completely winded. I also had an empty feeling in my chest. In order to breathe at all, we had to halt every ten steps, sometimes leaning on our alpenstocks, sometimes sitting down on the snow. When our panting for breath took our last ounce of strength, any further effort became impossible. For my part, if I had seen an avalanche descending upon me

then, I should not have stirred a step to get out of its way. I struggled to conquer my fatigue, but my legs refused their service, my stiffened joints would not function, vertigo seized me, and everything looked red before my eyes. My companion, less used to such exertions than I, was still more overcome. At times I was obliged to use force to make him go on, so demoralized was he by the cold, by weariness, and by the difficulty of breathing.

For two hours we had been walking thus, a few steps at a time, side by side, when I raised my eyes and saw that we were almost at the top of the slope, with nothing but sky beyond. A step or two farther and we were there. Then I looked around, fearing lest I was mistaken and should see some higher point still in the distance, for I should not have had the strength to climb it. But no; nothing higher anywhere in sight. I was at the end of the journey; I stood where no living being had ever before set foot; I was on the very top of Mont Blanc!

The lateness of the hour compelled the two explorers to descend after a half-hour's stay at the summit. They followed the tracks made by the points of their alpenstocks in the ascent, and toward midnight left the regions of ice behind them and set foot once more on bare ground. They halted for sleep beneath a high rock.

"It's rather queer," said Paccard the next morning on awakening; "I thought I heard birds singing, but it isn't daylight yet."

"Then your eyes are at fault," replied Balmat, "for the sun has been up a long time."

The doctor had, indeed, temporarily lost his eyesight from the blinding glare of the sun on the snow. As for Balmat, his eyes, too, were in a bad condition; and it was in this pitiful state that they reentered Chamonix, the one who could see a little leading by the strap of his knapsack the one who could not see at all. But rest cured this blindness for them both, and the following year Balmat guided Saussure to the top of the mountain.

CHAPTER XVI

SAUSSURE'S ASCENT

S AUSSURE left Chamonix the first day of August, 1787, accompanied by a servant and eighteen guides, carrying his
physical instruments and other necessary equipment. Jacques
Balmat led the guides. Saussure tells us:

> The first evening I pitched my tent at the top of Côte
> Mountain amid blocks of granite that had been brought
> down by the neighboring glacier. That is where Dr. Pac-
> card and Balmat passed the first night of their expedi-
> tion. This part of the ascent is easy and quite free from
> danger, the route running always over grass-ground or
> rock; but after that the going is wholly on snow and ice,
> clear to the summit. Consequently, the second day is
> very fatiguing. First one must cross Côte Glacier, which
> is extremely dangerous on account of the wide and deep
> crevasses intersecting it. To cross these, there is often
> but one way, and that is to pick one's course over sharp
> ridges of ice and arches of hardened snow, these latter
> extending like footbridges from one ridge to another. One
> feels the frail bridge cracking under one's tread; if it were
> to give way, one would go down with it. At other places
> the traveler is obliged to descend to the very bottom of
> the crevasse and then climb up the opposite side, cutting
> steps in the ice as he goes. Sometimes, after descending
> into one of these clefts between two vertical walls as
> smooth as crystal, one is at a loss how to get out. But the
> greatest danger of all is lest a thin layer of snow bridging
> some crevasse may conceal the peril lurking beneath and
> suddenly give way under the traveler.

As long as we were on good solid ice, my guides, clear-headed and sure-footed, showed no uneasiness, chatting together and laughing and flinging an occasional challenge at one another. But when we had to cross a bridge of snow over a yawning abyss, they advanced in complete silence, the first three roped together at intervals of two or three meters, the others in pairs, one guide in front, one in the rear, with an alpenstock held between them. Each adjusted his pace to the one ahead and planted his feet exactly in the tracks of his predecessor. Prudence on this perilous passage was all the more necessary as the day before one of my guides had almost lost his life here. In company with two others, he had gone ahead to make a reconnaissance, when all of a sudden the snow broke under him as he was halfway across a crevasse; but as the three guides had taken the precaution to rope themselves together, he escaped with nothing worse than a moment's anxious suspension over the abyss. We passed close to the chasm that had thus opened under him, and I shuddered at the sight of the danger he had run.

Although the glacier was but a quarter of a league wide, it took us three hours to cross it, after which we entered a ravine that winds upward to the foot of the final slope leading to the summit. This ravine lies deep in snow that is cut up here and there by enormous crevasses, of which one cannot see the bottom. On the precipitous sides or walls of these fearful chasms are very clearly to be seen cross-sections of the successive layers of snow, one layer to a year. Great blocks of granite, wrested from their foundations by descending avalanches, lie scattered all about. My guides were in favor of stopping for the night in the shelter of one of these rocks, but my plan was to go higher and pitch our tent on the Great Plateau. It was with difficulty that I persuaded them to yield to me, for Balmat's account of his night up there had frightened them. They greatly feared such an attempt would result in the death of us all. I assured them we should dig ourselves in, good and deep, and that our excavation would be covered with the tent, and that with the whole company snuggling under this shelter, the cold could not affect us very much. This plan finally dispelled their fears.

At four o'clock in the afternoon we reached the Great Plateau, where we held long and serious deliberations on the choice of a spot for pitching the tent. In addition to the cold, there were two other dangers to avoid, one menacing us from above, the other lurking beneath. It was important to find a spot sheltered from any avalanche that might come crashing down upon us, and at the same time not likely to be over a thinly concealed crevasse. We all shuddered at the thought that, laden with the weight of twenty men and softened with the warmth from their bodies, the snow might suddenly give way in the hours of sleep and drop the whole company into the abyss. Finally, we selected a spot that appeared to promise the desired security.

Straightway the guides began the excavation that was to serve us as shelter, but they were very soon affected by the rarity of the air at that altitude. Those robust men, who had made nothing of the ascent thus far, had not lifted more than five or six shovelfuls of snow when they found it impossible to continue and asked to be relieved. One of their number, who had gone back for a little water that had collected under the sun's heat in a crack in the ice, fell ill on the way and came back without any water. He passed the evening in extreme pain. All were impatient for the tent to be got ready, as it was their only hope of comfort. If they sat still on the snow, the cold cut them like sharp knives; and if they tried to warm themselves a little by exercising, fatigue and shortness of breath soon left them limp and with no courage to continue.

Finally, the canvas was stretched over the excavation and we made haste to get under its shelter. But we had a bad night, there being scant space for so many persons, and we could hardly find room to sit down on a little straw, even though each man sat between the legs of the one behind. At last we were falling into a doze when we were awakened by the thunder of an avalanche descending upon a part of the slope we were about to climb.

We rose, but the preparations for departure took a good deal of time. Snow had to be melted for breakfast and for the day's march. It was drunk as soon as melted. A burning thirst consumed us, and even those who scrupulously guarded the wine I had ordered brought with us stole repeatedly some of the water I tried to hold in reserve. Finally, we set out after veiling our faces in green crape to protect our eyes from the glare of the sun on the snow. The Great Plateau was crossed and we found ourselves at the foot of a slope strewn with what the avalanche had brought down. We all halted for some moments in the hope that after a good rest to legs and lungs we could cross the avalanche at a rather brisk pace and without pausing for breath. But that was impossible. Fatigue from the thinness of the air one breathes is something that cannot be contended against. When it takes full possession of you, the most imminent danger could not make you move a step. On the further side of this avalanche, the ascent became steeper and steeper, with a frightful precipice bordering it on the left.

Our foremost guides cut steps in the frozen snow with their hatchets, but these steps were so far apart that at every stride there was danger of missing one's footing and slipping over the edge of the precipice. As we approached the summit, the layer of frozen snow became thinner, breaking under our feet and threatening to drop us over the brink of the declivity if we lost our balance in the least. But I paid no attention to this danger, being determined to keep going as long as I had the strength to do so. My only concern was to watch my step and push on. At the points of greatest danger, two guides, one in front of me, the other behind, came to my help with a long stick which they each grasped at one end and held between me and the precipice. Thus we proceeded in single file, I in the middle with this portable railing to guard me.

Toward nine o'clock, we had only about three hundred meters more to climb, and that on firm snow without a crevasse. Consequently, I hoped to reach the top in less than three quarters of an hour. But I was too sanguine, the thinness of the air being much more of an obstacle than I could have believed. Every ten or fifteen steps my strength gave out and I found myself on the point of fainting, so that I had to sit down. After several deep breaths and a short rest, strength would return and I would fancy myself able to continue on to the summit without a halt; but it took only ten steps to convince me of the contrary. All my guides were in more or less the same condition as I. Noting with keen regret the rapid passing of the time that I wished to utilize in carrying out my experiments on the summit, I made a number of attempts to shorten these rests. For example, I tried the plan of not going to the limit of my strength but of pausing an instant every four or five steps. I gained nothing by this, however, and after a few repetitions of the scheme was forced to abandon it, my distress being no less than before. The only thing that revived my energy a little was the cold north wind. Whenever in my toilsome ascent my face was turned in that direction and I took in full breaths of air coming from that quarter, I could accomplish twenty-five steps without a halt. Two long hours were consumed in climbing this deadly slope of three hundred meters. Finally, at eleven o'clock, I gained the summit with all my guides.

First of all, upon reaching my goal, I turned my eyes toward Chamonix, where my family was. I knew that, with eye to the telescope, they had been following my every step with painful anxiety. It had been arranged that on seeing me at the top they should hoist a flag as a signal that their well-grounded fears were at an end. I now saw the flag flung to the breeze, and I cannot describe the comforting sensation this signal gave me. I could thenceforward give myself up to the majestic spectacle spread before me and take in hand my prearranged experiments, the chief object of my expedition.

The first moment of my arrival at the summit of Mont Blanc was not to give me the unalloyed satisfaction I might have expected. The long and fatiguing struggle, the vivid remembrance of the suffering this achievement had cost me, filled me with a sort of anger rather than with a feeling of pleasure that I at last trod the snow that capped the mountain's summit. I sat down on the ridge that forms the very tip-top of Mont Blanc and looked about me. The view was unquestionably worth what it had cost. Overhead the sun shone brightly in a sky of so deep a blue as to look almost black. Stretched out beneath was a veritable chaos of sublime horrors, an awe-inspiring confusion of ice needles, domes of snow, naked peaks. My glance swept the thousand mountain tops of the Alps, and I could scarcely believe my eyes. I thought I must be dreaming when I saw beneath me those majestic peaks whose bases even are so difficult and dangerous of approach. Here and there streaks as of glass glistened in the gorges under the sun's rays; they were glaciers and could be counted by the hundred. On the south the view extended across the plains of Lombardy as far as the sea, while on the north the eye met two spots of azure, the lakes of Geneva and Neuchâtel, and beyond these the monotonous blue line of the Jura range. To the right lay the Swiss mountains, all fleecy, and in the remoter distance, the Swiss meadows spread out like a green carpet. On the left, beyond the Alps of Dauphiné and fading away in the mist, stretched the plains of France.

I tore myself from this entrancing spectacle to proceed with the experiments I had planned. But when it came to setting up my instruments and taking observations I found myself obliged, every minute or two, to suspend my work and give my whole attention to recovering my breath. As long as I kept perfectly still I felt only a slight discomfort, a touch of heart trouble; but whenever I made the slightest exertion or fixed my attention for a few moments, and especially when in stooping over I compressed my lungs, I had to rest and pant for a little while. My guides experienced the same discomfort. They had no appetite and did not even crave wine or brandy. Cold water alone satisfied them and did them good. Some of them, unable to bear this kind of suffering, went down the mountain to find air less difficult to breathe.

The thinness of the air is the cause of this strange discomfort felt at great heights. On the summit of Mont Blanc the mercury in the barometer, instead of standing at the normal seventy-six centimeters, falls to forty-three, showing that the air is about twice as rare as down on the plain. Now, to support life a certain volume of air must enter the lungs in a given time. If the air breathed is twice as rare, the inspirations must be twice as frequent in order that the rarity of the air may be counterbalanced by the amount taken into the lungs. It is this forced quickening of the act of breathing that causes the fatigue and discomfort felt on high mountains.

We were all in a kind of fever, for at the same time that the breathing is accelerated, the circulation is also quickened. I obtained convincing proof of this on Mont Blanc. Not to confound the effects of our laborious climb with those due to the rarity of the atmosphere, I did not make my test until we had rested quietly for three hours on the top of the mountain. Balmat's pulse then beat ninety-eight to the minute, my servant's one hundred and twelve, and mine one hundred. At Chamonix, under like conditions of rest, these rates, in the same order, were reduced to forty-nine, sixty, and seventy-two. Thus are explained our feverish state, the thirst that tormented us, our aversion to wine and brandy, and our disinclination to take even any sort of nourishment.

The burning thirst that devoured us had still another cause, and that was the extreme dryness of the air. I proved conclusively with the hygrometer that at the top of Mont Blanc the air contained only one-sixth of the humidity prevalent at the foot of the mountain. Eating snow aggravated our thirst instead of quenching it; and so, to obtain a little water, my guides were constantly busy melting snow on a little charcoal stove I had taken the precaution to include in my equipment. But this was a vexatiously slow process, as the charcoal would not burn well for lack of air and continual blowing was necessary to maintain even a feeble combustion.

To the thinness of the air was attributable another fact that made a deep impression on my guides; and that was the extraordinary weakness of sound. At twenty or thirty paces' distance, we could hardly hear one another. I discharged a pistol, but the explosion was so faint that the smallest firecracker would have made as much noise in the plain.

It was an exceptionally fine day, with a higher temperature than I could have expected. At noon the thermometer, in the sun, registered two degrees below freezing. On the southern slope just beneath the summit, the temperature was very tolerable, and there most of the guides took their rest in the sun, sitting on their knapsacks, which they placed here and there on the snow.

On account of the extreme purity and transparency of the air at that great height, the sky has a deep blue and at or near the summit one is struck with a singular phenomenon: the visibility of the stars in broad daylight. But to get this effect the observer must be completely in the shade and even have this shade extend well above his head, as otherwise the brightness of the atmosphere overpowers the fainter light of the stars. This purity of the air and the resultant deep blue of the sky struck terror into the hearts of a party of guides in their first attempt to reach the summit of Mont Blanc. As they were toiling up a steep ascent, all at once they saw the sky through a gap in the top of the slope. The darkness of the heavens made them mistake this opening for the entrance to some chasm in the mountain, and they turned back in alarm, reporting at Chamonix that they had been unable to go on because a horrible chasm had opened before them.

I saw no signs of animal life near the summit except two butterflies, poor lost wanderers, swept away by a puff of wind and carried aloft to those fatal heights. Several times I have noted the way these insects get lost on the glaciers. In flying across the fields that border them they venture over the ice and, losing sight of their native heath, keep on indefinitely, not knowing where to alight. Upborne by the wind, they sometimes attain the loftiest peaks, where they finally fall from exhaustion and perish on the snow.

I stayed at the top three hours and a half; then we came down and on the afternoon of the following day arrived at Chamonix. Balmat and Paccard, my predecessors in this ascent, had returned from their expedition almost blind and with faces cracked and bleeding from the glare of the sun on the snow; but none of us met with any such misfortune, the crape we wore over our faces having protected us perfectly.

CHAPTER XVII

MONT PERDU

SETTING OUT from Barèges on August 11, 1797, Ramond, the learned explorer of the Pyrenees, arrived the next day with his guides at the foot of the glaciers of Mont Perdu (or Monte Perdido, as it is called in Spanish), in the highest sheep pastures in the world and confronted by stupendous ramparts of rock that formed a kind of enclosure. He writes:

> Here, we met two Spanish shepherds, of the number of those who rent these high-lying grazing grounds of our Pyrenees and drive thither their migratory flocks. These two men were reclining outside a stone hut just large enough to hold them, either sitting or lying down. That is all that is necessary for the half-wild nomads who frequent these rugged regions for only a few days in the summer. Elsewhere they dispense with even this accommodation, and if they can find shelter under some overhanging rock they do not take the trouble to put up any sort of shanty.
>
> Two men of this kind, familiar as they were with the neighborhood of Mont Perdu, seemed to us a most happy encounter upon our approach to the mountain, and the only question was, which of us should interrogate them. But shepherds have no concern with the realms of eternal snow, and the replies of these two were proving only moderately satisfactory when a smuggler of their nation joined them. He was an authority. Compelled by his calling to shun the highways and risk his neck on the most dangerous by-paths, he must have seen Mont Perdu at close range; and in fact he proved to be a much better informant than the two shepherds.

While the all-important question of what route to select was engaging the attention of these three Spaniards and my guides, I formed a plan of my own. The unanimous result of their consultation was that to reach Mont Perdu we should have to follow certain trails that seemed to me too roundabout.

I had been studying the glacier just above us, and had observed that it was still covered with snow, which ought to make the going not too difficult for us. It was true the incline was steep, but it did not appear to me too steep for climbing. Moreover, the glacier led to a gap that gave promise of affording access to Mont Perdu, which was invisible from where we stood. I announced my determination to risk the adventure. This project seemed foolhardy to the shepherds, and the smuggler was at first the only one to applaud my resolution. All the others merely smiled. But an end had to be put to this uncertainty, and I declared I would scale the glacier with whoever cared to accompany me. Firmness never fails to overcome indecision; they followed me. As for the smuggler, he had already gone on ahead and was soon out of sight.

We soon reached the stones and gravel brought down by the moving ice from the upper slopes and forming the moraine of the glacier, and here we had to take to the snow and enter upon the dangerous route that was expected to lead us to where we could get sight of Mont Perdu. At first it was mere child's play, the snow being firm and the grade only moderately steep. We started off in confident mood, but had not gone more than fifty steps before the incline became less easy. Looking ahead, we saw the steepness continually increasing. Our pace slackened and we halted from time to time for consultation. Then the snow hardened so that we left no footprints on it, notwithstanding the spikes in the soles of our shoes, and we were forced to cut steps in the ice as we advanced. Accordingly, we arranged ourselves in single file in order that we might tread in the steps prepared by the first three in the column. For an hour all went well. We carefully avoided the bare and slippery ice of the glacier, and by making numerous zigzags, prudently planned beforehand, we were successfully skirting the too steep slopes when suddenly we saw a man in desperate straits clinging to a rock and calling to us for help. It was our smuggler.

His misadventure was written on the snow in one long and significant trail. The unlucky fellow had boldly begun the ascent without spiked shoes or hatchet or any other safeguard, and had slipped down the steep incline for more than two hundred paces. Once started, it was inconceivable how he had managed to stop. We should have liked to fly to his aid, but were obliged to crawl. At last we reached him and received him into our company. He had lost jacket and cap, his pack of wares worth from fifteen to eighteen francs, and, worst of all, his alpenstock. This had gone on without him to the foot of the incline, and we could not recover it. The other things were scattered about here and there, and we soon secured the jacket and the little packet of merchandise. But the cap had lodged in a perilous position and it cost us a good quarter of an hour to get it, although not twenty feet away. The poor man had so lost his courage that our united exhortations were of little avail in restoring his nerve. Indeed, our reassurances produced less effect on him than his uneasiness produced on my companions, and already I began to read in their faces the signs of a faltering that boded no good. The question now was whether we should change our course by trying the rocks at the edge of the glacier. I was not in favor of this, but the men's uneasiness was increasing. Twice we turned aside to try to climb the rocks, and each time we were forced to return to the ice.

This part of the glacier was the steepest, with prospects of better going not far ahead; but we were almost at our last gasp. Higher up, the ascent became visibly easier and the ice was hidden under snow of a pure white that, standing out as it did against the deep blue of the sky, indicated the top of the ridge. The only question now was how to surmount the obstacle beyond which we saw in imagination the summit of Mont Perdu. We mustered all our remaining strength and zealously exhorted and encouraged one another. Every step upward lowered the walls enclosing us, and the gap, which had been hidden from view for a long time by a projection of the glacier, finally reappeared in gigantic proportions, and we could feel the cold wind coming through the wide opening. We pushed on at our best speed and presently reached our goal all out of breath. A cry of joy announced the change of scene.

A gloomy silence, however, succeeded this jubilation at sight of the deep gorge still separating us from Mont Perdu, of the glaciers on every side of it, and of the clouds that veiled it. The spectacle was both fearful and sublime, overwhelming us as we gazed. "There is Mont Perdu! There is Mont Perdu!" exclaimed one to another; and all the time no one could really distinguish the mountain in that chaos of rocks, snow, ice, and clouds. But it was not so absurd, after all, that my companions thought they saw Mont Perdu, for everything here is a part of it, even the crest that we had just surmounted, a height separated from the main summit by the subsidence or the erosion of a part of the mountainside. That summit was before us, though in deep shade and lost in the folds of a thick fog swirling slowly about it. But what was still more unexpected and could not have been seen except from the post of observation occupied by us was the indescribably majestic appearance of the buttresses to that lofty summit. As though chiseled out of the solid rock by an army of giants, they assumed the form of a flight of immense steps, some draped in snow, some bristling with glaciers that overlapped and went pouring over one another in great motionless cascades to the shores of a lake whose surface, frozen but clear of snow, shone with a somber luster heightened by the dazzling whiteness on all sides of it.

This lake, its desolate situation, the masses of ice bordering it, the black walls surmounting it, Mont Perdu towering over it in a stormy sky, and the rugged rampart, steep and bare, from one of whose battlements we were contemplating this spectacle, all combined to form the most impressive and the most somber tableau the Pyrenees have ever offered me.

But it was high time to decide what we should do about pushing on to the more easily accessible parts of the mountain. As to the summit itself, that was out of the question, the extreme roughness of its coating of ice and the steepness of its sides forbidding any attempt to climb it. We descended into the depression before us. The slope, although extremely steep, was not dangerous. Once on a level with the lake, its frozen surface offered us easy access to the lower steps of the giant staircase leading to the summit. But we were obliged to give some thought to our return. It was midday, and the appearance of the sky betokened an approaching change of weather.

"Let's stay where we are," said my companions, "and perhaps tomorrow we can manage to reach the top of the mountain."

"But how about the cold night ahead of us?" I queried.

"Oh, what is one night, with the hope of doing great things in the morning?"

"But we shall need something to eat, shan't we?"

"We can do without."

Foresight and caution were flung to the winds. The ice ceased to be formidable, and the dense clouds swirling about the summit no longer wore a sinister look. But just then, from the depths of those clouds, there came an awful detonation awakening the echoes of that vast wilderness. Even the boldest turned pale, and all thought a storm was about to burst upon them in those frightful solitudes, cutting off all egress. However, it was only an avalanche sliding down from the upper steps of the great stairway; but it left an unfavorable impression, and the only thought was to get away.

A month later, on the seventh of September, I again turned my steps toward Mont Perdu. To save time and thus put to good use the whole of the next day, I decided to pass the night in the Spanish shepherds' hut. It was empty, its owners having abandoned those pastures, where the grass was already withered by night frosts. The grazing grounds, so green not a month before, were now faded and desolate. In twenty-seven days I had seen spring and summer come and go on those mountain slopes. I took possession of the hut.

At break of day we were off. The glacier had greatly changed since my first visit. No snow was now to be seen, the ice presented only its bare surface, and there was not a spot where the foot could leave its print. Along the middle, the glacier was hollowed out, and two wide cracks or crevasses seamed it from top to bottom. Even in our spiked shoes we could obtain no foothold, and our ironshod alpenstocks, with our whole weight brought to bear on them, made hardly a dent with their pointed end. But we were equipped with good ice-cutting implements, and were obliged to use them from that point onward. The work was of the hardest, and we were not even free to direct it at our will. The glacier had assumed the shape of a gutter, and in the middle it was all full of holes and cracks, so that we had to avoid this part and at the same time keep at a sufficient distance from the excessively steep sides. Thus we were obliged to follow with nice discrimination a rather difficult course between the two perils that lurked on the right and on the left. It was a veritable ladder of ice that we had to climb, with no zigzags to ease the ascent and disguise its steepness, which became more and more pronounced as we went on.

We were nearing the big hump in the glacier above the depression I have just mentioned, and we were at a loss how and where to set about scaling this formidable mound. We found ourselves nearly at the end of our resources. One of the party suggested our getting around the obstacle by clambering up the edge which we had hitherto so carefully avoided. I must tell the reader just what this edge was. It took the form of a sharp ridge, almost as sharp as a knife, separated from the rock at the side by a wide space that opened like a funnel into the cavities of the glacier. This suggestion, which a little earlier would have seemed absurd, was now seen to be the only plan that offered any means, short of abject retreat, of extricating ourselves from our perilous situation. A dozen steps cut in an almost vertical line brought us to the top of this ridge, the sharp edge of which we were obliged to knock off before we could get any sort of foothold, and then we had to pound the ice with considerable force to make sure it would bear us.

By incessant hacking and pounding we succeeded in advancing thirteen steps in half an hour, balancing ourselves all the while on a slippery line with a precipice behind us and one on each side. Such a position and especially so slow a rate of progress were well calculated to damp our ardor. After these thirteen steps we were forced to halt and take counsel once more. In this pause I caught sight of a little bird flying from rock to rock; it was a wall-creeper. A gnat alighted near me and began to clean its tiny wings, whose powers of flight we could not but envy. What a humiliating incongruity between faculties and means! Man measures the heavens and is fettered to the earth; he weighs the air in which the eagle soars; he sends up his balloon, which bursts and drops the observer; a frail insect sports over my head, and I crawl on the ground.

I was aroused from this unpleasant reverie by an incident still more unpleasant. A guide near the head of our column declared he was dizzy and in danger of falling. We were obliged to place him in the middle of the line, and the reader will readily understand how difficult and dangerous this operation was on so narrow a support. Meanwhile, the ridge of ice was subjecting us every moment to fresh perils, and soon it became impossible to advance any further in this manner, the rocks on each side of the glacier blocking the way. We resolved to climb them step by step. The first man was hoisted up by the second, and as soon as he had secured a foothold he lent his hand in turn. The risks for those in the rear were at least equal to those encountered by the leaders, and perhaps they were even greater, for the men in front could not make a misstep without endangering the rest of the party, nor could they loosen a fragment of rock without sending it rolling down onto the heads of those behind. I was rather badly hurt by one of these fragments, being in a position where I could not dodge it when I saw it coming. But finally, after a five-hour climb, at constant risk to our lives, the enclosing wall that cut off our view of Mont Perdu was surmounted.

From our rocky perch we surveyed with mute astonishment the majestic spectacle of the mountain standing out in brilliant relief against the sky on account of the exceptionally favorable atmospheric conditions.

On my former visit, the mists shrouding the summit had cast a shadow even over objects that they did not cover. Today nothing was veiled, nothing deprived of the full benefit of the radiant sunshine. The lake, now completely thawed, reflected an azure sky, the glaciers gleamed like streams of crystal, and the summit of the mountain, all transfigured with celestial light, seemed not to belong to this earth. Here was a new world, a world governed by the laws of another existence. What repose in that vast enclosure, where centuries pass with a lighter step than do years down in the valley! What silence on those heights, where every sound is the ominous forerunner of some stupendous phenomenon! How calm the air, and how clear the sky as it flooded us with light! All was in harmony — air, sky, earth, and water; all seemed wrapped in contemplation in the presence of the sun, and appeared to receive his gaze with motionless respect.

Even after seeing Mont Blanc one should not fail to visit Mont Perdu. When one has seen the greatest of Europe's granite mountains there still remains to be seen the greatest of the limestone mountains. Those simple and solemn outlines, those bold and clean-cut silhouettes, those rocks so sound and whole in their wide layers aligned like walls, curving to form an amphitheater, or fashioned like a staircase, or rising like towers erected by the hands of giants — all these one looks for in vain in granite mountains, whose rent and jagged sides bristle with sharp points. Here, on the contrary, so harmonious are all the outlines and so modulated the gradations in height that the preeminence of the chief summit is due less to its elevation than to its shape, its mass, and a certain arrangement of everything around it, an arrangement that holds all neighboring objects in subordination. The top of Mont Perdu is only five or six hundred meters above the level of the lake, but it is the last and the highest of innumerable lofty rock masses piled one on another. From it as from their source flow the glaciers that pile themselves up on the shores of the lake; and from it descend all those sheets of snow that carpet the succession of rock terraces, clothe the upper slopes, break up as they approach the lower reaches, and remain intact only on the summit itself.

As for climbing that majestic summit, so bold an enterprise was not to be thought of. Indisputably the three thousand meters we had already ascended were by far the greater part of the journey; but no comparison is possible between the glaciers and the slopes we had surmounted with so much difficulty and those still to be scaled at far greater risk to life and limb. In vain did I study the imposing crest of the mountain; my scrutiny only strengthened my doubt as to whether it would ever be possible to find a way by which to ascend that tremendous pile of forbidding glaciers and rocky ramparts.

I restricted my activities to a second and more careful inspection of the basin in which lies the lake. We started to descend into the circular hollow without suspecting the difficulties in store for us. But we soon discovered that the thaw had greatly enlarged the circuit of the lake and water now covered what before had appeared to be its shores. Viewed from any quarter this lake, only a short time before so beautiful and now so annoying in that it barred our approach to Mont Perdu, was everywhere enclosed by rocks and by walls of ice. We looked at one another, took counsel together, gave vent to our vexation; but all to no purpose. We were forced to accept the inevitable and to trust ourselves to the perils of a very steep sheet of ice on which the slightest misstep seemed sure to send us into the lake. And this misstep was made by one of the guides, the one attacked by giddiness as we climbed the glacier. Down he went like a shot; but a slight depression, or perhaps a stone, or a mere nothing, stopped him within two feet of the lake. Except for this bit of good luck he would certainly have lost his life, as we had only our ropes to pull him out with, and these ropes he himself was carrying.

The part of the plateau surrounding Mont Perdu and not occupied by the lake is covered with enormous glaciers. One can have no idea of them without seeing them at close range, as we did this time. Nothing can take the place of a near view in these extraordinary scenes where the eye is constantly deceived in estimating distances.

Immense blocks of ice are piled up on the vast terraces of the mountain, and some of these terraces have peculiar undulations that can be likened only to solidified waves. The base of this series of waves is of enormous thickness, extending vertically downward into the lake, and from its cavernous hollows water spouts in torrents. As we were looking at one of these vaults of ice it broke before our eyes with a noise like thunder — the only sound to disturb the quiet of the place while we were there.

Though it was only three o'clock, the cold was becoming very uncomfortable. One look at those awful solitudes sufficed to convince us of the impossibility of remaining there. We often speak of the unsubdued wilds and conceive of them as places where nature shows herself in an abundance of life and movement. In imagination, we picture the dark forests in which savages hunt their prey, the desert sands crossed by caravans of laden camels, and the rocky shores where the seal disports itself and the penguin builds its nest; but here we were the only beholders of nature's more somber aspect. On one side loomed irregular masses of rock that appeared about to come tumbling down at any moment, and on the other, we beheld the subdued gleam of vast accumulations of ice. Beneath these lay the lake, calm and black by reason of its great depth, and enclosed by banks of snow, rock, or sandstone.

Not a flower, not a blade of grass was to be seen. In an eight hours' tramp, the only sign of plant life that had met my eye was the shriveled remnant of what had once been an anemone. No vestige of life showed itself in these uninhabitable regions. In the lake, not a fish was visible, not even one of those aquatic salamanders one finds in bodies of water that thaw out for only three months of the year. Not a lemming left its footprints on those fields of snow; not a bird varied the blankness of that azure vault. Everywhere the stillness of death held sway. We had spent more than two hours in that silent enclosure, and we should have left it without seeing any moving object but ourselves if two frail butterflies had not by chance preceded us in our explorations. They were strangers, outsiders, like ourselves, borne thither by a blast of wind from their native land. One of them was fluttering about its companion, fallen into the lake. It is necessary to view such solitudes as these and see the last insect die there if one would understand the importance of the part that life plays in nature. Depression had settled upon us, and we turned our backs on these somber scenes.

CHAPTER XVIII

WHERE SNOW NEVER MELTS

THOSE DESOLATE regions we have just visited with Balmat, Saussure, and Ramond, those desert stretches of snow and ice where all life ceases, those forbidding solitudes, eternal abodes of frost and silence, are in reality so many busy laboratories, always at work for the enrichment of the plains. In those domains of death are prepared the elements of life. There is held in reserve the wherewithal for renewing the soil of the lowlands. Thence the vivifying streams take their start, at first mere threads of water trickling downward in the cracks in the ice, then little cascades falling from the upper heights down into the gorges of the mountainside, still farther on calm streams dispensing fertility on each side as they flow, and finally majestic rivers swollen by numerous tributaries and emptying into the sea through wide mouths. Those accumulated snows on the mountaintops are rain supplies for every day of the year; those ice fields are sources of living water, indispensable to the soil's fertility.

The irrigation of the earth's land surface, a thing of the utmost importance for both animal and plant life, is accomplished exclusively by the precipitation (the sending down) of the moisture held in the atmosphere. This moisture falls here and there in the form of rain or snow. The atmosphere in its turn gets its water from the sea, whence the heat of the sun causes it to rise as vapor which ere long collects in clouds. All the watercourses of all the continents, all the rivers and brooks and springs, have but one source — the reservoirs of moisture stored up in the clouds and fed by the incessant evaporation of the oceans and other bodies of water. You are doubtless familiar with those allegorical figures representing rivers, leaning on their urns and crowned with reeds, and apparently turning an anxious ear to the babbling of their meager waters, which are always on the point of drying up. Real rivers, rivers of God's creation and not of man's imagination, have none of this anxiety; they know that their waters will never dry up because for source they have the atmosphere, which draws its supply from the sea, the immense, inexhaustible sea. The tiny rill that trickles between two mossy banks, the brook babbling beneath the alder trees in the meadow, the mountain torrent bounding from one jagged rock to another, the league-wide river that has for tributaries the watercourses of an empire — all have their source in the clouds and return to the sea whence those clouds came. A country's water supply comes originally from the ocean by way of the clouds; the source of sources is in the atmosphere and the sea.

Clouds gather especially about high mountaintops, guided thither by an invisible hand, and there it may happen that the mists slowly soak into the soil as into a sponge. This process, repeated again and again, causes the moisture to reach the very depths of the mountain, whence it issues through the mountainsides in the form of springs and brooks to water the plains below. Or the clouds veiling a mountain summit may discharge their watery burden as rain, which washes the slopes and greatly adds to the volume of the neighboring streams. At times, also, especially when the mountain is a very high one, the clouds send down snow, which melts only gradually under the sun's rays and so forms a most lasting and useful reservoir for irrigation purposes.

If the moisture in the atmosphere were always discharged as rain, the soil would suffer from an alternation of superabundant supply and disastrous drought. Our highways turn dry and dusty for lack of moisture, and when rain comes it forms little streams of muddy water in the roadbed. Something like this would be the result if nothing but rain were given us for irrigation. In the rainy season, we should have foaming torrents in our ravines, and these torrents would feed temporary muddy streams, destined to dry up to the last drop in the season of no rain. If, again, the soil were dependent for its moisture on the humidity of the atmosphere alone, we should have only streams of insignificant volume — puny springs and tiny brooklets. For a great river that is to continue running with but little diminished volume throughout the year, snow is indispensable, and the reason is plain. Rain, unless long continued, only washes the surface and runs off too quickly to soak into the earth to any depth and accumulate there as a reserve supply. A heavy rain can in a short time swell the volume of a river and even make it overflow its banks, but it cannot feed the river all the year through. Too violent and too frequent downpours cause disastrous floods, whereas not too abundant rains furnish a good supply of water; but as rain is not and cannot be continuous, it does not constitute the main source of water supply for a great river that never ceases to flow and always fills, or nearly fills, its channel.

With snow, the conditions are wholly different. Snow may be called solidified rain. Held in reserve and melting gradually, it alone is capable of furnishing streams with their needed supply of water for an indefinite length of time. The melting process is so gradual and economical that the ground drinks it up drop by drop and gives it out later in the form of springs. Under its moist blanket of snow, the earth undergoes a saturation that the sun cannot soon dry, the very depths of the soil having become soaked like a sponge, and the underground reservoirs being filled for a long time to come.

In the physical economy of the earth, things are ordered much as in our own domestic economy. What comes easily goes quickly, but what is earned by labor and perseverance is more profitable and lasts longer. In like manner, the water left by a sudden shower is quickly evaporated by the sun, whereas the slowly accumulating water supply furnished by snowstorms stores itself up in the ground as the snow gradually melts.

But the snow that falls on the plains is far from sufficient to feed the great rivers, coming as it does neither often enough nor in adequate quantity. More than that, melting soon under the heat of the sun and so not remaining long enough to soak into the ground, it produces little more effect than so much rain; the ground has not time to absorb it entirely. Here we have a good example in proof of the prime importance of mountains.

The temperature of the atmosphere falls rapidly as we ascend, and the average rate of this fall is one degree for every 150 or 200 meters of ascent. Accordingly, at a height of 2,000 or 3,000 meters, the temperature must often fall below the freezing point; and this has been proved to be so from the reading of the thermometer on high mountains. In those lofty regions, therefore, the moisture held in the atmosphere cannot be precipitated as rain on account of the cold, but must fall as snow, and that in summer as well as in winter. In their descent from the upper atmosphere where they form, the flakes of snow meet on their way ever warmer and warmer layers of air, melt as they fall, and finally reach the plain as raindrops. Hence, all rain starting from a sufficient height is snow in the beginning. This can easily be proved in mountainous regions: after every shower in the valleys, a fresh layer of snow is to be seen on the neighboring summits.

It snows, then, in all seasons even in the hottest climate, but with this difference, that whereas in the winter season, in a cool climate, the snow falls as snow, in warmer regions the flakes melt in falling before reaching the lowlands and are thus turned into drops of rain. To prevent this melting, whatever the climate and whatever the season — a melting that destroys the usefulness of the snow as a reservoir of moisture for feeding the rivers and other streams — what is necessary? Evidently, the snowflakes must be collected in a mass before they reach layers of air so warm as to melt them. They must, as they fall, alight on some resting place cold enough to admit of their accumulating there as snow and not as water. Well, these resting places for the snow, these reservoirs for holding immense stores of solidified water, are the high mountains, with their summits always swept by icy breezes.

Thus, both on account of the mists that often shroud them and still more on account of the snow that covers them for at least a great part of the year, lofty mountain chains serve as the starting points of great watercourses. From their two sides flow, like so many vivifying arteries, rivers born of the gradual melting of snow and the condensation of mist. Some flow down one slope of the mountain chain, others down the opposite slope. The name "watershed," given to the crest of a range of mountains, comes from this division of the waters. What its ridge-pole is to a roof, this crest or "divide" is to the mountain chain. Recall for a moment what occurs on a snow-covered roof when the snow melts; there you have a good likeness, in miniature, of a snow-capped mountain range with its double series of watercourses. On the roof, every conductor running down on one side has its little stream of water from the melting snow, and every conductor on the other side has its corresponding stream, while all these streams flowing in two opposite directions have the ridge-pole for a common dividing line. So in a mountain chain, the line of highest elevation marks the division of the waters, and the ravines running down the two slopes receive each its share of the total water supply for distribution to the plains below.

In our temperate climate, snow covers the plains only a part of the time in the winter season, but it whitens the mountaintops, if they are at least of medium height, a good part of the year. The plains of hot countries never see snow in any season, while the mountains of sufficient height in those countries are capped with snow that never wholly melts. In the polar regions, the summer sun manages to clear the plains here and there for a few months or a few weeks, but it cannot entirely melt snow that lies at the height of a few hundred meters; and this is the natural consequence of the lowness of temperature due to that altitude.

There is, then, from one end of the earth to the other, in the equatorial regions no less than in the temperate and the frigid zones, a height, varying with the climate, above which the sun's heat is insufficient to melt entirely the year's accumulation of snow. Above this height, rain is unknown even in midsummer, being replaced by snow and sleet. Bare ground and bare rock are never seen there; an eternal mantle of white covers all things. The height at which perpetual snow begins must, plainly enough, be greater in a hot climate than in a cold one; and therefore, as a general rule, this dividing line must become increasingly lower as one advances from the equator toward either pole. At the equator perpetual snow begins at an altitude of about 4800 meters; in the Alps and the Pyrenees at about 2700 meters; in Iceland at 936 meters; and in the islands of the Spitzbergen group at zero, or in other words at the sea-level.

We sometimes speak of the ice that clothes lofty peaks, but this use of the word "ice" is incorrect except in the sense of hardened snow. Real ice is impossible on very high mountains because there is never any water at those heights. Water could be there only as rain or as melted snow, but we have just seen that rain can never fall on those frigid mountain-tops, only snow and sleet being sent down from the clouds; and snow at that height can melt only very superficially if at all, and that only in the few days of unclouded summer weather. The little water resulting from this process freezes at nightfall and helps to bind the mass of snow all together; but in no case is the melting sufficient to supply the water necessary for the making of thick layers of ice. I will add, while we are on this subject, what has been learned through observations conducted at the summit of Mont Blanc.

The crest of the mountain is a long ridge, nearly horizontal, running from east to west, and so narrow that two persons cannot walk on it abreast. Each slope is an immense, monotonous sheet of snow of dazzling whiteness. On the crest the snow is thinly coated with ice, which cracks under the feet and easily breaks up. This coating results from a superficial melting occasionally induced by the sun's heat and followed the next night by freezing. On the mountain-sides, there is fuller exposure to the sun and the snow melts to a greater depth; hence, the crust that forms is usually thick enough to bear a person's weight. In every instance, however, underneath this surface crust of ice, there is snow, sometimes compact, sometimes dry and powdery. Deeper down is another icy crust, and under this, a fresh layer of powdery snow, and so on indefinitely. It is evident that each of these layers, separated one from another by a crust of ice, represents the snow of a single downfall or even the accumulated snow of a whole year.

The ice crust on the summit is so thin that a blast of wind is enough to break it and send the fragments flying to a great height, mixed with eddies of powdery snow. When this occurs, one can see from the neighboring valleys a kind of grayish smoke or mist rising from the summit and borne in whichever direction the wind happens to be blowing. The country people then say that Mont Blanc is smoking his pipe. Sometimes these puffs of flying snow have a reddish tinge in the light of the setting sun and suggest a volcanic eruption. As for measuring the thickness of the snow mantle covering the mountain, that would be no easy undertaking. It would require that a cross-section of the accumulated layers of snow should somewhere be exposed, and no such cross-section is anywhere visible. The white mantle drapes the entire mountain-top and its slopes without showing at any point what its thickness is. However, as the result of his various observations, Saussure thought this thickness might be reckoned at about sixty meters. That, then, would be the depth of the perpetual snow on the summit and upper slopes of Mont Blanc.

This depth, considerable though it is, by no means represents the whole volume of snow that has fallen on Mont Blanc. From year's end to year's end, there falls in the Alps about eighteen meters' depth of snow. Why is it, then, one might ask, that after all these centuries of accumulated deposits, there is no greater quantity now heaped up there? As the occasional melting of surface snow really amounts to almost nothing and tends to preserve the underlying layers by providing a protective covering of ice rather than to diminish the aggregate mass of snow, what has become of the thousands and thousands of layers that the mountain has received in the past and that ought, apparently, to be found there now, piled up in the order of their coming, the oldest at the bottom, the most recent at the top? Ought not the mountain to acquire in the course of time an indefinite height from the heaping up of layer after layer of snow, each year's contribution being added to that of the preceding year?

No; that is not the way it works out. In all things, the forces of nature are subject to an inviolable law of equilibrium, so that no one of them can enjoy an advantage over the others for a long enough time to bring about disorder. And there would be serious disorder if the moisture in the atmosphere were to solidify and accumulate endlessly on the mountains. Lofty peaks, continually piling up their snows layer by layer, would at last erect so monstrous a structure of snow and ice that the immediate consequence would be a general lowering of the temperature over all the adjacent territory. The regions of perpetual snow would become larger and larger, and thither would be borne the moisture evaporated from the oceans and the seas, to be precipitated and rendered forever useless, forever unable to fall in beneficent showers on the thirsty land. In course of time, all the oceans and seas, gradually depleted by evaporation, would be added to those deserts of ice, and sooner or later, the entire surface of the earth would present very much the same appearance as northern Greenland does today. Thus, for the general harmony of things in this world, the snow that falls on high mountains, and which we inaccurately speak of as perpetual snow, should not accumulate there indefinitely, but should melt and disappear, as snow elsewhere does, returning to the ocean after doing its part in the work of irrigation.

But it is not the sun that melts it, the sun's heat being insufficient for this at those heights; it is the heat of the earth, the heat of the great subterranean furnace. You know how rapidly the temperature rises as one descends into the bowels of the earth, and so you will understand that a little of this interior heat, by ascending into the body of the mountain, must reach the mantle of snow cloaking its surface and thus cause a gradual melting, in winter as well as in summer. Hence, it is from underneath and not from above that the melting of snow on lofty peaks is brought about; and while the surface snow, open to the icy winds at all times, receives year by year fresh deposits on which the sun has hardly any effect, the underlying snow, next to the ground and acted upon by the subterranean heat, remains somewhat above the freezing point and is liquefied and removed at a rate equal to the increase from above. Consequently, the total depth of snow is maintained with but little variation from year to year. This incessant melting of the underlying snow keeps the ground beneath in a moist condition and contributes greatly to the feeding of the streams flowing down the mountain-sides.

Another agency restricting the accumulation of snow on high mountains is the occasional fall of avalanches. When the slope it covers is steep, the sheet of snow, held in position very lightly, slips at the slightest disturbance of its equilibrium and slides down into the valley. A loosened stone, a puff of wind, the report of a pistol, the cracking of a glacier, the tread of a careless mountain-climber — any one of these may be enough to disturb the delicate equilibrium and start the downrush of the avalanche. This movement, once begun, is communicated to adjacent masses of snow until we have, perhaps, a vast field in motion and gathering speed as it slides downward with the roar of a torrent, crashing against intervening obstacles and breaking up into whirlpools of powdery white particles. An immense cascade of powdered silver appears to hurl itself furiously down the mountain-side. Fir-trees are uprooted and brushed aside like so many bits of straw. Great granite blocks are torn up and swept away. The atmospheric disturbance caused by the descent of this huge mass is sometimes so violent as to overthrow persons and even buildings at a considerable distance from the avalanche.

Nearly every day avalanches go rushing down from the snow-capped mountain summits into the adjacent ravines where, as we shall see in the next chapter, glaciers have their origin. These avalanches are seldom disastrous, their passage being over uninhabited territory. But now and then one slides down into some inhabited valley, and then the loss of life and property is lamentable. We hear of whole villages destroyed by these awful visitations, overturned from top to bottom or transported, almost intact, to another spot. There are heartbreaking accounts of persons buried alive, sometimes by the hundred, under the billows of the snowy flood.

In the spring, when the sun begins to soften the hard-packed snows of the preceding winter, any traveler obliged to make his way through some mountain pass overhung by snow-covered slopes does so only with the scrupulous precautions dictated by the imminent danger of avalanches. If possible, the journey is made before sunrise and while the snow still retains the firmness produced by the freezing of the preceding night, and if there is a company of travelers, they proceed in single file and at a certain distance from one another. In this way, there is some chance that if an avalanche carries off a part of the company, the remaining members will escape and be able to go to the rescue of their less fortunate comrades. Complete silence is observed on the way, even the bells of the mules being muffled, as a word, a sound of any sort, a slight movement of the air, might start an avalanche. If at any point advance seems especially perilous, a pistol is discharged to loosen and send down any threatening snow masses before the expedition passes that way. On some of the Alpine routes, it has been found necessary to build covered galleries or snow-sheds in the most dangerous parts for the protection of travelers from avalanches.

CHAPTER XIX

GLACIERS

HIGH MOUNTAINS serve as cradles for great rivers. In all seasons, midsummer as well as midwinter, clouds of vapor drawn from the sea by the sun's heat and carried to those lofty peaks by the wind send down their snow on the mountain-tops, where it accumulates, layer by layer, never leaving its rocky bed exposed for a single day in the year. This snow, renewed as fast as it melts and hence called perpetual snow, serves as a reservoir for holding the water supply of the surrounding region solidified by the cold; and it liquefies and begins to move again only with cautious slowness and in quantities suited to the needs of the land to be irrigated.

If too rapid, this melting process would in a few days exhaust the supply destined to feed various streams through weeks and months, and the lowlands would then be left exposed to drought after being laid waste by raging torrents. If it were too slow, we should have, instead of great rivers watering an empire on their way to the sea, only a few little brooks that would lose themselves in the gravel on their way oceanward or be dried up by the heat of the sun.

On lofty mountain-tops, snow melts too slowly, the sun having but little effect there, and the slight warmth from the earth's interior being insufficient to provide the needed daily supply of snow-water for the great rivers of the region. At the foot of the mountain, the melting would go on at too rapid a rate under the burning summer sun. Between these two extremes, a mean is required for the welfare of the surrounding country. It is necessary for the snow from the heights above to be brought down to lower levels, where it will find a warmer temperature to melt it in suitable abundance; but it is also necessary that this conveyance should be managed with extreme prudence. In other words, if there is need of lofty peaks, lifting their summits into the realms of perpetual frost and there receiving the waters of heaven in a solid form for retention until called for, there is also need of a special contrivance for slowly lowering the accumulated snow and bringing it under the rays of a warmer sun without risk of injury to valleys and plains by a premature melting. Well, this contrivance, so important for the welfare of our continents, is found in glaciers.

The accumulations of snow, as we have seen, slide down the steep slopes and into the neighboring valleys. Therefore, high valleys bordered by such snow-covered slopes are themselves filled with snow that has been piling up there for countless years and is continually renewed by avalanches. These beds of snow, hardened and solidified by the enormous pressure of successive layers, and finally turned into ice by alternate partial meltings and freezings, form what we call glaciers. Every valley in the regions of perpetual snow has one. In the Alps alone, more than a thousand can be counted. They are sometimes four or five leagues long and a league or more wide, while their thickness is commonly between thirty and forty meters, with occasional instances of unusual thickness measuring from two hundred up to four hundred meters.

There is nothing more varied in appearance than a glacier. In one place, it looks, perhaps, like a sea rendered motionless by freezing at the moment when, toward the end of a violent storm, it swells and rolls in heavy billows. At another part, all unevenness is smoothed out, and the surface is nothing but an inclined plane dotted with opaque beads or an immense shining mirror. Elsewhere, again, there are great folds of drapery resembling alabaster, cascades frozen and motionless amid billows of snowy foam, broken arches, fantastic structures of the purest crystal, obelisks, arrows, and upstanding ridges of what looks like stained glass, colored by the sun's rays. Here and there may be seen transverse clefts yawning in a threatening manner and exposing to view the very bottom of the glacier. Between their vertical walls shimmers a green or bluish light which, in the lower depths, fades away into darkness. From the bottom of these crevasses comes up the murmur of running water — a rushing torrent, in fact — making its way downward beneath the glacier. At still other points are ice grottoes which soften the daylight in such a manner as to give the ice the appearance of beryl. From these grottoes issue streams of cool, clear water, flowing in crystal channels and losing themselves in the clefts in the ice. Here and there, also, are large, round, shell-like formations, basins hollowed out in the transparent ice. A hundred streamlets flow into these basins without filling them, the water losing itself in the depths of the glacier.

At its lower end, facing down the valley, the glacier comes to an abrupt stop as if it had been cut off perpendicularly, with an excavation at the bottom in the form of a cavern which sometimes measures thirty meters in height. From the mouth of this ice grotto rushes a foaming torrent, its waters muddy, blackish, milky, or green, according to the nature of the rocks that the glacier gradually wears away under its enormous pressure as it moves slowly along in its bed. At the front of the advancing glacier is a belt of stones all heaped up and mixed together in disorder. This is known as the "terminal lateral," and over this natural dike pours the torrent, leaping from rock to rock.

One can make one's way for a considerable distance into these glacial grottoes. What a weird light there is in the crystal caves, fit abodes for the divinities of winter! From the translucent vault overhead is shed a blue light, softened by the ice through which it filters. In the limpid walls, which are of great thickness, may be seen the play of emerald and indigo hues. The illumination is not exactly that of daylight, nor yet is it darkness, but rather the sea-green twilight of the ocean depths. If by chance a ray of sunshine strikes through the entrance to one of these caverns, how brilliant the effect, how fairy-like the illumination! The twisted fringes, the ice prisms, the giant pillars supporting the vaulted roof — all these absorb the light, break it up, and send it out again in radiant streams of diverse hues. Rainbow tints are reflected from wall to wall, the stalactites hanging from the dome of ice suddenly light up, and every point gleams like a carbuncle, every edge sparkles with many-colored fires. All about are hung flashing mirrors, and everything is radiant with magic colors of iridescent splendor.

It is imprudent to venture under these vaults of ice, especially in time of thaw, as at any moment the rash explorer might be crushed by the falling in of the massive roof over his head. Two young men who visited the cave of the Rhone glacier took it into their heads to fire off a pistol, that they might hear the reverberation of the explosion. That was enough to bring down the ice roof, and the two imprudent youngsters were never seen again. However, bold explorers have defied the danger and pushed their way into these glacial caverns as far as possible, in order to see what they are like; and their report is that they extend long distances and have various ramifications, finally ending in narrow galleries, passages, and channels, impassable to the explorer and flooded with streams from the melting ice and snow.

Now let us return to the outside of the glacier. Its surface is, as a rule, not slippery like a sheet of glare ice but rough and granular, so that unless the slope is very steep, one is in little danger of catching a fall. Often it is covered with a layer of round, bead-like particles, into which the foot sinks as into sand. This granulated ice is old snow, somewhat resembling coarse salt in appearance. Its condition is the result of partial melting followed by freezing, which turns each water-soaked particle into a granule of ice. Finally, at the upper end of the valley, the glacier is lost under the drifting snow.

Nowhere in a glacier does ice form as on our rivers, in homogeneous, compact, continuous masses; but it is always composed of rather loosely united, small, transparent pieces, having so little cohesion that a block easily breaks into a multitude of fragments. At the lower end of the glacier, these fragments are about the size of a walnut, while higher up they diminish to that of a pea. This singular structure is very easily explained. If a glacier were formed by the sudden freezing of a great watercourse, its ice would be homogeneous and transparent; but that is not at all the way a glacier comes into being. It is gradually molded by the pouring of great masses of snow, in the form of avalanches, into the valley it is to occupy. This snow—watered in the daytime by rain and by the partial melting of its own substance, then frozen at night—finally, after these alternate meltings and freezings, is converted into ice of porous and granular structure. Moisten a little snow and then let it freeze, and you will have, in miniature, something resembling glacial ice.

Another feature noticeable in glaciers is this: on each side, extending its entire length, a glacier is bordered by a strip of fragmentary matter sent down from the adjacent slopes by the action of thunder, avalanches, and storms, and consisting of jagged rocks, coarse and fine sand, and quantities of mud, all mixed together. These bordering strips are known as "lateral moraines."

One cannot look at a glacier without receiving an impression of imperturbable repose and eternal immobility. Those immense masses of ice, old as the centuries, seem immovably and permanently established in their valleys. Those layers upon layers of frozen water appear to have the solidity and the strength of so many courses of granite, and one cannot but feel that nothing could move them short of a convulsion violent enough to shake to their foundations the mountains that dominate them.

But this first impression is deceptive, for glaciers do move. They are solidified rivers and, like the liquid rivers that they themselves feed, they flow, although with the slowness of the centuries. A glacier's daily progress down the valley it occupies is only a few centimeters. It moves in one solid mass, dragging over a thousand obstructions the burden of its enormous layers. Like a river, it wears away the valley that serves it as bed. A current of water softens and washes away earth from its banks; a current of ice grinds down the hardest rock and turns it into mud. A wet rag with a little fine sand on it will polish a stone if rubbed against it long enough. If the sand is coarse, it will merely scratch the stone. In the same way, a glacier, as it moves onward, either polishes the rocks along its course or cuts deep grooves in them. Here the rag is the glacier, a mass of ice weighing as much as a mountain, and the grains of sand are the mineral fragments that have tumbled into the glacier's yawning crevices and so found their way to the bottom.

Everything yields to this irresistible friction. On the floor of the valley, the exposed rock is scored with long and deep furrows running in the same direction as the glacier's movement. Channels extend in parallel lines of geometrical regularity. After these more violent lithographic operations, the engraving implements break up into smaller fragments, and these in turn into grains of sand of varying degrees of coarseness, which have for their office the tracing of fine lines such as a diamond point might cut on a pane of glass. At last, the grains of sand are reduced to fine powder, whose gentle friction wears away all remaining roughness and gives to the abraded rock surface the smoothness of polished marble. Meanwhile, the water running under the glacier is taking up, little by little, the mud produced by this immense grinding and polishing operation, so that the stream issuing from the terminal cavern is always turbid.

A river of water carries along with it pebbles, sand, and silt, which it deposits at its mouth. A river of ice, a glacier, also conveys its load of mineral matter; but its pebbles are fragments of mountains, and, instead of rolling them along at the bottom of its bed, it bears them on its back. I have just told you that on each side of a glacier, there is a moraine, a strip composed of mineral fragments sent down from the neighboring summits and slopes by the repeated action of storms, thunderbolts, and avalanches. As the glacier moves down the valley, these deposits move with it, the vehicle conveying them being strong enough to do so even were they solid blocks cut out of the mountainside. But as it moves along, the glacier enters a warmer atmosphere, and when it reaches a point where the heat is too great for the ice to withstand it, the glacier, as you already know, comes to an abrupt end in a sort of steep escarpment which is continually melting away and continually being renewed by the forward push of fresh ice.

It is here that the glacier, released from the restraining fetters of frost, becomes liquid, turns into a torrent, and takes its course in freedom down the valley. Every fragment in the two lateral moraines of a glacier advances slowly, with the part of the glacier that bears it, toward the terminal escarpment. It is a long journey, but that matters not; the fragment finally reaches its destination. Little by little, its support is removed, it overhangs the ice more and more as its props melt away, until at last, there remains nothing to hold it up and it falls into the midst of the fragments that preceded it. In this manner, there is formed in front of every glacier that pile of rocks and stones and other matter which we call a terminal moraine. As its alluvial deposit, then, the river of ice piles up this terminal moraine consisting of broken bits of the mountain whence it came.

We have just noted the chief effects produced by the movement of glaciers, and it now remains to inquire into the causes that originate these vast masses of ice, and to find out what power it is that pushes them forward down the valleys. The movement of a glacier may be ascribed to two agencies, the inclination of its bed and the expansive force of ice.

Nearly all glaciers rest on sloping ground, and between the mass of ice and the surface on which it lies, there flows, even in winter, a sheet of water resulting from the gradual melting of the ice. It is evident, therefore, that the ice, partly freed by this running water from its adhesion to the ground, will be propelled by its own weight down the slope on which it rests, and so will move toward the lower end of the valley at a slow but steady rate.

Now as to the second agency. Ice always fills a little more space than the water that goes to the making of it, and when it forms in an enclosed space, with walls resisting its increase in volume, it exerts on those walls a pressure that is all but irresistible and that we call expansive force. Furthermore, we know that the substance of a glacier is not perfectly compact and homogeneous but full of pores and other unfilled spaces, as it is composed of piled-up snow with cracks and crevices running all through it in every direction. In the daytime, when a superficial melting is going on, the glacier absorbs the snow-water, its pores and cracks becoming more or less filled with it. Then in the night, if the temperature falls below freezing, it is very clear what must be the result. The water freezing in the fissures pushes back the walls restraining it; every particle of ice in the process of formation acts like a wedge, and the sum total of all these internal thrusts is an irresistible expansion of the whole mass. Thereupon the glacier, held to its bed by the unshakable mountains on both sides, twists and squirms, so to speak, in the tremendous struggle going on between the opposing obstructions and the forces striving to overthrow them. There resounds the deep note of cracking ice far down in the glacier, ruptures make themselves visible, crevasses yawn, until at last, the frozen stream moves in the only direction that offers no hindrance, and that is down the valley.

The distance over which a glacier moves in a year varies greatly with different glaciers, as the rate of movement is evidently closely related to the incline of the valley down which the glacier makes its way. In some instances, the annual advance is estimated at twenty meters. But whatever the rate of progress, on reaching the point where the temperature is high enough to melt it, a glacier always comes to an end in the steep escarpment already described and turns into a torrent of water, the source or tributary of a river. At that point, the glacier is continually being destroyed by the sun's heat, while at the head of the valley fresh snow is piling up, packing together, and starting on its downward course so that the glacier is always maintained in a nearly constant condition.

It is to be noted that, in order to reach a part of the valley where its melting shall be complete, a glacier must descend far below the line of perpetual snow. This line, as we have already learned, is reached in our part of the world at an altitude of about 2700 meters above the level of the sea. Certain Alpine glaciers move down to 1100 or even 1000 meters above sea level. At this height, not only are large trees and green pastures possible, but crops can easily be raised and brought to maturity. Imagine the strange spectacle of these ice rivers flowing from the regions of perpetual frost to brave the sun's heat amid tilled fields and under the walnut trees of the valley. Right beside the blue walls of a glacier, there may be yellowing fields of grain, cattle grazing in grass breast-high, and bees gathering honey from the catkins of the alder trees. On one side, we have summer, warmth, and life, while a few steps to the other side we find ice that is being constantly renewed, winter, and death. No, I am wrong; it is life, after all, for from this mass of ice, continually melting on the surface from the warmth of the sun, and at the bottom from the earth's inner heat, there is born a rushing stream that ere long becomes a river or perhaps the tributary of a river that flows hundreds of miles and distributes its vivifying waters over vast stretches of territory. Yes, it is life, despite all appearances to the contrary; for a glacier serves as emissary of the upper reservoirs in which is stored the water supply of a whole region, a supply wisely held in restraint by the detaining hand of frost. A glacier is the providential vehicle conveying to the lowland, with prudent slowness, the snow and ice that would never have melted on the mountaintops. It brings this snow and ice down into the valleys where melting can take place.

CHAPTER XX

GREAT RIVERS

RAIN, MOISTURE in the atmosphere, melting snow — these it is that furnish water to our springs and brooks, which by their union in sufficient volume form rivers. The latter, flowing from various directions according to the natural slope of the ground, unite to make still larger rivers, and these in turn may pour their waters into some great artery that crosses a continent and empties into the ocean, its original source. In the sea begins and ends that vast circulating system designed for the irrigation and enrichment of the continents. From the sea starts the current of atmospheric moisture, and into the sea pours the current of terrestrial waters returned to their starting point. Just as the heart is the point of departure and of arrival of the nourishing blood that carries life to the different parts of the body, so the sea is the point of departure and of arrival of the continental blood, the vivifying waters of the earth.

There is great variety in the way a stream may take its start. Sometimes its source is beneath a glacier's massive layers of ice, whence by a thousand little channels the water finally reaches the terminal cavern and bursts forth in a foaming torrent. Or the stream may gush in a powerful current from the midst of rocks at the bottom of some valley far from the melting snow and ice that constitute the source of supply. In still other instances, the headwaters are seen trickling from a spongy soil or oozing drop by drop through the fissures in broken rock. Amid this great variety of origin, let us select two examples, one of them being of the kind already familiar to you — a spring issuing from a glacial cavern. The other instance shall be one

184

of the most remarkable springs to be found in all France — the fountain of Vaucluse.

I will describe in some detail this famous spring which gives its name to the department it waters. It gushes forth from the bottom of a wild gorge that ends abruptly in an immense vertical rampart of solid rock. The name Vaucluse, meaning a closed valley, has reference to this very rampart across the gorge. Picture to your mind's eye, then, a ravine with rugged walls of bare rock on each side, some lesser rocks at their base rudely fashioned in the shape of pyramids by the action of storm and flood, and a vertical reddish wall in front of you, cutting off all advance in that direction. This reddish wall or rampart is a rocky, precipitous mountain side. Such is the general formation of the celebrated valley of Vaucluse.

In the season of low water, the head of this valley is nothing but a pile of huge rocks coated with a fleece of black moss. From their velvety backs one might, with a little effort of the imagination, take these moss-covered shapes for a herd of aquatic monsters crouching in the cool shade of the place. Here and there amid this strange group, water gushes up in considerable volume, but calm and clear. The chief spring, however, is not here; it is at the foot of the terminal rampart. There, in the solid rock itself, opens a vast cavern with a rapidly descending floor. Going down this, you find yourself under a natural vault, its rugged arch bearing the weight of the mountain above, while at your feet is what appears to be a bottomless well filled with calm water of a beautiful blue.

In time of rain or thaw, this water rises, fills the cavern, mounts the steep slope, and overflows in an enormous flood at the rate of 2400 liters a second. It is then that the fountain of Vaucluse thunders and rages in tumultuous uproar as its waters, bounding and rebounding from one to another of those moss-covered rocks that we first saw dry and placid, plunge downward in cascades whiter than snow, break into foam with deafening uproar, and send up great jets of fine spray. Farther down the valley, all is calm, and one does not have to go a great distance before coming upon an important river, the Sorgue, which has its source in the fountain of Vaucluse, and which, after irrigating a portion of the department of that name, empties into the Rhone. Whence comes this great quantity of water that gushes up from the bottom of a gorge so bare, and in the dry season so arid, that one might almost take it for an old volcanic crater? It comes, by oozing and through underground channels, from the neighboring mountain chain, whose principal peak, Mont Ventoux, is capped with snow during a great part of the year.

The bed of a river is the channel that conducts it down a more or less steep incline to its place of emptying, its mouth. Abrupt inequalities in the earth's surface may cause sudden changes of level in the river's bed, and then we have waterfalls. These are also called cascades where the stream is of no great volume, and cataracts where they occur in large rivers.

Europe has no more deservedly celebrated cascade than that of Gavarnie. Near Mont Perdu, in the wildest part of the Pyrenees, is the semicircular plateau of Gavarnie, or Cirque de Gavarnie, as it is commonly known. It is a half-circle walled in by a vertical rampart of rock four or five hundred feet high. This rampart, with its glacier-filled embrasures, is itself dominated by a semicircular range of mountains rising in vast terraces white with perpetual snow. Ten or twelve streams come rushing down from this range into the plateau, the most considerable of them plunging from the top of an overhanging rock and falling 410 meters, touching the mountain side but once in its fall, that once being at about two fifths of its way down. Its peculiar setting gives it the appearance of a long streamer of muslin or of silvery gauze fluttering from the top of the rampart. It is less a column of water than a filmy cloud gliding through the air, having as it does all the whiteness and lightness and undulating motion of a fleecy cloud. In its translucent mist, the sunbeams play in wavering rainbow tints, ever on the verge of fading away and ever renewed.

At last this radiant ribbon of water reaches the ground, whereupon it breaks in foaming torrents over the rocks and throws up a glittering shower of spray as pleasing to the sight, as gracefully waving, as a spreading tuft of fine feathers. This is surmounted by a cloud of mist that floats upward against the background of the rocky rampart. In this part of the plateau, the ground is covered with perpetual snow, through which the cascade opens a way by undermining it in such a manner as to leave an arch called the Bridge of Ice. For some distance, the stream runs under the crust of snow and ice; then, swollen with the various cascades falling from the heights above, it comes to view again, its waters showing a tinge of deep blue, and rushes onward and downward where the plateau is uninclosed, and so into the valley in a foaming torrent called the Torrent of Pau.

In North America, there is a series of five great lakes flowing one into another and feeding the St. Lawrence River with their waters. In the defile between the last two of these lakes, Erie and Ontario, the bed of the river makes a sudden descent of fifty meters and thus creates one of the most famous of waterfalls. It is the cataract of Niagara, or Niagara Falls.

Where the stream takes its plunge, it is less like a river than a sea hurling itself into the abyss. A little island covered with verdure stands at the brink of the falls and divides the cataract into two branches, one on the Canadian side, the other on that of the United States. The first is shaped like a horseshoe, its circuit measuring 600 meters; the second, of only half this extent, has no curve. In this double cataract, Niagara, rightly called "Thundering Water" by the Indians, pours over the falls 250,000 hectoliters of water every second.

The spectator is struck dumb at this awe-inspiring sight. Dark and greenish on the surface as it flows over the brink, the moving mass of liquid becomes variegated lower down with a sort of crystal embroidery, losing itself finally in the abyss in an avalanche of foam. The thunder of the falling water as it strikes its bed is no mean rival of the thunder that accompanies the lightning flash in a violent storm. From the boiling flood rises a white mist that floats over the cataract like smoke from a fire.

A staircase built on the American side of the falls enables one to reach the foot of the cataract and even make one's way under it. To the frightful accompaniment of the thundering water, one can walk between the wall of precipitous rock on one side and the terrifying curtain of the cataract on the other. On this side of the falls, there is a populous town spread out on the rocky plateau from which the river takes its plunge; and farther down, a suspension bridge, the gigantic work of a people vying with nature herself in grandeur of achievement, spans the stream from bank to bank. It has two levels, or roadways, one over the other and eight meters apart. The upper is for the use of railway trains, the lower for carriages and pedestrians.

When the bed of a river, instead of making a vertical drop, is merely inclined so as to offer a steep grade, and is at the same time strewn with large rocks, we have what is called a rapid (or more often in the plural, rapids). These conditions give us, not a fall of water in one mass from an overhanging brink, but a succession of little cascades amid a labyrinth of islets and rocks.

Sometimes a river encounters in its course a barrier of rock obstructing its passage. If under this barrier the earth is of such a nature as to yield to the force of the stream, an underground channel is made and the river disappears from sight for some distance, reappearing sooner or later and running on as before. Such is the case with the Rhone near its issue from Lake Geneva. The Meuse likewise disappears underground near Bazoilles, and reappears ten kilometers farther down. The Guadiana, in Spain, filters down through spongy soil and comes to view again in greater volume at a lower point in its course. The ground under which the stream runs is called by the Spaniards a wide bridge, and it can give pasturage to one hundred thousand horned cattle. But there are rivers that disappear permanently, seeming to lose themselves in the ground. Sandy soil may absorb them or the sun dry them up before they reach the sea. Africa furnishes numerous examples of these incomplete rivers, these mouthless streams.

Sometimes a river encounters in its course a barrier of rock obstructing its passage. If under this barrier the earth is of such a nature as to yield to the force of the stream, an underground channel is made and the river disappears from sight for some distance, reappearing sooner or later and running on as before. Such is the case with the Rhone near its issue from Lake Geneva.

The Meuse likewise disappears underground near Bazoilles and reappears ten kilometers farther down. The Guadiana, in Spain, filters down through spongy soil and comes to view again in greater volume at a lower point in its course. The ground under which the stream runs is called by the Spaniards a wide bridge, and it can give pasturage to one hundred thousand horned cattle. But there are rivers that disappear permanently, seeming to lose themselves in the ground. Sandy soil may absorb them or the sun dry them up before they reach the sea. Africa furnishes numerous examples of these incomplete rivers, these mouthless streams.

In the lower part of its course, where the inclination of its channel is slight and its waters calm, a river deposits its burden of mineral and other matter that its swifter current has been carrying, and thus near its mouth there accumulates a mass of sand and mud and other alluvial refuse, obstructing the channel and dividing the stream into a number of branches or mouths. These deposits accumulating where a river empties into the sea give to the collective mouths of the stream a somewhat triangular form, and we call this triangle a delta, on account of its likeness to the Greek letter of that name, which answers to our letter D. The Rhone has a delta, and so have the Rhine, the Nile, the Ganges, the Mississippi, and other large rivers.

The delta of the Rhone is called Camargue Island. A little below Arles, about seven leagues from the sea, the river divides, enclosing between its arms and the Mediterranean a triangular plain of about 370,000 acres' area. This is Camargue Island, an indeterminate stretch of ground disputed over by fresh water and salt, by the alluvial deposits of the river and the sands of the sea. Three regions are distinguishable here as one goes from the banks of the river to the middle of the delta, which is occupied by a vast pond, the pond of Calcares. These regions are the cultivated, the grazing, and the pond districts.

The first, lying along the two mouths of the Rhone, is wonderfully fertile, made so by the rich annual alluvial deposits. Abundant crops of grain are raised here, the soil being kept clear of sea-salt by the constant infiltration of river water. Beyond this belt lie the grazing grounds, which are salt lands. There, shelterless and without keepers other than mounted herdsmen who at long intervals come to round up their wild herds with tridents for goads, wander thousands of cattle that have reverted to their primitive untamed condition. Black, small and stocky, wild-eyed and with threatening horns, they have resumed their native characteristics and thrown off the degenerate qualities of domestication. One mark, and only one, reminds the observer that they are still the servants of man, victims intended for his slaughter-houses and for the gratification of his love of cruelty: on their shoulders is the proprietor's brand, burned into the flesh with red-hot iron.

Over the same grazing grounds there gallop, heedless of rough weather and exulting in their freedom, herds of wild horses descended from those that the Arabs, at one time masters of southern France, left behind them in those regions. These horses are small, white, spirited, and wholly untamed. Their mouth knows not the bit, nor their hoof the iron shoe. At harvest-time they are driven from their pasturage to run back and forth over the threshing-floor and tread out the grain. That done, they are set free again.

The third region in the Rhone delta, the region of the ponds, may be considered as dry land in the making and in the unmaking, being the seat of incessant strife between river and sea, the former constantly bringing in material for fertile fields and the latter constantly washing it away. In some far-off future the river will get the better of the contest, its alluvial deposits having already reclaimed the whole upper part of the delta. The coast-line is being pushed out to seaward, but so slowly that it takes centuries to measure any progress. Water is the chief factor in the operation, earth being but secondary.

Across the shifting sands of the beach the sea makes for itself a thousand passages, and breaks in everywhere. Even land that appears to be high and dry enjoys no immunity from the infiltration of sea-water, the brine percolating the soil from beneath until the whole is water-soaked and the surface coated with a glassy crust of salt. Sandy flats with a sparse growth of pines lashed by the northwest wind, stretches of ground frosted with saline incrustations, swamps putrid with decaying vegetable matter, briny pools, stagnant lagoons, foul mud with malarial exhalations — such is the lower Camargue.

But this region, so unwholesome to man, is an earthly paradise to aquatic birds. The ponds are the wild duck's favorite resort, on the dunes is heard the cry of the little ring-necked plover, and from amid the bulrushes the bittern sounds its deep note. Skimming the surface of the water in untiring flight, the tern and the seagull pass swiftly to and fro. With eyes sharpened by hunger they inspect the water as they fly, and if a fish shows itself, that is the last of it. But what is this other bird, clad in red and having the appearance of walking on stilts, so disproportionately long are its legs? It is the flamingo, one of the strangest of birds. Its neck equals its legs for length and slenderness, and its beak, with its ungainly twist, has not its like in all the world. With this ungraceful implement the bird digs in the mud, gathers shellfish, and breaks them open. Its nest is a curious structure of clay, a veritable tower with a bowl-shaped top for holding the eggs. In brooding, the creature sits astride on its nest and lets its legs dangle on each side. Its instinct serves it wonderfully well, for what could the mother flamingo do with her stilts if she had to hatch her eggs in an ordinary nest?

It is difficult to form any estimate of the amount of sediment carried down by rivers and deposited at their mouths or washed out to sea. In the course of a year, the Ganges empties into the Bay of Bengal an amount of silt weighing 356,000,000 tons. The Brahmaputra, its neighbor, accomplishes as great a task. But of all these great levelers of continents, the most active are the Hwang-ho and the Yang-tse-Kiang, in China. The first amasses at its mouth every twenty-five days enough sediment to make an island one kilometer square, and it threatens sooner or later to fill up the vast gulf it empties into. The second carries to the sea three times as much matter as the Ganges. For conveyance by vessel of this immense mass of silt there would be required a fleet of two thousand ships, each with a capacity of 1400 tons, and they would have to descend the river daily and throw their cargo into the sea. In the rainy season, the Amazon is very wide and its muddy waters stain the Atlantic for a distance of two hundred leagues out to sea. Who can estimate the amount of silt wrested from the soil of South America and deposited in the ocean by this giant stream? The alluvial deposits of the Po and the Adige encroach on the Adriatic Sea at the rate of seventy meters a year. A number of towns near the mouths of these rivers were formerly seaports, but today are at some distance from the coast. Adria, the ancient settlement that gave its name to the sea on whose shore it stood eighteen centuries ago, is now eight leagues from that shore. Ravenna also was once a port; two leagues of dry land now separate it from the sea.

In most instances, the mouth of a river emptying into the ocean is daily flushed by the ebb and flow of the tide, especially if the tide is strong at that part of the coast; and it is thus kept more or less clear of silt. This action causes its enlargement into a sort of deep gulf where fresh water and salt water mingle. Such a mouth is called an estuary. The Rio de la Plata is the estuary into which empty the Paraná and the Uruguay, and it has a width of fifty leagues. The mouth of the Amazon, ten leagues wide, is likewise an estuary. The Gironde, formed by the union of the Garonne and the Dordogne, is another. Through these spacious channels, hollowed out both by rivers and by sea, the largest vessels can make their way well inland.

As a general rule, then, a river whose mouth is not kept clear by the tide has a delta. Of this kind are the rivers flowing into the Mediterranean. But if a river's mouth is kept unobstructed by the tide, it takes the form of an estuary. To this class belong the rivers that empty into the ocean. The Rhone, which empties into the Mediterranean, has its delta, the Island of Camargue. The Garonne and the Dordogne, flowing into the Atlantic, have as their estuary the Gironde.

LAKES AND SPRINGS

THE PRINCIPAL RIVERS OF THE WORLD
IN THE ORDER OF THEIR LENGTH[18]

Name of River	Kilometers
Amazon (South America)	5,660
Yang-tse-Kiang (Asia)	5,380
Yenisei (Asia)	5,180
Lena (Asia)	4,440
Amur (Asia)	4,380
Obi (Asia)	4,300
Hwang-ho (Asia)	4,220
Nile (Africa)	4,200
Irawadi (Asia)	4,070
Mackenzie (North America)	3,930
Cambodia (Asia)	3,890
Paraná (South America)	3,650
Indus (Asia)	3,630
Rio Grande (North America)	3,440
Volga (Europe)	3,340
St. Lawrence (North America)	3,300
Niger (Africa)	3,300
Brahmaputra (Asia)	3,200
Ganges (Asia)	3,110

18   The Missouri and the lower Mississippi combined form the longest stream in the world, the total length being about 3,900 miles or a little more than 6,240 kilometers. - *Translator*.

Euphrates (Asia)	2,760
Danube (Europe)	2,750
Orinoco (South America)	2,500
San Francisco (South America)	2,500
Columbia (North America)	2,400
Dnieper (Europe)	2,000
Don (Europe)	1,780
Elbe (Europe)	1,270
Senegal (Africa)	1,150
Rhine (Europe)	1,100
Rhone (Europe)	1,030
Loire (Europe)	960
Seine (Europe)	630

CHAPTER XXI

LAKES AND SPRINGS

IN ADDITION to its running streams, every continent has its stationary bodies of water, almost or sometimes entirely surrounded by land and having no immediate communication with the sea. These inland bodies of water are called lakes; or if they are very shallow, covering considerable surface and with shores not clearly defined, they are known as marshes or swamps. Lakes may be divided into four classes.

In the first class are those that have no stream emptying into them and no stream flowing out of them. Commonly, they are small and unimportant. Several craters of extinct volcanoes in Auvergne furnish good examples. Rain has filled these calcined bowls that once held liquid lava, and as successive downpours about balance the losses due to evaporation, the level remains nearly the same.

To the second class belong lakes that have outflowing but no inflowing streams. They are fed from underneath by hidden springs that fill the basin, or pour into it a great body of water, before the overflow begins. Many large rivers have such lakes as their source. Such a river is the St. Lawrence, with its headwaters in the Great Lakes between the United States and Canada.

The third class comprises lakes that both receive and give out running water. They may be regarded as expansions of the streams flowing through them. Of this number are Lake Constance, traversed by the Rhine, and Lake Geneva, traversed by the Rhone.

Finally, we have a fourth class of lakes that receive streams, even great rivers, but have no visible outlet. How is it, you will perhaps ask, that these reservoirs, always receiving water and never letting it flow out, do not at last overflow? The answer is simple: evaporation takes from them, first and last, as much water as runs in. All that is necessary for this result is that the exposed surface of water and the temperature shall be such as to produce sufficient evaporation to balance the inflow. Some of these lakes are salt, and if they are large enough they are regarded as inland seas. Of this kind are the Caspian Sea, the Dead Sea, and the Aral Sea. The Caspian receives the Volga, the longest river of Europe. Its level and that of the district around it is twenty-five meters lower than the neighboring seas, the Black and the Mediterranean. An immense hollow in the ground holds the waters of the Caspian, and this hollow is due to a bending of the earth's crust.

The Dead Sea fills a depression still more extraordinary than that of the Caspian, the level of its waters being four hundred meters lower than the Mediterranean. This caving-in of the earth's crust is supposed to be the ancient site of the five biblical "cities of the plain" destroyed by fire from heaven. In approaching it from Jerusalem, the traveler descends a steep incline, as into some vast volcanic crater. The water of this accursed sea, despite the lugubrious name and unhallowed associations of the sea itself, has nothing mournful or mysterious in its aspect. On the contrary, it sparkles in the sunlight and is of a beautiful blue color; but, too heavy to be rippled and ruffled by the wind, it preserves a monotonous calm and has no margin of white foam along its pebbly beach. It is a silent, motionless, dead sea. Salt is everywhere: the waters are saturated with it, the soil is permeated with it, puddles and ponds hold it in crystallized form, and whole hills are composed of it with hardly any clay to soil its whiteness. Calcined rocks and lava fragments encumber the shore.

Nevertheless, the environs of the Dead Sea are not altogether sterile. Wherever there is fresh water, plant life does not fail to show itself. Rushes grow to a man's height, great clumps of reeds are seen, and here are found thickets of that singular bush bearing the fruit known as apples of Sodom, or Dead Sea apples.

They look somewhat like our green apples, but have a very hard skin. As soon as you open them, however, a fine white powder comes out, and if you blow this away you will find nothing left but a pinch of seeds wrapped in down like that of young birds. With the exception of these few spots of verdure, the surroundings of the sea have such a character of gloomy desolation that one cannot fail to recognize the marks of God's wrath.

Having now considered the most noteworthy peculiarities of rivers and lakes and other inland bodies of water, let us turn our attention to a few secondary but nonetheless interesting details of the same general subject. I will tell you something about springs; but first, we must acquaint ourselves with a principle of hydrostatics that will help to explain what follows.

Take a goblet-shaped glass vessel and nearly fill it with water. This vessel, A, is furnished with a metal tube, B, at its base; and to this metal tube can be attached various glass tubes, D, D', D'', of any form and caliber desired. A cock, R, closes the metal tube and thus cuts off communication between the vessel and the glass tube attached. If this cock is opened, the water in the vessel immediately enters the glass tube and rises to exactly the level of the water in the vessel, whatever the shape of the tube may be, whether sinuous like D, straight and erect like D',

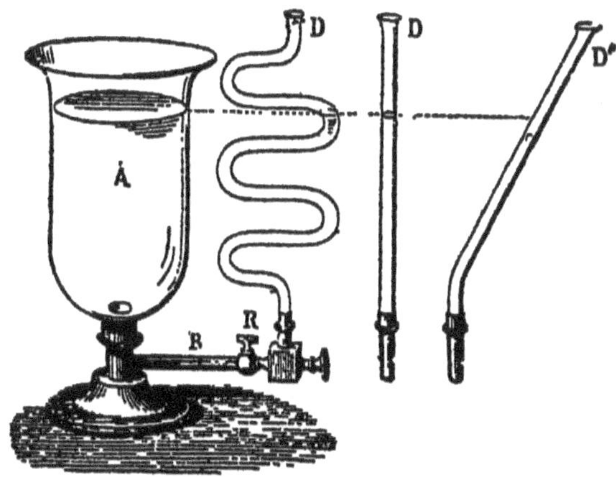

FIGURE 17

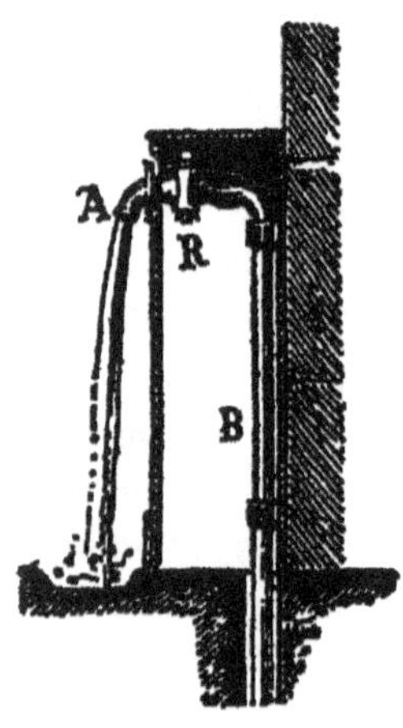

FIGURE 18

or inclined like D". In all three cases, the water rises to precisely the same level, as represented by the dotted line in the accompanying illustration. Hence the law known as the law of communicating vessels: when several vessels or containers of any form communicate with one another, if water is poured into one of them, the others likewise receive water, and the liquid rises to exactly the same level in all. That is what makes the fountains play in our public squares. Conducted through underground pipes from a reservoir at a distance, the water seeks its level by rising in a conduit built into the masonry of the fountain and flows out if the orifice of the fountain is not higher than the level of the water in the reservoir whence it came. If it is higher, no water will flow, for water ceases to rise at the precise level of its source.

Now suppose that to the metal tube in our illustration, no glass tube has been attached, and that the cock is opened; what will happen? Well, the water will spurt up into the air in a jet that will nearly reach the level of the water in the vessel. That it does not quite reach this level is due both to the unsupported weight of the water itself and to the resistance it meets with in the air through which it rises. In this way is to be explained the spouting of water in natural as well as in artificial fountains. Imagine an elevated reservoir communicating through underground pipes with an opening directed upward. If this opening is small enough and is lower than the water level in the reservoir, the water will come out with some force and the jet will rise to nearly the height of that level. Its failure to attain that height is to be explained as in the preceding instance. The height attained by a jet of water depends, then, on the vertical distance of the jet's orifice from the level of the water in the reservoir whence the spouting water comes.

To sum up: water, like all other liquids, tends, by virtue of its

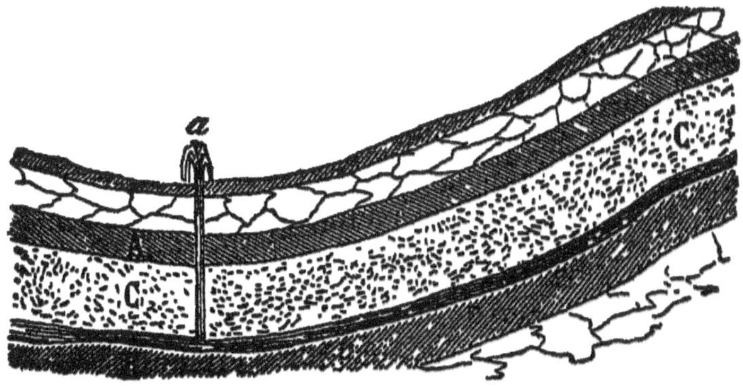

FIGURE 19

great mobility, to reach the same level in all vessels and conduits of whatever form to which it is admitted; and if there is a small opening pointing upward in any conducting pipe, the water will spurt out through this opening to a height approximating that of its source.

The various layers composing the soil differ in the ease with which they let water pass through them; or, as it is expressed in more learned language, they are not equally permeable. Some layers, especially those of clay, offer much resistance to the infiltration of water, while others, particularly those of sand, absorb water very freely. Let us suppose a soil to be composed of two layers of clay, A and B, with a layer of sand, C, between them, as represented in Figure 19. These layers, as we have already learned, may be situated at different depths at different places because of certain dislocations, bendings, and foldings undergone by the earth's crust in which they lie. A layer that is far beneath the surface in one place may appear on the surface in another. Let us suppose, then, that the sandy layer lying at some depth in the part of the ground here represented rises to the surface somewhere else, — as, for example, at the right of our picture. This cropping out may occur in the bed of a stream, lake, or other body of water, or on a mountain where there is perpetual snow. It may, again, occur in some hollow where rainwater collects or on a hillside where the mists of night condense. In each of these instances, the layer of sand, on account of its great permeability, absorbs water, which collects between the two impermeable layers of clay. Thus is formed an underground body of water, more or less abundant, more or less extended.

Now, if this layer of sand comes to the surface somewhere, as on the side of a deep valley, or if some natural fissure in the soil, some crevice or other opening, offers it communication with the outside, at this point we have a spring fed by the underground reservoir. But it may be that the saturated layer of sand does not come to the surface or find any communication with the outer world, and in that case, the existence of the underground water remains unsuspected. Unknown to us, it is there nevertheless, under our very feet perhaps, and beneath the driest of soil. To bring it to the surface and so make it of use, an opening must be effected. Suppose, then, at the point a in our picture, a boring is made: as soon as the boring penetrates the upper of the two layers imprisoning the water, it will rise through the opening thus offered and will tend to reach the level of the reservoir, pond, lake, or river whence it came. It will spout up to a greater or less height if the mouth of the well just bored is lower than the reservoir; if not, it will rise in the well to the height of its source.

To reach the layer saturated with water from some neighboring stream, lake, or pond, it is often sufficient to dig to a moderate depth; and in this way, wells are commonly dug which fill up to the level of the stream, lake, or pond that feeds them by a process of infiltration. If the water level rises or falls in the source of supply, it also rises or falls, to the same degree, in the wells. But if the underground body of water lies at a great depth, it is customary to bore artesian wells, so named because they have long been known in Artois. With the aid of a powerful boring instrument at the end of an iron rod, to which other rods are added, one by one, as the boring goes deeper and deeper, a round hole from one to two decimeters in diameter is drilled through the various layers of soil — gravel, marl, clay, perhaps limestone also — until water is reached, it may be at a depth of several hundred meters. If rock of extreme hardness is met with, it is customary to cut through it with an instrument somewhat like a surgeon's trepan. Then for clearing the hole of any mud, gravel, sand, bits of stone, or other obstructions, a special kind of spoon is used as a scoop. Finally, to keep the walls of the cylindrical well from caving in or crumbling, and also to prevent any sideways escape of the water as it rises in the well, the hole is fitted with a metal tube as a lining jacket.

I will call your attention, in closing this subject, to the high temperature you have probably noticed in some artesian well water. This is due to the earth's interior heat prevailing in those lower depths whence the water comes.

In certain localities, we find springs or fountains that give water for some days, perhaps some months, without interruption, and then stop for a while, after which they again begin to flow. These curious springs, whose waters dry up and then resume their flow at regular intervals, are known as intermittent springs. To take only two examples, I will mention the Colmars fountain in the department of the Lower Alps, which comes to a stop every seven minutes and then goes on again, and the Puis-Gros fountain near Chambéry, which flows every six hours, — at sunrise, midday, sunset, and midnight. The explanation of the curious behavior of these intermittent springs is found in the principle of the siphon.

A siphon is a tube bent over on itself, either in a curve or with two elbows, as ABC in the picture here given, and with one arm longer than the other. The shorter arm is plunged into the liquid that is to be drawn off, which we will suppose to be water. If you apply your mouth to the end C and suck until the siphon is full, and then leave it to itself, the water will begin to flow from that end and will keep on flowing until the level of the water in the reservoir sinks below the end of the short arm of the tube. It is the pressure of the atmosphere, the downward push of the air on the surface of the water in the reservoir, that causes this flowing.

In the science called physics, it is

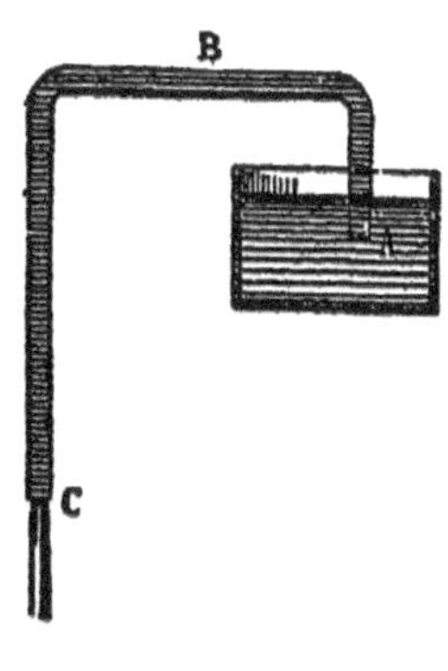

FIGURE 20

shown that the atmosphere exerts pressure on all objects and in all directions, and that this pressure will hold up, in a tube, a column of water about ten meters high. For the sake of clearness, let us suppose the short arm of our siphon to be one meter long and the other three meters. The atmospheric pressure exerted on the surface of the water in the reservoir and transmitted to the opening A of the short arm is sufficient to hold up a column of water ten meters high; but as the column of water in the short arm of the siphon is only one meter high, there remains an unused pressure represented by a column of water nine meters high. In like manner, the atmospheric pressure at the opening C is capable of supporting a ten-meter column of water, but as it has to support only a three-meter column, there remain seven meters to represent the unused surplus of that pressure. Therefore, as we have at A an unused pressure represented by nine meters and at C a similar pressure represented by only seven meters, the water in the siphon cannot remain at rest between these two unequal pressures, but will run out from the end of the longer arm, where the pressure is less than at the other end; and as it runs, its place will immediately be filled by more water from the reservoir. Thus, there will be a continuous flow as long as the short arm of the siphon has its end in water. It is clear, then, that when a siphon is filled with a liquid, no matter how, the liquid will immediately flow from the short to the long arm on account of the inequality in the pressure at the two ends of the siphon.

Suppose now (see Figure 21) there is a natural cavity far down in some mountain, and that water filters in and collects in this cavity, which communicates with the outside through a fissure, ABC, roughly shaped like a siphon; and suppose, further, that this fissure lets more water run out in a given time than the cavity receives. At first, water will collect without flowing out as long as its level remains below the dotted line passing through the siphon's elbow; but when the water reaches that height, it will be forced from the shorter into the longer arm of the siphon so that the latter will be filled and the outflow will begin. As, however, the siphon discharges water faster than the

FIGURE 21

reservoir receives it, the level of the water in the reservoir will gradually sink until it reaches the line AG passing through the opening of the short arm of our natural siphon. Then the flow will cease, the siphon's short arm no longer reaching the water. But as infiltration continues uninterrupted, the water level will rise again to B and the spring will resume its flow, stopping again when the water sinks to AG, and so on indefinitely. Thus, you see, the mystery of intermittent springs is no great mystery after all.

Water in limy soil always contains a little carbonate of lime in solution. If the water is allowed to stand a while, this substance is deposited until it forms on the inside of the containing vessel an earthy coating difficult to remove. Sometimes, indeed, the pipes of fountains fed with this limy water become obstructed with limy incrustations, and certain springs are so charged with lime that they petrify, to all outward appearance, anything sprayed with the water. The spring of Saint-Allyre, at

Clermont-Ferrand, is of this kind. In a few days, it covers with a beautiful stony coating birds' nests, baskets of fruit, or other objects exposed to its spray. In this mineral crust, these objects look as if they had come from the hands of a sculptor who had chiseled them out of stone.

Water containing medicinal properties is yielded by certain springs, the most important of which are gaseous, chalybeate, and sulphur springs. The first contain carbonic-acid gas, have a slightly acid taste, and effervesce like cider and certain white wines. Nieder Selters, in the Prussian province of Hesse-Nassau, and Vichy, in the French department of Allier, belong in this class. Chalybeate springs contain iron in solution and have a taste like that of ink. If you drop a few pieces of gallnut into the water, they will turn black. The springs at Forges, in the department of Seine-Inférieur, at Passy, near Paris, and at Spa, in Belgium, are of this sort. Lastly, sulphur springs owe their peculiar quality to the sulphur compounds they contain in solution. They have an odor of rotten eggs, and they turn silver black. Springs of this class are those at Barèges-les-Bains, Bagnères-de-Bigorre, and Bagnères-de-Luchon, in the Pyrenees.

Thermal springs are those whose waters are warm or hot, their temperature varying with the location and sometimes being as high as 100° centigrade, the boiling-point. You already know that this temperature is due to the earth's inner heat. Most thermal springs are also mineral springs; that is, they contain in solution various substances like those I have just named. I will mention a few of the thermal springs of France, with the temperature of each.

Name of Spring	Temperature
Chaudes-Aigues (Cantal)	88 degrees
Dax (Landes)	60 "
Bourbonne (Haute-Marne)	50 "
Mont-Dore (Puy-de-Dôme)	44 "
Vichy (Allier)	40 "
Barèges-les-Bains (Hautes-Pyrénées)	40 "

CHAPTER XXII

THE SEA

THE SEA! at this word the murmur of waves fills your ears, and you think of those beautiful shells, white and pearly, that the tide casts up on the shore amid tangles of seaweed. Perhaps, too, you think of the boundless expanse of waters, today smiling, smooth as a mirror, blue as the sky; tomorrow dark, threatening, its billows rising and falling in rhythmic surges; and, still later, stirred to fury, with white-capped waves breaking in foam and spray against the cliffs. Or it may be that the word arouses no associations, that you have never seen the sea, are utterly unacquainted with it. Then let me tell you what little I know about it, what little I have seen.

The total area of all the oceans and seas is about three times that of all the continents. Soundings taken at many places prove that the ocean floor is as uneven as the land. In certain parts, it is cut up with deep ravines whose bottom can hardly be reached with the plummet, while in other parts it abounds in mountain chains whose loftier summits project above the sea level and form islands. In still other regions it is a vast plain or a broad plateau. Freed of its watery covering, it would be like any other stretch of dry land, naturally enough, for the underground forces that carved out our valleys and piled up our mountains also fashioned the ocean bed. The sea, despite its immensity, is but a puddle when compared with the stupendous mass of the globe. The earth's inner fires, then, have caused folds and wrinkles and other irregularities in the floor of the ocean no less than in the surface of the continent. What is a continent but a patch of what was once ocean floor?

Changes in the earth's crust have pushed the continents up out of the water, and like changes may push them back under the water and raise other continents in their place. The bottom of the sea, therefore, has the same inequalities as the land, and hence it is clear that the oceans must vary greatly in depth at different places, with the corresponding variation in the sea bottom, which is diversified with mountains and valleys and low plains and high plateaus.

To take a sounding, we drop into the sea a small leaden weight attached to the end of a very long cord. The length of cord unreeled by the fall of the weight shows the depth of the water at that point. The deepest part of the Mediterranean appears to lie between Africa and Greece, where the plummet pulls after it from four thousand to five thousand meters of cord before touching bottom. In the Atlantic, still greater depths are found. South of the Grand Bank of Newfoundland, the sounding indicates about eight thousand meters of water, and around the South Pole, where there is very little land, the sea is so deep that there are places showing depths ranging from fourteen thousand to fifteen thousand meters. Between these mid-ocean abysses and the shore, where the waves lap the sands, all the intermediate degrees of depth may be found, sometimes with slow gradations, sometimes with abrupt changes, according to the character of the sea bottom. Off one shore, the sea may deepen with frightful rapidity, which means that this shore is on the top of some precipitous escarpment whose bottom is under water. Off another shore, the depth may increase so gradually that one has to wade out a long distance before reaching even moderately deep water. In that case, the sea bottom is a plain with hardly any slope, being a continuation of the plain not under water.

The mean ocean depth appears to be from six to seven kilometers; that is, if the sea bottom were all leveled off so as to be like the bottom of a basin made by man, the water, while still retaining its present surface area, would form a layer having a thickness throughout of six to seven kilometers. In this shape, the total volume of seawater can be approximately calculated, and it is found to be three million cubic myriameters[19]. Let us translate this colossal figure into other terms, terms that shall mean something to our imagination. Let us suppose all the seawater to be drained off, and then let us imagine some great and inexhaustible river to empty its waters into the collective sea basin until it is full. This river shall be the Rhone, if you like, the largest river in France. The flow of its water at Lyons is commonly about six hundred cubic meters a second, but it sometimes increases to four thousand cubic meters and even more. Let us fix it at five thousand cubic meters a second and suppose the river to keep up this copious flow indefinitely. Well, this king of rivers, always swift of current and always at its highest level, will at the end of twenty years have poured into the ocean basins only a thousandth part of the water they at present hold. If you have ever seen the Rhone, you can perhaps form some conception of the sea's immensity. No, I must take that back; it is impossible for any mind to conceive of the vastness of all the oceans and seas taken together. Who shall flatter himself that he can grasp the immensity of that stupendous body of water, even though it be but a dewdrop from the infinite resources of the Creator?

Can the sea level change? Can it rise and fall? It is often said that the sea retreats and leaves new land exposed, or that it encroaches on the land and invades it. Do its waters really shrink one day and swell the next? No.

It is an elementary law of hydrostatics[20] that the level of liquids remains uniform. At no point on the surface of a body of water can that surface, whatever its extent, become permanently depressed below the general level; for as soon as the cause of the disturbance of the equilibrium ceases to act, the water necessarily returns to its former level by virtue of its fluidity. Only through an increase or a decrease in the volume of water can the level be made to rise or fall. But note well that this rising or

---

19   Expressed in cubic meters, roughly equivalent to our cubic yards, the number would be three followed by eighteen ciphers. – *Translator.*
20   The branch of physics that treats of the pressure and the equilibrium of fluids. – *Translator.*

falling is not local and restricted; on the contrary, it takes place over the whole surface and is proportioned to the quantity of water added or withdrawn. If the volume of water remains the same while the level changes, this must be due to some distortion in the walls or the bottom of the containing basin, the total capacity of the basin remaining unchanged.

We know of thousands of places where, since the beginning of historic time, the level of the sea has never varied. Such and such a reef, such and such a rock, barely covered by the waves as far back as can be traced in geographical archives, are washed by the waves in the same manner today. These natural gauges of the sea level tell us, then, that after at least forty centuries the total volume of water has not changed. That is a fact placed beyond the slightest doubt by the testimony of the ages. Every drop of water in the ocean is counted by Him who has girdled the earth with the sea as with a sash. Not a drop is lost, not a drop is added.

If the form of the dry land and that of the sea basin have not changed, we ought to find the sea level everywhere the same as when the first observations were made and recorded. But both dry land and sea basin have undergone considerable changes, and the lines separating land from sea have thus been shifted. In one place the water has retreated, exposing great stretches of shore, and this new shore has soon become covered with vegetation. In another place, extensive tracts of land have been submerged together with their buildings, their forests, and their harvests.

But appearances are often deceptive. Interpreted by reason, they lead to conclusions the opposite of those arrived at by the senses. Appearances would have us believe the earth to be stationary in space, whereas reason tells us the contrary. Appearances, again, seem to show that the sea is a variable body of water, constantly swelling and shrinking in volume, flooding certain regions at one time and then retreating; but reason teaches us that the general ocean level cannot vary, and that the dry land, erroneously regarded as fixed and invariable, lacks stability, and that it is this solid substance of the earth's crust that causes all the changes attributed to the fluid ocean. The water does not change its level; it is the basin enclosing it that changes and so causes the apparent change in the level of the water.

Recall the examples already cited by me on this important subject — the gradual rise of the coast of Sweden and Chile's enormous increase in area within our own time.

Let us, then, relegate to the class of false notions the common belief in the fixity of the rock-bound coast, and the changeableness of the ocean that washes it. Ever since land and water were created, the waves of the sea, rolling hither and thither, have never departed from their same general level; and the so-called *terra firma* is continually rising here, falling there, breaking open in another place, and so on.

The waters of the sea hold in solution a great variety of substances, which impart an extremely disagreeable taste and make seawater unfit for domestic uses. Of these substances, the most abundant is common salt, its office being to prevent putrefaction in water abounding in remnants of plant and animal life, not to speak of all the filth of every sort constantly poured into it as into a common sewer by inflowing rivers, those sanitary agents so indispensable to our continents. The sea's saltness varies, being in general more pronounced where but little fresh water is received from rivers and where evaporation is rapid. A liter of water from the Caspian Sea contains about six grams of saline matter, a liter from the Black Sea has about eighteen, from the Atlantic about thirty-two, and from the Mediterranean forty-four. The Dead Sea is altogether exceptional in this regard, a liter of its water holding as much as four hundred grams of saline residue. The salt dissolved in seawater is of great help to navigation: by making the water heavier, the salt gives it power to support greater burdens. A person can float on the surface of the Dead Sea without making a movement.

The attempt has been made to estimate as nearly as possible the total amount of salt contained in the oceans and the seas, and it is worth our while to note the result. If the oceans and the seas should all dry up, the salt left behind would be enough to build a mountain at least fifteen hundred meters high and having a base as large as all North America; or, in other terms, the mass of salt, if spread evenly over the entire surface of the earth, would form a layer ten meters thick.

In small quantities, water appears colorless, but in greater volume, it shows its natural color, which is greenish blue. The sea, then, is blue with a greenish tinge and darker in mid-ocean than near the coast. But this color varies greatly with the state of the water's surface, the way the light strikes it, and the clearness of the sky. Under a bright sun, the calm sea is of a brilliant azure or a rich indigo; but when the sky is stormy, the sea turns bottle green, shading into black. Old ocean can show other tints also, these being due to purely local causes, as, for example, the nature of the sea bottom, colored sand, animalcules, and microscopic algae thickly dispersed in the water. Hence the tinge as of blood in certain parts of the Red Sea, caused by innumerable filaments of purple-colored microscopic algae. The vermilion hue in a certain part of the ocean near California is due to red animalcules.

If some microscopic creatures tint the sea red, others make it luminous. You are familiar with the glowworm, that curious little insect which in summer evenings shines amid the grass like a spark fallen from the stars. This insect, notwithstanding its bright light, does not burn like a live coal; it is no warmer when it glows than when it remains dark. It can, moreover, shine or not, as it chooses. The name "phosphorescence" is given to this light of animal origin, not because it is due to phosphorus, there being no trace of that in the glowworm's fireworks, but because of its resemblance to the gleam of phosphorus in the dark. The ocean waters, especially in tropical regions, are extremely rich in all sorts of phosphorescent animalcules, of which the most noteworthy are the noctilucidae (night shiners, if we translate the Latin word literally) and the pyrosomes (fire bodies). The noctilucidae are very small jelly-like specks, transparent and ending in a movable filament. Five of these animalcules placed end to end would measure only a millimeter. A pyrosome is shaped like a hollow cylinder about as large as one's finger, and it also is jelly-like and transparent. Hear, now, what travelers tell us about the sea turned to a lake of fire by myriads of these phosphorescent animalcules.

In one place, the surface of the ocean is all luminous, and its waves appear to be of molten metal. The prow that cleaves these waves sends red and blue flames spurting up from the cutwater. One would think it was plowing a furrow in burning sulfur. Sparks fly up in myriads from the water, so brilliant that our fireworks would look pale beside them. Phosphorescent clouds and ribbons of light are seen here and there in the waves. Elsewhere on the dark sea are clusters of pyrosomes cradled by the deep. Grouped in garlands and of resplendent brightness, they look not unlike chaplets of white-hot iron ingots. Like steel as it cools on coming out of the furnace, they vary in tint from one moment to another, passing from brilliant white to red, gold-color, orange, green, azure blue, then suddenly lighting up again and flashing brighter than ever. At intervals, one of these fiery garlands undulates like a piece of serpent-form fireworks, folding and unfolding, coiling itself up, and plunging like a ball of fire into the waves. Elsewhere, again, the ocean as far as can be seen is all one milky plain, glowing with a soft light as if phosphorus were dissolved in the water.

The marvelous spectacle of a luminous sea attains its full magnificence only in the warm waters of the tropics, though it is not altogether unknown in our part of the world — even so far north as the northern coast of France. You will read with interest the following account of what was witnessed by Monsieur de Quatrefages in the harbor of Boulogne.

> The calm water was still perfectly dark, but the slightest disturbance caused emissions of light. A grain of sand thrown on the dark surface produced a luminous spot, and the concentric ripples that followed were so many glowing circles, well-defined on the dark background. A stone as large as your fist produced the same result, and moreover, the drops of spray that splashed up were sparks like those thrown off by red-hot iron when hammered on the anvil. The coming of a steamboat into the harbor, each stroke of its paddles arousing the slumber-

ing phosphorescence, was a fine sight. But as soon as the surface of the water resumed its calm, all was dark again except the shore, which was always bordered with a phosphorescent band caused by the lapping waves.

The waves, on rolling toward the shore, assumed the appearance of billows of melted silver strewn with an infinite number of tiny stars and having crests of bluish flame. In breaking on the nearly level sandy beach, they swept over a broad expanse, and this entire space then took on a uniform appearance, white and shining, sprinkled with myriads of sparks, brilliant white or green and blue. Then the water retreated and the beach was left in darkness; but at the slightest disturbance, as for example the tread of the observer, it became so luminous that it appeared literally to burn. The damp gravel all about the foot as it trod the beach assumed the appearance of red-hot coals. A stick drawn quickly through the water left behind it a furrow of white light. Hands plunged into the sea came out as luminous as if they had been rubbed with phosphorus. Water dipped up at random and poured out from a certain height had a very deceptive likeness to a stream of melted silver. When a dog came barking at my heels, I threw a glass of water at the yelping animal, and it ran off to escape what it took to be a baptism of fire, and after that was content to threaten me from a distance.

According to this learned observer, the sea's phosphorescence was here produced wholly by noctilucidae, those animated specks of which a drop of water might contain hundreds. How many of these lowest forms of animal life must it take to give a phosphorescent glow to a considerable surface of water, or to saturate with light whole regions of the ocean? That is a question that arithmetic would not dare to try to answer, so fabulous would be the number. After the marvel of the burning waves, another marvel offers itself for our contemplation — the incomprehensible power that in a few days can generate these animalcules in myriads of legions; it is the boundless fecundity of the infinitely little.

CHAPTER XXIII

CORAL ISLANDS

O F ALL the rocks that were formed at the bottom of the pre-historic seas, the most noteworthy is limestone, carbonate of lime. Limestone is the offspring of the ocean waters as granite is the offspring of the underground fires. Today, whatever height we reach in our mountain-climbing, or whatever depth we attain as we descend into the bowels of the earth, there we find, embedded in limestone, fossils without number; that is, the petrified remains of creatures that once lived far down in the water where this rock was formed. Marble is, in many instances, made of what formerly had life; and often our building-stone is nothing but a charnel-house, a pile of shellfish and broken corals, so that one can hardly take up a piece of it that does not show the imprint left on it by animal life.

To these catacombs of the prehistoric world, it was not always the largest animals that made the greatest contribution. Number here makes up for smallness of size. The massive layers of limestone whence Egypt obtained the material for her pyramids are composed of tiny shellfish known as nummulites and resembling lentils. Those that Paris uses for building purposes are almost wholly an agglomerate of tiny granular shells, milliolites, less than a millimeter in diameter. There is nothing more striking than the apparent inadequacy of the means employed by these tiny creatures for obtaining stupendous results. But, as an offset to this seeming insufficiency of means, consider the countless centuries during which the results were being reached.

In the prehistoric ocean, then, the minute creature we are here studying was a veritable limestone factory. Artificer of the

213

infinitely small, this tiny animalcule contributed to the infinitely great; for by bequeathing to future ages its dead body, it brought its atom of lime to add to the solid framework of this earth of ours, thus offering, in its puny corpse, a particle of cement for laying the foundations of the Andes or the Himalayas. Unceasingly and untiringly these humble builders, these providential cleansers of an impure atmosphere, solidified the carbonic-acid gas that had been washed out of the air with the falling rain, by clothing themselves in it after uniting it with the lime dissolved in the sea; and so, out of their calcareous coats, their limestone shells, accumulated in unimaginable profusion through a limitless fecundity, they built up the underlying strata of the ground on which we now walk. To comprehend the gigantic task of these humble artisans who actually sweated limestone through the pores of their skin and built with it the terrestrial edifice, let us glance at what is going on today in the waters of the sea.

The atmosphere in our day contains but a minute quantity of carbonic-acid gas, estimated at one-half of one thousandth; that is, in two thousand liters of air there is only one liter of carbonic-acid gas. And this proportion remains constant, despite a number of causes always tending to increase it, the chief of which are combustion, animal respiration, decomposition of organic matter, gaseous springs, and volcanic eruptions. The amount of carbonic-acid gas generated merely by the breathing of the great human family is something enormous. At an approximate estimate of the earth's population, this amount is found to be, annually, 160 milliards of cubic meters of carbonic-acid gas, which means 86,270,000,000 kilograms of pure carbon burned up every year by mankind in the act of breathing.

An incredible quantity is also produced by the decomposition — that is, the slow combustion through decay — of organic matter. Further, we must take account of the carbonic-acid gas given off by our burning of wood, coal, oil, and other fuel, especially in the various manufacturing industries. In Europe alone, the combustion of oil yields an amount of carbonic acid estimated at 80 milliards of cubic meters annually. Nor is this all: numerous springs contain this gas in solution and discharge it into the atmosphere, and volcanoes throw it up in prodigious torrents, certain occasional eruptions producing it in quantities that make the foregoing figures insignificant. What then becomes of this immense volume of carbonic-acid gas that is continually pouring into the atmosphere without any lasting increase to the fixed proportion? How is it that the ocean of air, though constantly receiving this gas, does not at last become unfit for breathing?

In the first place, a great part of this carbonic-acid gas is appropriated by vegetation, which breaks it up into its elements and keeps the carbon for its own sustenance, giving out the breathable element, oxygen. It is plain that if vegetation as a whole maintains its vigor undiminished, which appears to be the case, then the amount of carbonic acid active in the vegetable kingdom forms what may be conceived of as a torrent that is forever pouring back into its original source and so providing for its own uninterrupted production. In fact, both through natural processes of decay and through the respiration of animals supported directly or indirectly by vegetation, the vegetable kingdom produces as much carbonic acid as is needed for making new plant life to take the place of the old. Hence, if animal respiration and the decomposition that is always going on in both the animal and the vegetable kingdoms supply as much carbonic acid as is taken from the atmosphere by growing plant life, the world of living matter is forever moving in a circle, taking back today what it relinquished yesterday. Organic decay supplies the materials for organic renewal, and death and life are in constant equilibrium, the first furnishing sustenance to the second.

But after full acknowledgment has been made of the part played by vegetation in maintaining the existing state of the atmosphere, it is still necessary to take account of the carbonic-acid gas discharged by volcanoes and gaseous springs in quantities so immense that sooner or later these copious additions, if allowed to remain in the atmosphere, would make it a deadly poison for all breathing creatures. There must, then, be some other agency operating to preserve the purity of the atmosphere and prevent the accumulation therein of the unbreathable gas discharged from the bowels of the earth. Well, this agency, one of the marvels of Providence, is found in the humblest creatures of the sea, creatures that by clothing themselves in limestone turn into solid form all excess of carbonic acid, make it into stone, and so wrest it from the atmosphere in such a manner that it will not soon return thither. Legions of ocean's tiny inhabitants enclose themselves in a stony shell that is about one-half composed of carbonic acid washed out of the atmosphere by rain and by running water; and with these mineral shells that hold the harmful gas permanently captive, they lay the foundations of future continents.

Now, of all these tiny masons dedicated to the building up of new land and the sanitation of the atmosphere, the most important are mollusks and polyps. Mollusks you are familiar with, but under another name — that of shellfish. Do not be deceived by this name, however, and think that the mollusk is a fish. The popular term arises from the fact that so many mollusks live in the water. In the first part of the word shellfish we find emphasized the peculiar shell-like nature of the mollusk's outer covering, a covering that the creature has made out of its own inner resources, literally sweating limestone through the pores of its skin.

A few words on the snail will make it clear to you just how a mollusk's shell is produced; for the snail is a mollusk, even though it lives on land and not in the water. It does not find ready-made for it the shell it lives in; it does not move into it as we move into a house built by other hands than ours. The snail is, in a very real sense, the owner of its habitation, and all the more so that it is both architect and builder of it. Nay, more; a builder merely puts together certain materials in conformity with the architect's plans, but these materials are not made by himself; neither does the quarrier make the stone that he gets out of the mountainside, nor the lumberman the timbers and boards that he helps to produce. But the snail is not only architect and builder of its shell; it is also the maker of the material composing the shell. This material is a part of its own body, the building-stone and the mortar being first in the blood that flows through the mollusk's veins. It should be noted here that the snail, like all mollusks, has a heart, arteries, and veins, in which the blood circulates; but the blood is colorless instead of being red. Well, then, it certainly cannot be denied that this dwelling, made out of the dweller's body, is his very own piece of property.

Would you like to see the storehouse whence the snail gets the material for enlarging its shell as fast as needed by the growing body? That is easy enough: tease the animal a little to make it withdraw into its shell, and you will see, all around the opening, a fleshy swelling dotted with a great number of little white spots, each of which is a particle of limestone kept in reserve for future additions to the shell. From this swelling, the stone is sweated out as fast as it is required, and it is added on to the edge of the shell so that the latter grows longer and wider with each fresh layer.

But whence comes this limestone? It comes from what the creature eats, which contains particles of carbonate of lime — that is, limestone — just as the shell of a hen's egg comes from limestone particles eaten with the grain fed to the hen. If hens were fed with grain carefully sorted and cleaned, and were kept in poultry-houses where no carbonate of lime could be found, they would lay eggs without shells, or rather with shells reduced to a flabby membrane like thin parchment. In like manner, the snail, if deprived of limestone in its food, would have but a fragile and transparent covering of coagulated slime.

Sea mollusks follow the same method as the snail that lives on land: to build their shells they sweat stone. But the sea must furnish them with limestone, or at least with its constituents, carbonic acid and lime. Carbonic acid cannot fail them, for the enormous amount of this gas that volcanoes and other agencies tend to accumulate in the atmosphere, to the great danger of all breathing creatures, is washed out of the air by rain and carried to the sea by all the rivers. Indeed, streams in general contain more or less carbonic acid in solution. Lime cannot fail the mollusks, either, for if the waters of the ocean do not contain any of it in a free state, they do contain a number of substances into whose composition it enters. For example, a liter of water from the Mediterranean contains 44 grams of saline residue, of which chloride of calcium constitutes 6 grams, sulphate of lime 1.5 grams, and carbonate of lime 0.114 gram. We have seen, also, that fresh water often holds limestone in solution, and that it sometimes contains enough to coat with incrustations any object sprayed with it. Hence, all streams must be considered as more or less generous contributors of lime to the waters of the sea, and so the oceans are always sure to contain, in proportions we cannot measure, either carbonate of lime or the elements of which it is composed. The marine species that clothe themselves with stone — the polyps and the mollusks — accordingly, have for their shells and their coral formations materials as inexhaustible as are these prolific creatures themselves.

Now let us consider those most curious builders of islands, the polyps; and as you probably know not very much about these strange little creatures, so frail of structure that the slightest touch is enough to kill them, yet so strong by reason of their multitudes that they do not shrink from the task of building a large island, I will describe them in some detail.

Coral is known to you, at least in the form of those beads resembling drops of petrified blood that are used for making necklaces and bracelets. Before being made into beads, coral has the shape of a diminutive red tree, with trunk, branches, and twigs. Nevertheless, it is not a member of the plant world, despite its form and the blossoms with which it is covered as it lies at the bottom of the sea; and still less is it a mineral, notwithstanding its stony hardness; nor, again, is it an animal. What is it, then? It is the dwelling place of frail little beings living in a sort of community, a city in which each lives for all and all live for each; or it might be called a republic with a communistic form of government so radical that man in his wildest moments has never conceived anything similar.

The organism or bodily structure of these little creatures is of the simplest sort. Imagine a hollow globule of jelly-like matter, a tiny sac having its mouth bordered with eight scalloped

FIGURE 22

points, eight feelers that can spread themselves like the petals
of a flower. Such is the inhabitant of the coral formation familiar
to you. The feelers — or tentacles, as they are called — serve
for seizing the tiny prey brought within reach by the moving
water; they answer the purpose of arms and hands. The opening that they surround, which we may call the little animal's
mouth, swallows the prey when it is caught; and the sac next
to this opening and serving as stomach digests the food that is
swallowed. After digestion — But we will not continue; there
is no other opening than the one surrounded by the tentacles.

These curious creatures are called polyps, and their no less
curious dwelling is the polypidom, or madrepore, or coral. Thousands of polyps inhabit the same polypidom, each occupying
a special cavity sunk in the exterior of the common dwelling
place. Established thus in their cells, the numerous polyps, while
preserving each its own individuality, are not strangers to one
another. All the stomachs of the community are linked together

FIGURE 23

by a series of little channels or pipes, so that what any one member of the colony digests contributes to the sustenance of all the others. Expanding like so many little flowers on their bush-shaped polypidom, the polyps catch and appropriate whatever nutritive particles the waters of the restless sea may wash their way. Chance does not favor them all equally: one may have a fine catch while another does not once have occasion to close the net of its eight tentacles. No matter; at the end of the day all will have fared alike for food, both those that caught something for their stomachs to digest and those that caught nothing.

But how is this intercommunication kept up between stomach and stomach? In this way: Every polypidom is in the beginning a single polyp, wandering at large in the water until it settles down and anchors itself to some rock on the ocean floor, there to found a new colony. It has the curious faculty of multiplying by budding, as do certain plants. Thus a new polyp comes into being beside the first one, of which it is a sort of prolongation or branch, and it maintains stomachic communication with its parent, this being necessary for its development, just as a vital connection between the stem of a plant and its offshoot is necessary for the distribution of sap. The birth of this first polyp is followed by that of a second, a third, and so on, always in the same manner. But the children in their turn beget children, and these likewise become parents in due course; and so on, with no break to the network of intercommunicating stomachs. As to the polypidom, the common home of the tribe, it is built up as the result of exudation or sweating on the part of the entire community, which perspires limestone just as the snail perspires the material for its shell. And so it comes about that, as the population increases, the domicile grows in the same proportion, each new-born member contributing its share of material to the common abode.

From this mode of propagation you will readily understand how a polypidom is built up and peopled; but that does not account for the founding of new communities isolated from the first, since all the inhabitants of one of these colonies remain forever joined to one another. By the budding process a polypidom can grow indefinitely, but it cannot by this process start new colonies. There is the difficulty. However, when nature takes a notion to give an animal the faculty of imitating a plant and of multiplying by budding, she can also restore to it, on occasion, the usual means of propagation, so that the race may be disseminated. At a certain stage in their development polyps cease to bud and begin to lay eggs, which are carried off by the sea to some more or less distant part of the sea bottom, there to develop into polyps, starting points for new communities.

There are a great many species of polyps, and the dwellings they construct take very varied forms. As a rule they are pure white, the natural appearance of the carbonate of lime composing them; less often they are red, like the coral you are familiar with. There is nothing more pleasing to the eye than the various forms they take. In one place they are bushes of stone, branching with the same agreeable effect as real shrubs, while in another place they have the shape of parallel tubes grouped like organ pipes. Elsewhere they are clusters of cells that remind one of honeycomb, or they may be loose agglomerations of tiny bladders resembling soap suds. In still another specimen the polypidom is rounded like a cauliflower or a mushroom, its surface rough with scales arranged in regular order and showing a multitude of stars or a network in geometrical pattern or a labyrinth of folds and wrinkles. Once more, the polypidom may be flattened out like a sheet of paper and as thin as such a sheet, with a cut-out pattern that gives it the appearance of lace. On all these countless forms are thousands of animal flowers, or polyps, opening their tentacles so as to give the appearance of rosettes, and at the slightest alarm abruptly closing them.

A polypidom grows with extreme slowness. Countless legions

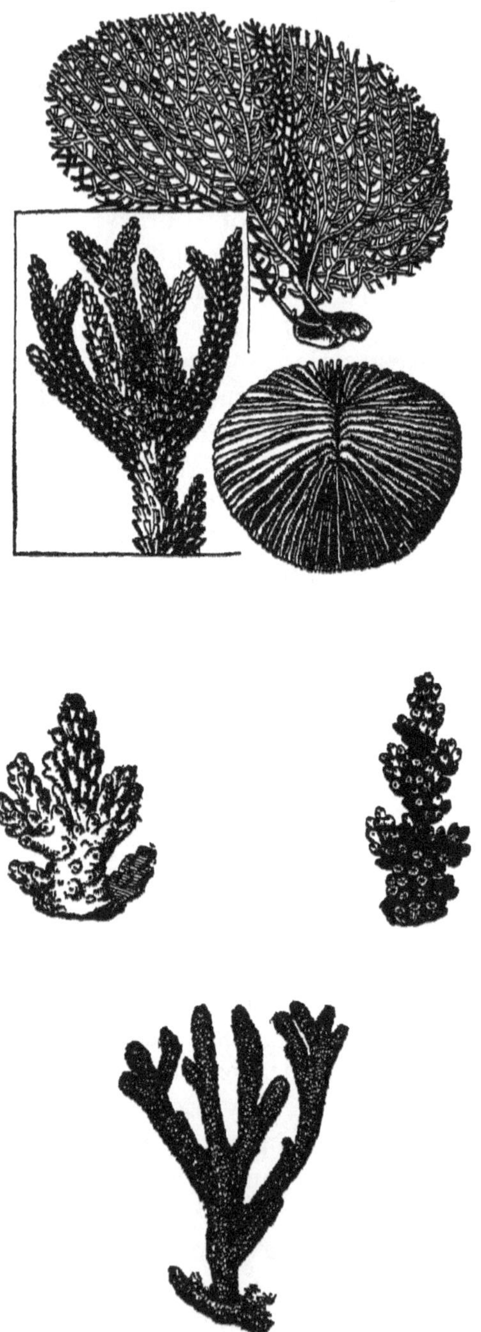

Figure 24

of workers and centuries of time are required for building up a coral structure of any size, as each animalcule adds only a tiny particle of limestone to the common edifice. Ehrenberg observed some isolated coral formations in the Red Sea, all belonging to the same family and measuring two or three meters in diameter. These formations must have been begun in a remote antiquity, their first layers dating back perhaps to the time of the pyramids, and their inhabitants, still active, being the contemporaries of the Pharaohs. There is no reason, then, why these frail workers should not build up structures far beyond man's power to erect. Time, numbers, materials — these are at their unlimited command. In the warm seas of the tropics, in every spot favorable to their activities, these colonies set to work and build up layer after layer, one structure upon another, with a slow perseverance that is greater than strength, until they reach the surface of the sea and so are obliged to discontinue their towering scaffolds. But even then their edifice, though halted in its upward growth, continues its enlargement horizontally. The top of the coral structure becomes a reef, the reef an islet, the islet an island, and the ocean has one more stretch of land planted in its waters.

A coral island is, therefore, the terminal plateau of a vast cluster of polyp dwellings, the foundations of the plateau being laid on the bottom of the sea. At first the island is only a barren stretch of limestone, but sooner or later the winds and the ocean currents bring seeds and vegetation tones down the dazzlingly white surface of the land. A few lizards, a few insects, borne thither on floating wood, are commonly the first colonists; then sea birds build their nests, and land birds that have gone astray seek refuge there. Finally, when these have fertilized the soil, man makes his appearance and builds his hut.

Coral islands rise but little above the level of the sea. They usually consist of circular or oval strips of land surrounding a shallow lake that communicates with the sea. Their appearance is as remarkable for its singularity as for its beauty. Imagine a circular strip of land covered with palm trees, their dark green foliage standing out vividly against the light blue of the sky. In the center of this wooded zone slumber the waters of a salt lake in which

FIGURE 25

mollusks and polyps continue their work of construction. On the outer side of this verdant ring extends a beach of the purest white, formed wholly of sand made of crushed coral, while parallel with it runs a line of reefs against which the ever boisterous ocean breaks in eddies of foam and spray. In their furious assault the waves threaten to engulf the island at any moment; but the island, small and low-lying though it is, nevertheless offers stout resistance, thanks to the energetic intervention of the polyps. These take part in the struggle, and toil night and day in repairing the imperiled structure, fortifying it with a rampart of reefs built up atom by atom and subject to an incessant wearing away as fast as it is constructed. With their soft, jelly-like bodies these tiny creatures, so insignificant individually, withstand collectively the ocean's onslaught; with their patient architecture they make headway against the fury of the waves, against which granite walls would be powerless.

And now if you would like to get an idea of the extent of the earth's land area that is made of coral, turn to a map of the world and look at the string of archipelagoes consisting of little islands running across the Pacific Ocean from the southern part of South America to southern Asia. Many of these archipelagoes are wholly of coral formation, while those of a different origin are at least encircled with a string of coral beads. The

Maldive Archipelago alone, in the Indian Ocean, comprises twelve thousand reefs, islets, and islands, all of coral structure, the largest of these islands being two leagues around. A single bank of coral in Dutch East India has a surface of eighty-eight square kilometers. Oceania, which comprises a fifth part of the earth's surface, is in great part the work of polyps.

The service rendered by these world-builders was no less important in those prehistoric waters whence our continents have emerged. Certain terrestrial strata, certain mountain chains, are the creation of polyps. In some districts of interior France one walks on nothing but old coral. The town[21] where I am writing this book is built of a kind of stone that contains, even in its smallest fragments, coral remains; and the mortar in the walls of the house now sheltering me is made of coral sand.

---

21   Probably the city of Orange. - *Translator*.

CHAPTER XXIV

TIDES

A LIQUID at rest in a basin remains at rest as long as nothing disturbs it. The waters of the sea would be forever calm and motionless if no disquieting agency troubled their repose. But this repose would lead to an unwholesome condition, as these waters need to be violently and unceasingly stirred up in order that they may not become putrid, but may take up in solution the air demanded by their countless forms of animal and vegetable life. Thus the continual movement of seawater is as essential to the world's welfare and as interesting to us as is the movement of the earth's atmospheric envelope. For the ocean of water no less than for the ocean of air, there are required those violent agitations that prevent stagnation and ensure a sanitary condition. Now, the all-important duty of stirring up the oceans is entrusted to the atmosphere, to the attraction of the heavenly bodies in our neighborhood, and to heat.

Atmospheric disturbances ruffle the surface of the sea and set the water in motion. If the wind comes in sudden gusts, it causes waves that jostle one another with a great display of foam and froth; if strong and continuous, it lifts the water in long billows that move shoreward in parallel lines, one after another in stately regularity, and finally dash themselves on the beach. But these disturbances affect merely the surface of the sea, leaving the water tranquil thirty meters below, even in the worst of storms. Off our coasts, the largest waves are rarely more than two or three meters high; but in some parts of the southern seas, as around Cape Horn and the Cape of Good Hope, the waves, in exceptionally severe storms, rise to a height of ten and twelve meters. These waves are veritable chains of moving hills, with a wide and deep valley between one wave and the following. Lashed by the wind, their crests throw off showers of spray and foam until they finally collapse with a terrific force that is enough to wreck the staunchest vessel.

The momentum of ocean waves as they dash on the rocks is something almost beyond belief. Against a rugged shore exposed to these assaults, the billows hurl themselves with a shock that fairly makes the earth tremble. Dikes and breakwaters of the solidest construction are demolished and swept away, enormous blocks of stone being tossed hither and thither and rolled about like so many pebbles. It is this incessant action of the waves that creates cliffs or vertical escarpments such as are so often seen along the seashore. Escarpments of this kind are conspicuous along the coasts of the English Channel, in both France and England. Unceasingly these cliffs are undermined by the waves so that pieces are every now and then falling into the water, where they are rolled about and worn into smooth pebbles. Thus the ocean encroaches more and more on the land. History tells us of lighthouses, towers, dwellings, villages even, that have had to be abandoned because undermined by the sea, and that are now quite buried beneath the waves.

At other parts of the coast, the sea brings new material to add to the land, washing ashore great quantities of sand, the finer grains of which are caught up by the wind and piled in long low hills called dunes. On the seacoast of France, in Pas-de-Calais, there are dunes running along the shore from Boulogne; also in Brittany near Nantes and Sables-d'Olonne; and in the Landes from Bordeaux to the Pyrenees over a stretch 240 kilometers long. In the department of the Landes alone, the dunes cover a surface of nearly 75,000 acres.

What a singular spectacle is presented by these dunes! From the top of one of the sandhills, which is reached only by wading knee-deep in the sand, the eye takes in with delight the wide view extending to the distant yellowish horizon and embracing countless undulations of surface, with the rounded dunes everywhere a conspicuous feature. One feels lost amid this chaos of gleaming white hillocks, their crests swept by the wind and sending up puffs of fine sand with much the same effect as that produced by the ocean waves when they are lashed by a storm. We behold the same monotonous undulations, the same heaving billows as at sea, but with the difference that here the waves are of sand and immovable. Nothing breaks the silence of these gloomy solitudes except, at times, the hoarse cry of some seabird passing overhead and at regular intervals the breaking of the ocean waves beyond the farthest line of dunes.

Woe betide the rash adventurer who should push forward into these wild regions on a stormy day; for then the sand is lifted in dense clouds and driven onward by the wind with irresistible force. Sand-spouts, not unlike waterspouts, attest the fury of the storm, and the air is full of flying particles. When the squall has subsided, the appearance of the surrounding region is altered: what was a hill is now a valley, and what was a valley is now a hill.

In every storm, the dunes advance a little farther inland. The wind from the sea gradually pushes a dune over into the next depression, which in turn becomes heaped up into a dune, and so on as far as the foremost dune, which is blown over onto tilled land. Meanwhile, the sea has been piling up on the shore fresh material for another line of sandhills, which takes its place behind those already formed. In this manner, the dunes slowly invade the cultivated territory and cover it with a deep layer of barren sand. Nothing can check the persistent activity of wind and water and sand. If a forest stands in the way of the invading sand, it is buried, only the tops of the tallest trees remaining visible like little bushes above the wide-stretching yellow surface. Whole villages, even, are swallowed up, houses and church and everything disappearing beneath the sand. What can one do in the face of such a foe, a foe that advances with irresistible might and unpitying steadiness, gaining each year nearly twenty meters of cultivated land and respecting nothing — neither ripening harvests nor human habitations nor majestic forests? Human ingenuity has nevertheless finally found a way to control this formidable scourge, and a very simple way it is: the dunes are made to stand where they are by being planted with pine trees.

Such fluctuations of the sea as are caused by the wind are purely accidental and as irregular as the shifting of the wind itself; but in addition to these movements, there are others of great regularity and of periodic occurrence. These are the tides. On all ocean shores, the sea at certain hours recedes from the beach and leaves exposed considerable stretches that were covered with water. This receding of the water is known as the ebbing or falling of the tide. A little later, the waves return and again take possession of the beach. This movement is known as the rising tide or the flood tide, and these alternations of ebb and flow succeed each other about every six hours. Hence, in twenty-four hours, there are two ebb tides and two flood tides.

To a person unfamiliar with it, the tide is a very mysterious thing. At a fixed time and without any apparent cause, in the calmest as well as in the stormiest weather, the waves cease to beat the shore that seemed to confine them too closely; they recede with more or less haste as if a great hole had been opened in the sea bottom and the waters of the ocean were being drawn off. This recession halts at some distance from the high-water line, the distance depending on the slope of the beach. Then it is possible to walk dry-shod where before one would have been forced to wade or swim.

What fun it is for you, my young readers, to run down across the beach at low tide and see the little fishes and other creatures that have been left stranded by the retreating waves and now lie amid the tangled seaweed and the pretty shells and smooth white pebbles. But do not linger too long over the treasures of the deep, for once more the tide is rising fast, its white-capped waves advancing with an ominous murmur. There are shores where the swiftest horse could not keep pace with the inflowing tide. As it comes in, it rapidly covers the sand, the pebbles, the rocks, everything that was laid bare by its previous retreat until it once more dashes against the cliffs that bar its further progress.

Now let us seek an explanation of these rising and falling tides. You know that the various heavenly bodies attract one another, that the sun in particular attracts the earth and makes it fall toward that great luminary, and that the earth in its turn exerts a like attraction on the moon. You have not forgotten that from this attraction, this incessant falling, combined with the initial impetus, results the revolution of the smaller body about the larger, — of the earth about the sun and of the moon about the earth. The attraction is always mutual; that is, the smaller body attracts the larger at the same time that the larger attracts the smaller, though in a lesser degree. If the earth attracts the moon, the moon also attracts the earth. The latter, being the larger, dominates its satellite; but it is nonetheless true that the satellite exerts its force of attraction on the earth. If two persons take hold of a rope, one at each end, and pull in opposite directions, trying to draw each other over a line midway between them, the stronger will win. But the weaker has not been pulling without effect: he will have shaken, more or less, the sturdiness of his opponent's stand. So it is with the moon: in the contest of mutual attractions, it yields to the earth and revolves about that body; but, even while yielding to it, the moon causes disturbance to its oceans, which by reason of their mobility are more easily shifted from their position of equilibrium than are the solid parts of the globe.

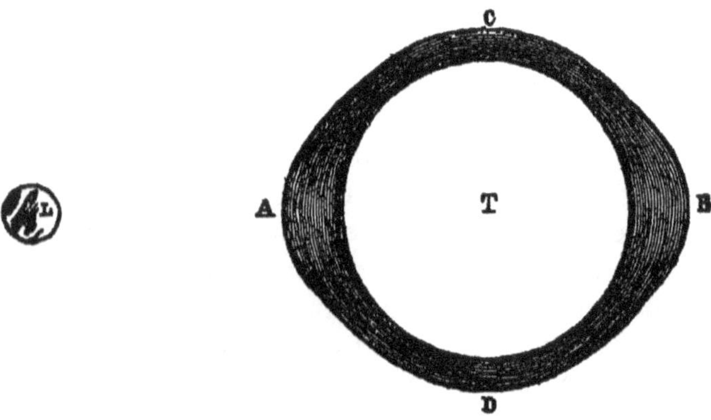

FIGURE 26

To make the matter clearer, let us imagine the earth to be completely covered with water; then, bearing in mind that the force of attraction diminishes with distance, let us consider what effect the moon's attraction will have upon this universal sea. In the accompanying diagram, L represents the moon, T the earth, and the shaded portion is the ocean. Now, it is clear that the moon's attraction is strongest at the point A, which is nearest to the moon, and weakest at B, which is at the greatest distance. Hence, there is a flow of water toward A and a rise in the ocean's general level at that point and in its neighborhood. But this flow of water toward the point of greatest attraction is not everywhere the same; you can see that at the point B, where the moon's attraction is weakest, the water will be slower than elsewhere in yielding to the pull exerted by the satellite. By thus hanging back, the water will form a swelling, exactly opposite the first. But these two swellings must be compensated for by corresponding depressions in the ocean-level elsewhere; and these depressions will be greatest at the two points halfway between A and B; that is, at C and D, where the lunar pull is neither at its maximum nor at its minimum, but midway between. At A and B, then, the tide will be high, and at C and D low.

To an imaginary observer at A, the moon is high in the heavens — directly overhead, in fact, and exactly opposite the point of highest water. An observer at B would have the diameter of the earth between himself and the moon. Finally, for the points C and D, the moon is on the horizon, rising in respect to one point and setting in respect to the other. The waters of the ocean are heaped up in that part where the moon is directly overhead, and also in the part lying on the other side of the globe; and they are depressed in the parts where the moon is on the horizon, whether it is in the east or in the west. In twenty-four hours, the earth, because of its daily rotation, presents its different parts successively to the moon, or, what comes to the same thing, the moon appears to revolve about the earth from east to west once in about twenty-four hours; and the two ocean swellings, A and B, which must always be, respectively, one nearest to and the other farthest from the moon, follow the satellite's apparent movement and likewise go around the earth from east to west at the same rate as the moon. Of course, this is also true of the two depressions, C and D. You see then that in twenty-four hours' time, there are for every part of the ocean two high and two low tides, with about six hours between ebb and flow and between flow and ebb. And so we find an explanation of the wonderful regularity of the tides: they are controlled by the great clock of the heavens.

Even if you have not quite understood what I have just been saying, you must at least have been impressed with the attraction exerted on the earth by the sun, that immense heavenly body to which we owe light and heat; and you may therefore have been wondering whether this colossus of the skies, this center of our planetary system, holding as it does our earth in its regular yearly orbit, must not also affect the tides even more than does the moon. Unquestionably, the sun's attraction does affect the tides, but we must remember the enormous distance at which the sun acts. So far away, so very far away is our sun from us that, on the whole, despite its prodigious size, it makes the waters of the ocean rise only two meters where the moon raises them five. Therefore, in our study of the tides, it is the moon's influence that must receive chief attention.

Nevertheless, the solar tides must not be left out of account; their explanation is exactly the same as that of the lunar tides. The effect of the two heavenly bodies on the waters of the ocean is sometimes a combined effect, sometimes one in which the two forces act in opposition to each other. If the sun and the moon are on the same side of the earth, they act in unison, and the tide resulting from the sum of their actions is the highest possible. A like effect is produced when the two are in opposition, one on one side of the earth and the other on the other, because, as we have seen, the ocean waters are heaped up at two opposite points on the globe when an attraction is exerted from without. The highest tides, then, occur at the time of the syzygies; that is, when the three bodies, sun and moon and earth, are in a straight line, no matter what their respective positions. At such a time the moon is either full or new. But if, when the moon is high in the sky, the sun is on the horizon, the solar attraction tends to produce a low tide while the moon is acting to the contrary effect, and the result of these two discordant attractions is a considerably lowered lunar tide. The name *quadrature* is given to this position of sun, moon, and earth with respect to one another; and in this position, the moon shows but half its face, being in either its first or its last quarter.

You must not imagine that the tides act as do running streams and that the two opposite swellings that revolve about the earth every twenty-four hours are merely surface currents and sweep away with them any floating objects in their path. Far otherwise: the sea rises and falls in its place; it palpitates, as we might say, its bosom heaving when the moon is overhead and subsiding when it has passed on. Vessels are not carried along by the tidal wave any more than are straws by the ripples produced when a stone falls into still water. An alternate rising and falling, this motion advancing from east to west, is all that takes place in the open sea; and it would be the same everywhere if, as we have been supposing, the earth were completely covered with water.

But one-quarter of the earth's surface is land, and so these interspersed obstacles to the free movement of the tides greatly modify their action. In the first place, intervening islands and continents hinder the advance of the tidal wave to such an extent that the moment of high tide is not precisely that of the moon's passage overhead or of its like movement on the opposite side of the earth. The tide, therefore, is found commonly to lag behind the moon, this delay varying with the configuration of land and water in any given region. At Gibraltar, for instance, the retardation is zero; at the mouth of the Gironde, it is three hours and fifty-three minutes; at Lorient, on the Bay of Biscay, three hours and thirty-two minutes; at Saint-Malo, six hours and ten minutes; at Cherbourg, eight hours; at Dieppe, eleven hours; at Dunkirk, twelve hours and thirteen minutes; and it increases with further advance up the narrowing English Channel. The exact amount of this retardation is called the establishment of the port, because of the importance to navigation of knowing the precise time of high tide at any given seaport. When the amount of retardation has been ascertained for any part of the coast, the hour and minute of high and low tide can be calculated in advance, the calculation being based on the time of the moon's passage.

In the open sea, the tide rises but little. In the South Sea Islands, it rises not higher than half a meter. Our diagram illustrating the tides is therefore much exaggerated, the heaping up of the ocean waters having in reality no such prominence, but being merely a slight swelling extending over a great extent of surface and attaining only very little height even at its highest part. Near land, and especially in narrow channels, the tidal wave, retarded in its course, increases in volume and therefore rises much higher than it does in the open sea. Thus at Saint-Malo, with conditions varying somewhat from day to day, the tide rises to a height ranging from six to seven and one-half meters above the mean water level, and falls correspondingly at its ebb so that the difference between high tide and low tide is from twelve to fifteen meters. Except in the English Channel, the tides on the French seacoast are not more than two or three meters high.

At a distance from land, the alternate rising and falling of the water does not create any current, but near land, it is otherwise. When the sea rises, it quickly overflows a gently sloping beach; and in falling, it recedes as quickly, leaving the beach dry. Hence, we have the two tides, the incoming and the outgoing, moving alternately toward the shore and toward the sea.

Lakes and landlocked seas like the Caspian can have no tides. Look back at our diagram (Figure 26) and you will see that if the water rises at A and B, it falls at C and D. For every upheaving of the ocean's bosom, there is somewhere a corresponding depression. The volume of water in the ocean being virtually invariable, if it is heaped up at one place it must be lowered at some other place; if it gains here, it must lose there. But the swelling at A, meaning a high tide at that point, and the corresponding depression at C, meaning a low tide there, are distant from each other a quarter of the circumference of the earth. Consequently, in order to have tides, a body of water must extend at least a quarter of the way around the earth. No inland body of water, not even the Caspian Sea, meets this requirement. The Mediterranean itself does not, and its communication with the Atlantic through the Strait of Gibraltar is too narrow to admit the tidal wave formed in the open seas. Hence, there is no tidal movement beyond a scarcely perceptible oscillation.

In entering the mouth of a river, the rising tide produces what is called a bar. The river is stopped, is barred in its course, and thrown back by the push of the sea and by the accumulated sand at the river's mouth. The channels where this struggle takes place between fresh water and salt, each pushing against the other, are dangerous to navigation. At its mouth, the Adour, for example, always presents the appearance of a turbulent sea. Here the ocean knows no rest. Even in the calmest weather, even when not a breath of wind ruffles its surface, the ocean checks the river, and the result is a wide semicircle of white-capped waves. This semicircle, the seat of perpetual conflict, is the line of separation between the ocean and the river; it defines the bar at the Adour's mouth.

The tidal thrust can even push the water of a river upstream and make it flow back toward its source. This movement is known as the tidal bore. In France, it is especially noticeable in the Dordogne and in the Seine. The rising tide, after entering the Gironde, that gulf-like estuary extending from Bordeaux to the sea, arrests the waters of the Dordogne, which then roll back in three or four great billows of remarkable height, filling the whole width of the river. These billows surge up the Dordogne with extraordinary rapidity and a deafening roar for eight leagues from its mouth. On their way, they even uproot trees, sink boats, destroy dikes, and hurl stones to a considerable distance.

The most remarkable tidal bore is that of the Amazon River in South America. The natives call it the *prororoca*. In this giant of rivers, the tide goes up as far as two hundred leagues. The prororoca announces itself by a thunder of conflicting waves that can be heard for two leagues around. At the river's mouth, the titanic struggle of the two currents, with their mountains of water dashing against one another in a frontal assault, makes the neighboring shores fairly tremble. Deep and prolonged is the thunder of the waters. Sailors and fishermen hasten to seek safety. Very soon, from one bank of the river to the other, in an expanse as wide as an arm of the sea, there rises a wave that rears its crest four or five meters above the general level. It is closely followed by a second, a third, and sometimes a fourth. It is the vanquished river rolling back toward its source. These waves, rushing with prodigious speed, overthrow everything in their path. On their surface, pebbles of the beach are seen swirling about, carried away like so many bits of cork. In the wake of this terrible prororoca, the river banks are left stripped to the bare rock.

Besides the fluctuations due to the moon's attraction and to the winds, the sea has other movements, caused chiefly by the uneven distribution of heat over the earth's surface. When the different parts of a fluid body do not all have the same temperature, currents form that tend to distribute the heat evenly, and thus there is set up a circulation of the warmer liquid toward the colder, and of the colder toward the warmer, until the temperature of the whole is uniform. But if for some reason this equalizing of the temperature is impossible, the circulation continues indefinitely. Therefore, it is that a continual interchange is going on between the tepid seas of the equator and the ice-cold waters of the polar regions. From the tropics start currents that go to the very ends of the earth, carrying with them the warmth stored up in their waters; and at the same time, there come from the poles other currents that warm themselves at the tropical fires, to return then to their starting point.

Now, of the numerous currents that thus keep the oceans stirred up and in a sanitary condition, the most important for us is the one in the Atlantic known as the Gulf Stream, a current starting from the Gulf of Mexico and running in a northeasterly direction. It is a wide river of warm water in the middle of the ocean, its bed and its banks being the ocean's colder waters. Those two giant rivers, the Amazon and the Mississippi, do not flow with a thousandth part of its volume, and the heat stored up in its waters would suffice to melt mountains of iron. The

Gulf of Mexico is an immense boiler heated from above by the tropical sun and from below by the earth's interior fires. Its islands and its shores are riddled with volcanic mouths whose frequent activities bear testimony to the existence of subterranean fires under the floor of the gulf.

That explains the enormous accumulation of heat in the Gulf Stream — heat that it gives out on its way to colder climes, though still retaining enough at the end of the journey to melt some portion of the vast sheet of ice around the North Pole. The Gulf Stream flows northeasterly as far as the Newfoundland Bank, where a part plunges downward and flows along the ocean floor toward the pole, while the remaining portion continues on the surface, turning eastward. At about the latitude of the Azores, a part of this great warm current splits off and, after skirting the African coast, reenters the Gulf of Mexico by following the equator, while the part that continues eastward washes the coasts of France, Ireland, England, Iceland, and Norway, finally disappearing at the North Cape, where it plunges beneath the polar ice.

At its starting point, the Gulf Stream is fourteen leagues wide and about three hundred meters deep. At first, it moves about two leagues an hour, but this rate gradually lessens, though it continues to the end to be considerable. The waters of the Gulf Stream are of a beautiful blue tinge, clearly defined against the green of the rest of the ocean. This strange current, running through waters of a lower temperature, nevertheless keeps within its liquid banks, and as far north as the Azores, there is no mingling of the blue waves with the green. Farther on, it widens, its tepid waters spreading out and softening the climate of northern Europe.

If it were not for the additional warmth brought from the sunny south by this wonderful current, the winters on our channel coast, as well as in England, Ireland, and Norway, would be very much colder. The thermometer shows us how considerable is the amount of heat brought from Mexico by this oceanic hot-water heater; for if the thermometer is immersed first in the Gulf Stream itself and then in the water that serves as bed for that current, it shows a difference ranging between 12° and 17° centigrade. In latitudes where the temperature in winter falls below freezing, the Gulf Stream is found to have a temperature of 26° centigrade above the freezing point.

But it is not only warmth that this current brings to the lands of the colder North; it also brings fuel. Tree trunks washed away from the shores of Florida and Louisiana drift northward and eastward in the Gulf Stream and are thrown upon the beach in Iceland, at the North Cape, and in Spitzbergen. The inhabitants of these cheerless regions hasten to gather in this driftwood for heating. Pieces of bamboo, carved wood, and trunks of a species of pine unknown to Europe, borne to the Azores by the ocean current, contributed to the discovery of America by confirming Christopher Columbus in his suspicion that there existed a new world in the distant West.

The Gulf Stream, with the branch splitting off from it in the latitude of the Azores and running along the African coast before turning west to reenter the Gulf of Mexico, circumscribes an area in the Atlantic larger than the Mediterranean. In this immense basin encircled by the ocean current just described, marine plants collect and multiply to the extent of forming floating fields, entangling tapestries through which vessels have difficulty in forcing a passage. The first explorers of the Atlantic ventured not without apprehension into this strange region of marine plants. Columbus himself, on his first voyage, was much struck with this sight, then new to him, and it needed all his firmness of soul to induce him, despite the murmurs of his demoralized companions, to cross this insidious sea that threatened to entangle and hold his ships in the network of floating seaweed.

CHAPTER XXV

THE POLAR REGIONS

A T THE far northern and the far southern ends of the earth lie redoubtable realms of cold, where water takes, as a rule, the solid form, making a firm ground of ice, with boulders and islands and mountains of ice that are equal in size and solidity to boulders and islands and mountains of granite. The sea, freezing to a great depth and taking on the hardness of rock, becomes firmly attached to the neighboring stretches of land, so that the whole forms a continent of snow and ice, its outlines expanding or contracting according to the season but never entirely melting. Let us devote this closing chapter to some of the more remarkable peculiarities of these terminal regions of the globe, half rock and half ice, beginning with the Arctic regions, which are better known than the Antarctic.

Navigators who in summer push their way into the Arctic seas encounter, first, great blocks of ice detached from the polar mass and borne southward by ocean currents. These icebergs take all sorts of shapes, - ruined castles, dismantled towers, walls with window-like openings, tall columns, graceful spires, massive obelisks. Sometimes the iceberg looks like a hill with two opposite sloping sides, or like a crater with a deeply notched rim, or a great fragment of a mountain, or an island with precipitous cliffs, or a promontory with steep escarpments; or, again, it may take the shape of a vault or a cupola built by the hand of man, or of a rustic bridge with a number of arches, their insecure keystones retaining their position by some miracle of equilibrium. Not seldom, the iceberg assumes the form of an edifice more fantastic than the wildest imagination could ever have conceived, or it may be a deep grotto, fitting lair for some sea monster.

Icebergs have been seen that measure three kilometers across, their lofty turrets attaining a height of fifty meters, and their bases extending down into the sea for two hundred meters. It is no rare occurrence to see, on one of these floating islands of ice, a bear embarked for unknown shores. Passenger on a craft worthy of it, the polar monster explores the sea in quest of prey. Still less rare is it to note fragments of rock, bits of some Arctic promontory, wrested from the shore and embedded in the side of the iceberg.

By no means all floating ice comes from the breaking up of the frozen surface of the sea; it may also be broken off from some glacier that takes its start far inland. In our part of the world, glaciers come to a halt with the melting of their ice at a height of at least a thousand meters above the sea level; but in the climate of the polar regions, they continue their downward course to the level of the sea, and even there they do not melt. In Greenland, for example, there are rivers of ice larger than those of the Alps. These rivers move slowly; they make progress, but they never run, retaining their solid form from source to mouth. Instead of pouring their waters into the sea, they cast into it mountains of ice. The solidified river pushes its way into the ocean all in one piece, with its moraines, its rocks and stones and pebbles gathered up on the march and incorporated in its mass. Sometimes its advancing end overhangs the sea like a promontory undermined by the waves; but sooner or later there is a resonant detonation awakening a thousand echoes, with a tremendous disturbance in the sea. It is the end of the glacier breaking off and falling into the water after being sapped by the action of the waves and rendered no longer able to support itself. A great upheaval of the sea caused by its fall spreads in all directions, announcing that the fleet of icebergs has added to its number one more colossus.

When the polar sea freezes, the ice, which is of great thickness, extends all along the coast and into every bay and inlet; and when this ice breaks up, every fragment of any considerable size carries away with it the rocks and stones embedded in its mass. Sooner or later, in the warmer waters farther south, these floating islands of ice melt, and their mineral cargoes sink to the bottom of the sea. Icebergs sometimes float about on the ocean separately, and sometimes they move in great fleets extending as far as the eye can see. It is the strangest spectacle: one seems to see, dancing up and down on the waves, the ruins of some city of giants, built of crystal, alabaster, and marble. But the danger, too, is great. These colossal masses, turning about and swaying this way and that, approaching one another and then receding, as the waves may impel them, often clash one against another with a tremendous grinding and crashing. Woe to the vessel that finds itself between two icebergs when they collide, for it is crushed to pieces like an eggshell in the grasp of a vise!

The English navigator Scoresby, who made many Arctic voyages, relates that in a single summer more than thirty vessels were lost in this way. Under his very eyes, one was crushed between two icebergs, only the tip of the mainmast remaining visible above the united masses of ice. Another, tilted up by collision with an iceberg, stood on its stern like a rearing horse. Two others were pierced clear through by the pointed ends of icebergs. But floating icebergs are not the most terrible danger that threatens the navigator in these inhospitable seas. Occasionally there come down from Baffin's Bay floes incomparably larger than any iceberg and known to whalers as ice fields. Scoresby encountered some that were thirty leagues long and ten leagues wide. Often broken up and then rudely united again, these ice fields show a thousand irregularities of surface, which sometimes even take the shape of mountain chains such as might be found on a large island. A deep layer of snow completely covers the floating fields, and one might imagine them to be Swiss cantons wrested intact from their foundations in midwinter and cast into the sea, where some mysterious force keeps them afloat, with their plains, their ranges of hills, and their valleys. They move with alarming speed, and when they encounter any obstacle, the shock is indescribable. Imagine, if you can, the momentum of a body in rapid motion when that body weighs 10,000,000,000 tons. Hence, it is that the ship sighting one of these formidable moving islands on the horizon, and seeing that it is approaching and not receding, has but one chance of safety: that is, to turn about and sail away with all speed, so as to leave a free passage for the death-dealing raft.

What can the force be that, especially in Baffin's Bay, sets in motion all these trains of ice and sends them southward? Again, it is that great current in the Atlantic, the Gulf Stream, chilled and on its way back from the pole to the gulf.

Salt water subject to evaporation gains in weight because, the salt not evaporating, this water becomes richer in salt as its volume is reduced. Now, in the Gulf of Mexico, where the Gulf Stream starts, evaporation is rapid under the hot sun of those latitudes. In consequence of this evaporation, the water becomes more saline, and, hence, heavier. But, on the other hand, heat increases the volume of water and so makes the water lighter; and as this latter effect more than counterbalances the other, the result is that the warmer water, even though it contains more salt, floats on the colder and forms a surface current. It is plain, furthermore, that this current, rich in salt and floating only by virtue of its high temperature, must be directed downward as soon as it loses enough of its heat to destroy its buoyancy. Accordingly, as long as the warm water from the gulf retains sufficient warmth, it continues on its way as a surface current, while the counter current, originating at the pole and consisting of much colder water, flows along the sea bottom. But when the warmer stream has parted with a certain amount of its heat on its course, so that it can no longer float, it plunges downward under the weight of its extraordinary proportion of salt and gives place to the current of cold water, which in its turn rises and flows on the surface.

In the northern seas, then, there are found to prevail conditions contrary to those observed farther south; that is, the cold current from the pole flows on the surface, and the current that was warm when it started from the Gulf of Mexico flows along the ocean bottom. Floating icebergs show in a striking manner the presence of these two opposite currents, one above the other.

The smaller masses of ice, their immersed portions bathed only by the surface current, all move from north to south; but among the larger, there are some whose bases occasionally reach down into the lower current, and when this occurs, these icebergs may be seen to turn back and go northward until they escape the invisible force that drew them in a direction opposite to the general movement. Thus it is that the trains of ice coming down from Baffin's Bay are borne along by the polar current — that is, by the chilled Gulf Stream returning to warm itself in the Gulf of Mexico after giving up its last degree of warmth to the polar seas.

The meeting place of these warm waters from the gulf and the icy current from the polar regions is at the north of Newfoundland; there, the Arctic stream and a branch of the stream from the south meet and pass each other, exchanging their relative positions in the ocean, the one that was on the surface being now in the depths, and the one that was in the depths being now on the surface.

The great submarine plateau known as the Newfoundland Bank, or the Grand Bank, is the result of the meeting of the two currents. On encountering the warm water from the south, the ice carried along by the current from the pole melts and discharges into the sea the mineral matter, such as sand, pebbles, fragments of rock, and so on, that it brought away from the shores of Greenland. At the same time, the miscellaneous marine population — including mollusks especially — that the warm current has carried thus far perishes upon being suddenly immersed in the icy northern waters; and the shells and skeletons that in this manner find their way to the ocean bottom add to the deposit already there. Thus, the Newfoundland Bank is built up both with the mineral matter brought down by icebergs from the Arctic regions and with the shells and skeletons of marine life suddenly extinguished by contact with the ice-cold waters from the north.

Let us penetrate farther into the Arctic regions, into the labyrinth of islands and straits that abound in the polar seas to the north of North America. As danger has its seductions for men of courage, there have long been and there always will be stout-hearted explorers who, for purely scientific ends, are ready to venture into those forbidding regions and to pass the winter there, and then, in defiance of all obstacles and perils, to approach as nearly to the pole as the limitations of human strength and endurance permit. Among these brave men, I will mention Sir John Franklin, who perished there in 1847 with his companions, 137 in number, and with the loss of his two ships, the *Erebus* and the *Terror*; also Kane, more fortunate in his expeditions, and assured of undying fame by having his name inscribed on the map of those far-northern regions. The first navigators to make their way into these perilous seas gave to the southern extremity of Greenland, which commands the entrance to these polar waters, the name of Cape Farewell, as if in crossing the threshold of the Arctic seas they felt that they were saying goodbye to life. Here, indeed, the danger is enough to frighten the boldest.

If the sea is not frozen over, if it offers a passage to the navigator, he advances slowly amid icebergs that bear down on him if the current sets that way, and threaten every moment to crush his frail craft. Then, in a few hours, the frost may do its deadly work and the icebergs may unite in a firm ring about the ship, cutting off all escape. The vessel is then icebound and becomes incorporated with the frozen sea itself, which might almost be taken for one mass of solid quartz. So there the ship and crew are stuck fast, it may be for days, it may be for months, or even for a whole year; and no human power can open a way out.

Meanwhile, the vessel's timbers creak and groan under the tremendous pressure of the encompassing ice. Will the good ship stand the strain, or will she be crushed to pieces? Often, there is nothing to be done but abandon the ship that is thus frozen in and set out on foot over the ice, which may at any moment crack open and swallow up the luckless mariners. But even if the ship's company succeeds in reaching land, safety is by no means assured. In that inhospitable climate, with nothing but snow and ice underfoot, the men will almost certainly die of hunger, cold, and despair.

Indeed, on land the peril is not less than on the sea, especially in the terrible Arctic winter when the sun disappears for months at a time and the thermometer registers 40° and 50° centigrade below zero. Muffled in furs and equipped with wide snowshoes, which support the wearer on the unstable snow, the men start out under the feeble glimmering of a wan twilight that makes one shiver with apprehension. It is not the darkness of night, nor is it the light of day; it is the uncertain gleam that penetrates a dungeon through a small grated window. He who for the first time finds himself plunged into this lugubrious half-darkness for months together, with nothing by which to distinguish midday from midnight, is tempted to believe himself transported to some imaginary world far from the abodes of humankind. Even such domestic animals as may have been brought from home to these forsaken regions, utter cries of terror and not seldom die of their fright.

Amid these scenes, where nature herself appears to be in mourning, man has nevertheless one faithful servant that vies with him in courage and fears neither the intense cold nor the long Arctic night. This servant is the Eskimo dog, the inseparable companion of those scattering tribes that give the sweet name of native land to those frightful regions and live there all the year through, in winter under snow huts, and in summer beneath sealskin tents. With a team of these hardy animals to drag the supply of provisions on a sledge, one sets forth. But the north wind lashes the traveler's face as with leather thongs and makes deep cuts in the skin; the blood seems to freeze in the veins; and the flesh turns blue with cold, then dead white, and loses all feeling. An energetic rubbing with snow every quarter of an hour is necessary to revive the sluggish circulation. One's breath turns to needles of frost around the nostrils; the beard, stuck to the clothing by a varnish of ice, can be detached only with the scissors; tears freeze on the eyelashes and stick them together; and the wretched traveler stumbles along as if seized with vertigo.

But fatigue compels a halt. A hut must be built in Eskimo fashion. Snow is piled up to form the walls, and a large slab of ice serves as roof. It is under this shelter, the only one possible here, that the explorers dispose themselves as best they can for a night's sleep after partaking sparingly of a slice of frozen fish thawed out over a lamp. When it is time to rise, a signal is given, and immediately, around the hut, little mounds of snow begin to move and to shake themselves. They are the Eskimo dogs; the animals have slept outside and become buried in snow while sleeping. A meager ration is given them, which they devour in a trice, and then they are harnessed to the sledge and the party pushes on once more.

Will the destination be reached? It seems highly improbable when one considers all the obstacles to be overcome. Any day the cold, already so terrible, may redouble in severity and freeze every man in the company within a few minutes. The dogs, so indispensable for the transport of supplies, may perish, or food may give out. Who knows how soon it may be necessary to divide up into mouthfuls what remnants of fishbones or tallow there may be left? Who knows, too, whether the ice may not at any moment give way under the travelers' feet — for their way is over the frozen sea oftener than on land — and plunge them all into the water? May Heaven protect you, noble explorers, who thus strive to wrest its secrets from that Northern realm!

No one has yet reached the North Pole[22]. In 1854 some brave Americans, Kane and his companions, after abandoning their ship, the *Advance*, which had been frozen in, continued their expedition with sledges and Eskimo dogs. They had resolved to reach the earth's northern extremity even if they should perish there to the last man. Now, when they arrived within two hundred leagues of the pole, do you know what they found, after crossing those vast fields of ice that had arrested their progress by water? They found an open sea; they found warmth and life. Flocks of aquatic fowl sported on the water; sea-gulls, ducks, geese, and other winged frequenters of ocean waters circled about in the air, while certain unknown birds of white plumage and a wide span of wing flew around them with piercing

22   The reader will understand that this was written before Peary's famous achievement of 1909. – *Translator*.

cries. Never had these explorers beheld so many birds together. Seals played on the rocks, fishes swam in the water, and flowers blossomed on the shore. In short, life once more showed itself in its varied forms.

This unexpected sheet of water stretched northward as far as the eye could see, open and free from icebergs, its greenish waves rolling at the explorers' feet like our ocean waves. A strong wind blew from offshore for fifty-two hours without bringing the smallest piece of floating ice. Every indication pointed to the probability that this sea was deep, open, and of great extent. Ah, if Kane then had only had his fine ship, the *Advance*, held captive forever by the ice, with what ardor he would have set sail on this miraculous sheet of water which, though it seemed to be encircled by a ring of perpetual ice, yet rolled its waves in freedom on toward the coveted pole! He would have reached and passed the earth's northern extremity.

What can it be that, at least during the summer, keeps the polar sea open within its enormous ring of ice? It is probably the Gulf Stream, which at different points plunges under the circum-polar ice and carries the last remnant of its warmth toward the pole.

Even less known than the Arctic regions are the Antarctic. They are covered as with a cap of ice a thousand leagues across. A few slightly explored points of land, such as Adélie Land, Victoria Land, and Louis Philippe Land, reveal here and there layers of granite under equally hard layers of ice. Louis Philippe Land and Adélie Land were discovered in 1838 and 1840 respectively by that glory of the French Navy, Dumont d'Urville, the dauntless explorer who, after escaping the perils of the Antarctic icebergs, and after hoisting our flag on the confines of the known world in those perilous polar regions, lost his life in 1844 in an accident on the Versailles railway.

The great cap of Antarctic ice is bordered with abrupt cliffs broken by a number of narrow winding channels.

Dumont d'Urville recounts:

The appearance of this insurmountable wall, stern

and impressive beyond the power of words to describe, fills the soul with an instinctive fear. Nowhere does man feel more keenly the sense of his own weakness and helplessness. It is a dead world, silent and lugubrious, where everything threatens man with annihilation. To the farthest limits of the horizon nothing but a chaos of ice is to be seen. Here and there an iceberg attains a height of thirty or even forty meters. They might be taken for rectangular buildings in a city of marble. The usual color of the ice, as seen through an almost permanent fog, is grayish; but occasionally, when the air is clear and the sun shines, there may be observed the most wonderful play of glancing light. A profound silence reigns over this domain of ice.

Life is represented by only a few seabirds circling about in noiseless flight, a few whales whose resonant blowing is the only sound to break, at intervals, the desolate silence, and by stupid herds of seals lying prone on the polished surface of the ice.

The two sloops of war comprising the expedition, the *Astrolabe* and the *Zélée*, made their way into one of the open channels intersecting the cliff. One might have imagined oneself in some narrow street of a city of giants. On the right and on the left towered vertical ramparts of ice, reaching far above the masts of our vessels. Beside these enormous masses of ice the two sloops looked absurdly small, their hulls appearing so fragile and their masts so slender that we could not suppress a feeling of fear. At the foot of these walls of ice yawned caverns into which the waves rushed with tremendous uproar, and on the clear and polished ice surfaces the sun's rays played with magic effects of light and shade. Down from far above there poured into the sea cascades fed by the snows melting under the January sun, this being the summer season in those latitudes. The officers' commands, reverberating from one wall of ice to another, awoke a thousand echoes that for the first time in those frozen solitudes repeated the human voice.

For an hour the vessels advanced thus between the two ramparts of ice, a falling fragment of which would surely have sufficed to sink them. But at last, they came out into an immense basin, closed on one side by the ice they had just penetrated, and on the other by land, a precipitous coast a thousand meters high and covered with a thick mantle of ice, its whiteness emphasized in a striking manner by the unclouded brilliance of the sun. It was Adélie Land, perhaps a part of an Antarctic continent. Boats were launched and, to the accompaniment of lusty cheers, the national tricolor was unfurled on this land at the confines of the globe, a land of reddish granite buried beneath three or four hundred meters of perpetual ice.

A few outcroppings of rock in the side of the icy cliff were the only evidences furnished to Dumont d'Urville that he had discovered a polar continent. Everywhere else the land, buried under ice, was indistinguishable from the glacial cap surrounding the pole. In 1841 Ross, of the English Navy, penetrated somewhat farther into this Antarctic ice cap and discovered, not far apart, two enormous volcanoes, which he named Mount Erebus and Mount Terror, after his two vessels, the very ones that were destined to be lost with Franklin amid the ice of the North Pole. Mount Erebus is 3750 meters high. When Ross visited this volcano, it was in full activity, a spreading tuft of flames and smoke surmounting it, and a lake of lava of dazzling brightness boiling in its snow-encircled crater.